The Long Road

Jennifer Loren

Books by Jennifer Loren

The Devil's Eyes Series

THE DEVIL'S EYES

THE DEVIL'S REVENGE

THE DEVIL'S SON

THE DEVIL'S MASQUERADE: THE POISON

THE DEVIL'S MASQUERADE: THE REMEDY

The Finding Ava Series

FINDING AVA

RECKLESS

THE LONG ROAD

Short Story

THE HAND THAT HOLDS MINE

http://www.jenniferloren.com/

Published by Jennifer Loren, 2013

ISBN: 0988802724
ISBN-13: 978-0-9888027-2-8

Acknowledgements

Copyediting: Erinn Giblin, Yours Truly, The Editor

Cover Design: Hang Le, By Hang Le

http://byhangle.com/

Prologue

Dani

Dear Dillon,

Everyone always asks me the moment I fell in love with you. When was it that you captured my heart for good and never let it go? There were many wonderful moments together, but I remember that moment perfectly. How could I not? It was with you. Honestly, I remember every moment I have spent with you, but this one is my favorite. The moment when I knew I would love you always; the first time you asked to spend forever with me.

"So, what if I asked you to marry me?" you asked suddenly as we sat watching my cousin getting married.

It was a shocking question, of course, not something I had ever considered before. You were my best friend, so much so that you even agreed to put on your best clothes and go with me to the family event so I wouldn't be bored. But did you really mean the question you just asked? I had to think for a second, trying to remember what my mother had said to my stepdad when he asked her only a week prior. It was a confusing conversation for me at the time, but I did my best to recall it before looking back up at you. "I would say that is a very serious question, and I would hope you considered all the points of concern, such as, do we enjoy the same things? Can we agree on the important things in life, um…money, children and …" The first part was easy, then I couldn't remember anything else my mother had said, so I added in what I thought was important at the time. "We would have to be husband and wife and not just friends anymore. We would have to live together in the same house and share stuff. And what about vacations Dillon? We would have to go together every single time. We would have to spend a lot of time together. We would have to be together forever!"

You looked at me with your eyebrows scrunched together and your sweet, crooked smile. "But that's why I would ask you, Dani," you said simply with a shrug of your shoulders.

I smiled and nodded. Your argument made perfect sense. I don't know why I even questioned you; however, after a few minutes, I realized maybe the time wasn't quite right for us. "Okay, but I don't think our parents will let us until we are at least twelve. They might kill us if we got married now."

"Oh yeah," you said, nodding in agreement. "So, can we go back to being just friends then? I don't wanna be killed." I nodded and held your hand, which you weren't too keen on back then, but you did it for a few minutes to renew our friendship and to please me.

No matter the time that has gone by, or the agony we have been through, I still love you with all my heart, and I always will.

Forever I am yours,

Dani

Chapter 1

Dillon

Shane has never been good with goodbyes. When I left to visit my grandparents in Florida, which was right after finishing up a pretty rough third-grade year, he looked like a puppy that was just taken away from its mother. And today, as he drops me off at the airport to return to North Carolina, he looks the exact same way. "Would you please lighten up? I'm not dying; I am simply leaving New York. I will only be a phone call away."

"I'm fine; although, I am not all that excited to be working with Parker, the over-enthusiastic brownnoser. You could have at least done one last horrible thing to get me into trouble so I can hate you before you go," Shane says to me.

"I tried, but once I quit, they no longer cared that I super-glued Parker's office door." I sit back thinking about Parker screaming for help on the other side of his door as we all sat ignoring him. "You know it took four hours for anyone to even call maintenance? The Partners had to have seen him whining on the other side of that window. I know it's not a big window, but his face was pressed so tight against it that you couldn't tell if it was his butt cheeks or the ones on his face. I don't think the Partners like him that much. Jenkins has to pass by there to get to the elevators; he walked right past and went to lunch for two hours. Maybe I should have asked to open a branch office in North Carolina rather than quit," I laugh.

"I don't think Jenkins appreciated the two thumbs up you gave him when he came back from lunch though." I look over at him confused. "Dillon, he said, *get out of my way, jackass*," Shane says with a snarl.

"That's only a pet name he gave me after I got caught stuffing all those granny panties in Parker's file drawers. He likes me. I know it," I say with a large smile.

Shane begins laughing. "That was hilarious. Where the hell did you find all those panties anyway?"

"Dollar Store, ten for a dollar. They were all irregular; they had an extra leg hole." I nod as we both laugh thinking about Parker finding a pair a year later in the back of his drawer as he searched for a file to give Jenkins. "I am really going to miss Parker," I say with a sigh.

"Well, I am going to miss you." Shane says, briefly glancing my way.

"Ahhh, I love you too, Shane." I reach out and hug him while trying to fight to kiss his cheek.

"Stop it, you sick fuck. People are staring at us," he says, smacking me away for the last time. "Anyway, tell your Dad I said hi, and let me know if you need any help. You know I will be there if you need me." I nod, suddenly feeling a little lonely myself. "Oh damn, it is going to really suck here without you."

"It's going to suck in Carolina without you too," I say and quickly suck it up and gather my bags. "Now go, and I will see you for Thanksgiving at your mom's house, like always." I jump out of his car and head straight through the airport doors, towards the life I thought I left behind.

My father has run his furniture factory as one to be envied. It's not huge, but it has always been successful, no matter what minor role it plays in the industry as a whole. Everything has gone well, never great, but good enough. That is, until my mother got sick. I lost my mother to breast cancer a few years ago, and my father was the one who helped her every step of the way; he gave up everything to be at her side. In the process, the business has been taken advantage of and nearly destroyed. My father would never ask for my help unless he was desperate. He has told me not to worry about it more times than I can count, so for him to now ask for help, it must be serious. He called me a few weeks ago, and I wasn't about to let him down. He said he would sell the factory and retire, but I know damn well that is the last thing he wants to do. That factory has been in the family since my great grandfather. Though we have never become rich, we were always able to survive, even through tough times thanks to my father. He is the strongest, smartest, and most noble man I have ever known. My father has been working himself too hard, trying to keep up with technology, and his crooked employees take advantage of his gullible kindness. There aren't many people left or even much to salvage, except the Conrad name, from what my father has confessed to me so far. Somehow, I have to figure out a way to build on that once great name and get my father's factory back to its respectable position.

I find it astonishing how I have to get from New York City to Greenberg, North Carolina via Chicago, Illinois. *That's the wrong direction!* My flight was late getting in, and now I am running through this huge ass airport trying to make my connection. I run up to the gate and quickly notice that no one is lining up to board. Checking the screen and frantically scanning the long list of departures and arrivals, I notice the word *Delayed*, flashing under my flight number. I check with the attendant who tells me to please sit until further notice. *At least I didn't miss my flight.* I find a decently comfortable spot across the aisle from a bar so I can watch ESPN on the TVs and people watch at the same time. One quick glance at a hottie walking by and I swear I see, *her*, simply gazing at sports magazines at a shop next to the bar. *Can't be. Nope, it can't be.* I take a quick look back, and she catches me. *Damn it. Don't look at her. Don't even turn. Just pretend you didn't see her. Why is she here? I can see her smiling towards me out of the corner of my eye, but there is no way I want to talk to her right now. I don't want to ever talk to her again.* The gate attendant suddenly announces my flight is cancelled due to the snow storm that caused me to be late in the first place. I should have stayed in New York. Now, I am stuck in Chicago's first unexpected snow storm. I quickly jump up and run to the flight boards to search for any hope of leaving this city and getting home today. While I search, I hear my name called out from behind me by a familiar voice. I briefly think about running, but instead, I stay in place arguing with myself on what to do. *Why? Why now? Try to do the right thing and this is what happens, your past comes back to smack you in the face. Because when bullshit can happen, it always does.*

"Dillon?" I turn slowly towards the sweet voice behind me, and there she is. "It is you," she says, smiling wide as if I should be happy to see her again.

"Hi, Dani. Long time no see, but I guess that's how you preferred it." I turn away from her snarling expression and back to the board in front of me. *Of course I see her now, just before I move back to the city of all things Dani. It would only make sense that I have a clear picture of her everywhere I go … for the rest of my damn life.*

Dani steps to my side, smelling annoyingly wonderful. "So, did your flight get cancelled too?" she asks.

"Yep, but I am trying to figure out another way out of here," I say, avoiding looking her way as best I can.

"Like what? All flights out are being cancelled for the day."

"I don't know; maybe I will rent a car or something."

"From Chicago to North Carolina in the middle of a snow storm?" she says with a laugh.

"Yes. Do you have a problem with that?" I sigh, walking away from her.

"No, not if that's what you want to do, but I wouldn't think it would be safe."

I turn towards her and look her dead in the eyes. "Oh! Now you're worried about what happens to me? Thanks for your concern, but I'm good." I walk away from her once again and go in search of a rental car kiosk. I spend an hour going from one place to the next, unsuccessfully searching for an available car. Of the fifteen plus rental car companies, either they were closed early or out of cars. *Wonderful.* After checking the boards a few more times and talking to the airline, I give up on the idea of getting out of here anytime today. The only thing to do now is get some food and some sleep, but the line at the airport hotel does not look promising. I wait anyway, hoping for the best.

While in line, Dani sneaks up to my side and seems to enjoy my instant frustration at seeing her again. "They are out of rooms, and pretty much all the nearby hotels are booked up. I did, however, manage to get a room if you would like to share?" Sighing hard, I grab my bag and head to some seating where I begin to make myself comfortable for a long night. "Are you going to sleep here?"

"Are you following me? Go away before I scream harassment."

Dani huffs, "Dillon, come on. Don't be ridiculous."

"Go away, lady. I am not interested." I turn away, and she taps me on my shoulder, whispering my name. "I told you, lady, I don't have that kind of money for one night," I say loudly enough to pique a nearby man's interest and piss her off at the same time, which makes me so happy.

"Dillon, stop it. I am trying to help you. You know what? Never mind! You can sleep here on a hard hotel lobby settee, rather than a pull out bed in a cozy room."

I look at my seat beneath me in confusion, "What the hell is a settee?"

"It's a couch you dumbass."

"Then call it a couch, you pretentious snob," I say back at her rolling eyes. "Go away, Dani. I am going to be fine sleeping here on my, *settee*."

"Oh! I am sure you will be just fine, until they kick you out for not having a reservation. Then you will be forced to sleep in the airport. Hmmm, I am not sure which would be worse: hard curved seating digging into your back or disgusting airport floor that people walk on, vomit on, spill their food on, and leave it sitting there all day and night, molding until someone comes and sweeps the crusty part away?"

The picture in my head becomes increasingly horrifying with every word she says, but I continue to smile wide at her. "Sounds wonderful," I say, turning my disgusted expression away from her.

"Dillon! Damn you. Stop being ridiculous, and come to my room with me. I promise, you will enjoy sleeping in my room much more than this."

"I'll room with you," two men say from behind her. One stands, waving his wallet at her, while the other eyes her inappropriately.

I stand up in between them and her, pushing one away while daring the other to make a move. "You both can forget it!" I yell at them.

"Hey buddy, if you aren't going to take her up on her offer then we are more than happy to." He and his friend approach with their chests out, trying to prove they are worthy of her time. "Baby, I assure you, I have enough money to keep you working all night long," he says, reaching out for her.

I step into his chest with fearless intimidation. "I'm not going to tell you twice. Walk away before we have a problem." They back up slowly, shaking their heads but still eyeing her way too much for comfort. I look back at her sternly.

"Don't look at me that way. All of that was your fault. Now I guess I have to make sure I have my Mace out when I walk to my room, and hopefully, I remember to lock my door. Not that it matters with these new key cards. I hear they are really easy to copy now."

"Use the latch. That would be the big metal thing that keeps people from coming in," I suggest.

She huffs, crossing her arms, while I sit down and go back to ignoring her. "Hmmm that's a good idea, but I hope I don't forget when I go out all alone to get ice in the middle of the night."

I jump back up in shock. "Who goes to get ice in the middle of the night?" I ask her.

"You know how I like my ice-water when I go to bed."

My anger turns to frustration, and I curse under my breath as I grab my bag. "Fine, show me to *our* room." She looks infuriatingly satisfied as she leads me to the room, which actually seems nice aside from the one bed. "So, this sofa pulls out right?" She nods and pulls the cushions out to reveal no pull out sofa. She looks up confused, and I smile. "Thought this one through, did ya?"

"Shut up, Dillon. You will simply have to sleep on the sofa as it is. I will call for some extra blankets and you can have one of the pillows."

"How the hell am I going to fit on there? It's five feet long, and I am six-two, Dani."

"Better than the chair in the lobby, isn't it? Not to mention free!"

I instantly back off my argument, *oh yeah*, "I'm good." She shakes her head and moves around the room arranging her things before touching up her makeup and grabbing her purse. "Going somewhere?"

"Yes, I'm hungry. Aren't you?" I think about it for a second and realize I am starving. I don't usually go this long without food, but I can deal until tomorrow. I don't need to torture myself by being around her any longer than necessary. "Come on, Dillon. I know you can't make it more than a couple of hours without food of some kind. Your metabolism is ridiculous. I'll buy if you come with me." I jump up to lead her out the door and to one of the hotel restaurants. Neither of us even think to question the choice: nice elegant restaurant or the sports bar? Sports bar for us both. The one thing I always did like about Dani was her appreciation for a great game.

We sit down, grab menus, and thoroughly screen them. I finally have to order something before my stomach growls one more time. Once we order, I concentrate on my drink and stare at every television in the room as long as it is in the opposite direction of her. She allows me to sit quietly but smiles anytime I accidently look her way. I order another drink and keep it near my mouth, just in case she thinks to ask me a question. *Where the hell is the damn food?* As soon as I spot the waitress, I sit up straight and wait patiently as she places our plates down in front of us before digging in and filling my mouth. Dani sighs and turns sideways to let me know she is done trying to talk to me. I down another drink while I eat and look her over more carefully for the first time since she popped out of nowhere to ruin my life again. She hasn't changed much other than a more stylish haircut and clothes. She still looks like an athletic tomboy with an incredible body, auburn hair, cute freckles across her nose, soft pink lips, and the longest eyelashes I have ever seen. It always melted me when she smiled and blinked her amazing doe eyes at me, and now … *she is doing it to that guy over there!* I watch as he smiles back at her, and she tilts her head and crosses her legs towards him.

"So are you two together?" the man, motioning towards me, asks Dani.

She glances my way and laughs, "Who, he and I? No, definitely not," she says right in front of me.

"What the hell are you doing?" I ask her.

She turns to me, seeming surprised by my question. "What is your problem?"

"Are you going to talk with that guy right in front of me?"

"Oh, I'm sorry. I didn't realize I wasn't allowed to talk at all. I thought I was only not supposed to talk to you?" I sit back in my seat and roll my eyes. "Not true? I can talk to you? I don't know what your problem is, but I have gone out of my way to be nice to you …"

"My problem?! My problem is that you show up out of nowhere after I haven't seen you in eight years. I haven't heard a word from you since you disappeared. And now you want me to jump up and down and scream for joy to see you again? I don't know how in the world this has happened, but I assure you, I am not excited to see you again." As soon as the words leave my mouth, she sinks down into herself and looks as if I just ran over her dog. *Great, I hate that she can still make me feel like an asshole that easily.*

"I'm sorry, Dillon, I am. I didn't want to leave … I didn't realize …" she says with tears forming. I can't stand to see her cry any more now than I could when we were kids, and just like then, I reach over and press my fingers in between hers and take hold of her hand without saying a word. Damn those eyelashes, and damn those lips for smiling right back at me and instantly grabbing my heart. I need another drink, and I order her one too, in hopes she won't want to talk as much. "So, you forgive me?"

"Sure, why not. Might as well. It's not like we will see each other again after tonight anyway, right?"

"Sure," she says with a suspicious expression. With the clink of our glasses, we move on with our night and manage a few laughs between us. Every glance her way reminds me of another moment, another time—a better time. She teases me like she always did, and I tease her right back with a little flirtatious touch in between. Another drink, another smile, and we head back to our room.

I feel light-headed and horny as hell. I watch her walk into the room and remove her shoes. Her slight sway and giggle means she is feeling good, too. She turns and smiles. "You're drunk," I say, laughing at her.

She steps forward and leans into my chest. "Remember the first time I was drunk and you carried me home on your back?" I laugh, recalling that time as I look down at her and feel my cock getting harder with every second I am near her. "Although, that was nothing compared to the time you came home crawling up the driveway and I had to help you into your house. You won one football game, and you boys went completely stupid."

"It wasn't just one football game! It was the championship, and you know it."

"Oh yes, and you scored the winning touchdown." She holds up her arms, laughing, "Whoo-hoo Dillon Conrad! Super tight end scores!"

"If I recall correctly, we both scored that night," I say, looking down at the doe-eyed beauty pressing against my chest.

"It was hard to say no. You looked so good in that uniform … running down that field and …hmmm," she says, stepping back and looking me over with a look of desire I have never seen from my high school love before. My body tingles, and my pants begin constricting.

"What was that?" I slide my fingers down her face and remove the hair as she moves into my hand and moans. This is not the naïve girl that I once knew. I run my hand down her side, searching for the right place to grasp and squeeze her closer to me.

Her breathy gasp against my lips only makes me want her

more. Dani grazes my face and caresses the back of my neck as she lightly kisses the side of my face and breathes, "I have missed you so much, Dillon." My head begins spinning as her lips take hold of mine. My shirt comes off and so does hers. "Wow, French underwear?" I say, admiring the sexy bra that holds her breasts perfectly in front of my face. She laughs and slides her skirt down, showing off the matching panties that barely cover her. I smile and pull her in close. "Who are these for?"

"I might have a boyfriend," she says, unzipping my pants and pulling out my erection with a long, respectful rub.

"You might, huh? Well, I hope he doesn't mind if I rip them." I take hold of her panties with a full grasp, grazing her pussy and feeling her tender wetness against my knuckles. I look her in the eyes and easily tear through the delicate fabric. I lift her up onto me and feel the tight clutch of her wetness pull me in deep. I groan, and she releases her breasts from her bra, wrapping her arms around me and encouraging me to go further. A whimper, a bite of her lips, and I take her and fall onto the bed. Her hands seem to know exactly what I need, and with every movement of them, I recognize precisely what she needs. It feels good to be near her, but it feels even better to be inside her again. She doesn't deny me any part of her; she lies back, fisting my hair and wrapping her legs around my hips to keep me on top of her. Every feeling and emotion I have built up since she left begins to surface and form into an energy driven fuck like I have never had. Our heated breaths blend in with our lips. Our tongues twist into one another's mouths before tasting our bare skin. The bed is a disaster, and our clothes are strewn all over the floor as we make full use of every part of the small hotel room. I use every piece of furniture to maneuver her body into a new desired position. Whether laid out in front of me on the bed or bent over the tiny desk, I find my way inside her, and I thrust my hardened cock right where I know she likes it. With a tender rub of her ass, I kiss her lips one last time as I watch her orgasm; it's a pleasurable sight, so much so it pushes me to come myself. I collapse hard and can barely move from her arms. Her gentle fingers run through my hair and down my back, causing me to relax even more and drift off to sleep without another word being said. My dreams carry me back to a time when things were much simpler.

The first time I saw her was at my ninth birthday party. As a June baby, I always had my friends over for the day, all day. There was no school to worry about and most of my friends lived nearby, so it was easy to invite everyone. My parents never complained and always provided an abundance of easy-to-grab junk food to satisfy our growing hunger between the rowdy play and the need for bandages for someone. My mother would keep an eye on us but usually stayed out of sight, so when she called out to me, as my team was about to take over the ball, I knew it must be important.

I run to my mother and immediately spot the strange girl sitting next to her with her arms folded and hair pulled back in a ponytail. I have never seen her before, and I know pretty much everyone in our small town thanks to my father's business here. My family has run a small, but well-known, furniture business and factory in Thomasville since before my grandfather was born. If I don't know them from my father's factory, then I know them from church. I, however, have never seen this girl before, and I don't know of anyone missing a girl. Oh no. I hope they didn't take that request for a sister seriously? I was only trying to guilt them into letting Shane spend the night so we could play video games all night. My parents have asked me many times if I would like them to adopt a brother or sister for me, since my mother isn't able to have any more, but … Oh no, I don't want a sister. Please Mom… this has got be a joke, I silently beg her as she looks down at me with that, 'be on your best behavior Dillon,' look.

"Dillon, this is Danielle …"

"Dani," the girl reminds my mother who smiles with a soft hand on the girl's back.

"Dani and her family moved in next door, and I thought it would be nice if you would introduce her to some of your friends."

"Right now? Mooommm! Lucas is ahead, and he is being a real jerk about it. We only need one more score to win."

"I'm fast, I really am," Dani says annoyingly. My Mom tilts her head slightly, the wordless symbol for 'Dillon let her play or you are going to be having a long boring talk with your father later'. I hate those talks.

I glance over at the girl and sigh, "Fine, you can be on my team." I quickly toss her the football, expecting her to drop it so I can glare at my mother and gain some sympathy for my honorable behavior, but Dani catches the ball easily and runs out in front of me, babbling away about what position she should play.

"Great! I can play running back or a receiver or …"

I stop her and take back the ball. "Wait, these guys are pretty rough. We don't hold back. We are all nine or ten except Shane, and he is eight but just as big and tough as the rest of us. Now, you can play, but if you get hurt, *you can't cry to my mom. Okay?"*

"I'm eight, and I can out run any of ya. Just you watch." I roll my eyes with a sideway glance her way. "Just throw me the ball, skinny boy," she says, poking me hard in the chest.

"I'm not skinny! You're skinny!" I say, rubbing my chest. She ignores me and gets into position as the other guys throw their hands out, waiting for me to explain. I wave them back and ignore their huffs and sighs. "Alright, I am going to throw long, so Shane block for me, and Rich, make sure you open up a lane for Joey."

"What about her?" Shane asks.

"Dani. Her name is Dani, and she can block or something, I don't know. Just let her play otherwise my mom is going to get mad at me."

"I said I can run," she says, putting her hands on her hips.

"I heard ya, so run then." She's annoying me already. Thanks Mom. We break our huddle and line up. Once I take a step back, I search for Joey who is covered, and they are coming after me strong. The only option is Dani, who is yelling at me to toss it to her — wow she's irritating, but I toss it to her anyway, and she takes off. Dang she's fast. I get buried under two guys as I watch her run it in. "Yes!" I yell. Dani dances around the ball while I, and the rest of our team, run up and high five her. I turn around and point at Lucas, the head of the other team. We have been friends forever, and unlike my best friend, Shane, Lucas and I enjoy anything competitive, especially against each other.

"Alright, come on. We still have time to beat you," Lucas says. I put my arm around Dani's shoulders and walk with the rest of the guys to line up, only to have to wait while Lucas huddles with his team to come up with a game plan.

"*Come on. You can't win. You only have time for one play,*" I remind him, as my father steps outside pointing at his watch. "*Hurry up! My dad made cheeseburgers, and I got a birthday cake to eat.*" Lucas huffs as he and his team line up against us. I watch his eyes and wait for him to pass to Ross, the fastest and tallest on his team, but he isn't fast enough to out run me. I run him down and stop him, jumping up with a smile only to watch Lucas run at Dani with full force. The hit was harsh, even by our standards. He stands up laughing while I run at him and knock him into the ground. "*What was that, jerk?*" I yell at him until my father pulls me off of him.

"*Dillon, stop it,*" my father says as he separates us. "*Lucas that was unnecessary what you did to Dani. This is supposed to be touch football, boys. Now, Lucas, you need to apologize to Dani.*" Lucas grumbles and turns to Dani who has a grass stain all down one side of her and a skinned up chin. He shakes her hand with a muffled apology that she seems to accept. Lucas and I shake hands, and my father escorts us back to the house to eat.

Dani is a little bruised and cut up, but it doesn't seem to bother her as she makes herself a single hotdog and sits down at one of the tables by herself. None of the guys will sit with her though. They all gather at the other table and pretend she doesn't exist. I assume it's because of Lucas. She looks up at me with sad eyes as I try to decide where to sit myself. I climb in right next to her, "*Can I sit with you, superstar?*" I ask, receiving an excited nod in return. Shane follows as do some of the other guys from my team.

Dani taps me on the arm. "*I didn't cry, so your mom won't get mad at ya.*"

I nod with a smile. "*Cool, thanks.*"

Later that night, I crash onto my bed, tossing my football, when I notice a light come on in the room across from mine. No one has lived in that house *for months, and before then, it was only an older lady and her husband. The old lady moved in with her daughter after her husband died, and the house has sat empty ever since, that is, until Dani and her family moved in this week. Dani moves in front of the window and notices me staring. I wave, and she lifts her window, to which I follow. "Thanks for sticking up for me today," she says.*

I shrug, "It's no big deal." She shrugs back, looking around like she wants to say something else. "So, what are you doing tomorrow? Shane and I were going to do stuff, if you want come with us?"

She looks up with a smile, "Sure, that sounds like fun."

"Cool." I smile back.

Chapter 2

Dillon

The sun comes in and nearly blinds me, even with my eyes closed. I roll away from the bright window and see her next to me. She is just as beautiful now as she was when we were kids, but we aren't kids anymore.

Dani opens her eyes and smiles up at me. I have to fight myself to keep from smiling back at her, so I quickly sit up in bed and scramble to think of the right thing to say. "I should probably get out of here. I have a flight home to find." Dani sits up next to me, holding the sheet over her naked body as if she is suddenly embarrassed. *Don't look at her, Dillon. Don't look at her.* "So yeah, thanks for the ... ummm, sharing the room and the bed, and well ... okay, I gotta go." I get up and frantically search for my pants or my underwear or something as my bare ass hangs out in front of her, prolonging the awkwardness. "Found them," I say, turning around and looking into her big, brown, innocent eyes. *Damn it! Don't look at her. Don't look at her!* Great. Now I feel like a jackass. "Do you want to get some breakfast or something? I'll pay."

"Breakfast is free with your stay at this hotel, Dillon."

"Right. Well, then ... feel free to order whatever you want." I smile wide, causing her to laugh.

"You can go, Dillon. Don't worry about it. I don't want to force you to spend any more time with me if you don't want to." I look around the room, trying to decide if she is setting me up or not. "Go Dillon, I'm fine."

Oh no, she said she's fine. "Well, I can at least help you with your bag to check out," I say, hoping she gives me a way out of this.

"No. No reason to bother yourself doing that. You have a flight to book," she says with a dejected sigh and knowing exactly what she did to me.

I sit down in the chair, honorably accepting my defeat. "I guess I can call from here and book a flight while I wait for you to get ready."

She stands up, wrapping the blanket around her with a smile. "If that's what you want to do," she says proudly, walking into the bathroom.

"If that's what you want to do," I mock her. *Where is my phone?* I search around the room, and think I find it when I realize it is actually Dani's phone with several missed messages. *Probably her dad. Oh how I would love to take a picture of my dick right now and send it to him.* The idea is almost too good to pass up. I quickly unzip my pants and maneuver her phone just right, and … we are a go. I laugh to myself when she gets a call.

Dani comes running out of the bathroom, soaking wet in a towel. "That's mine! Don't touch it. Don't answer that! It's mine," she says, taking her phone from my hand. "Hello. Hi. No, I'm fine. Yeah …" She disappears back into the bathroom and shuts the door so I can't hear the rest of her conversation.

By the time Dani steps back out, all prim and proper, I am ready to go myself, but not before I ask one question. "So, did

Thomas enjoy that picture I sent him?" I say, enjoying her scrambling to look through her phone. She slowly looks up at me, shaking her head. "Just kidding. I didn't get a chance to send it before you took the phone away. So, he's the boyfriend. Hmmm, good to know."

I grab her bag and mine and head out the door without another word. I follow her to check out and wait with her, smiling all over myself. She tries to ignore me, but as soon as we step out of the hotel and back into the airport, she slugs me in the arm. "Would you stop?"

"Stop what, Dani?"

"Acting like that. Like you just got away with stealing the cookie from the cookie jar."

I lean down into her face, "Mmm… it was a good cookie, too."

"My relationship with Thomas is complicated. What we did last night was after a huge argument he and I … I don't have to explain myself to you!" Dani says, taking hold of her bag and walking away from me.

"Hey, it doesn't bother me. It was simply a one night-stand with someone I knew once and will never see again," I say after her. I take my bag and my handful of breakfast goodies I grabbed from the hotel on my way out and head for my gate. Dani suddenly stops in front of me and turns towards me with a big, knowing smile. "What?"

"Nothing," she giggles with glee before walking on her merry way. *I don't like the sound of that.* I look her over for any signs of deception but find nothing. *Ignore it. Nope, I don't care. I do not care.* I move on and lose her in the crowds. Once at my gate, I glance around to make sure she is completely gone and then make myself at home with a new magazine, a bag of fruit gummies, and a large Gatorade. "Some things never change. Fruit gummies, really?" Dani says, snatching my magazine out of my hands. She sits down next to me and begins reading. "I cannot believe they traded him. He was all they had," she says, shaking her head, taking some of my gummies, and grabbing for my Gatorade. I pull it away from her.

"Why are you here? Go away. And I mean that in the nicest possible way, or whatever will get you away from me faster."

"Oh, Dillon. You are so funny," she laughs innocently.

"Go away."

"Can't, sorry. I am on this flight."

"What? No. Why?!"

"I have business in Thomasville. The funny thing is that I am actually meeting with your father." She looks up at me and makes a sweet, obnoxious expression to piss me off.

"I don't believe you. You're doing this to get back at me. I can't help it that you found me too irresistible and cheated on your boyfriend with me. That is not my fault. I tried to contain my handsomeness, but apparently, it just wasn't enough for you. Now, give me my magazine and my fruit gummies!" I take them back and squeeze in between an elderly woman with a walker and a man overly enjoying his Cinnabon. But it's a seat away from her, sort of. There are only so many seats and few open ones, so I am forced to face her. I hold up the magazine so I don't have to look at her, and all is good again until I suddenly begin to get pounded by rubber bands. I look up at her, and she begins looking around as if she has no clue. When she finally looks my way, I mouth harshly, "Stop it." She shrugs, but as soon as I move my magazine up, she pegs me with another. Alright that's it. I grab a few thrown my way and peg her back.

"Excuse me! Could you please stop that, Sir … Ma'am?" a lady from the airline says to us.

We manage to keep cool, but when it's time to board, she purposely cuts in front of me. I trip her as she gets on the plane, causing her to fall into the lap of the man in the first row. I think I was the only one who laughed, but I wasn't the only one that enjoyed it.

"I am so sorry sir. My feet must have gotten tangled with someone's big, boat-sized feet," Dani says to him.

"Oh no problem. I didn't mind at all," the man says, winking at her.

Dani quickly moves away from him, turns, and punches me. "I can't believe you did that."

"What? You didn't like him? He looked very nice."

"He looked a hundred years old," she grumbles as I laugh. I sit peacefully down in my seat, but then she changes seats with the gentleman next to me and sits down with a large smile.

"I am not sure if you heard me before, but … *go away*," I pronounce clearly for her.

"No, I think, instead, I am going to discuss my menstrual

cycle with you the whole way there."

"You wouldn't dare?"

"Wouldn't I?"

"What do you want?"

She turns completely towards me with a serious expression. "I want you to actually forgive me and for us to start over and get along."

I shake my head. "Sorry, can't do that." I turn away and go back to my magazine, stopping only to put my headphones on to make sure I don't have to hear anything about any cycle of hers.

She huffs and asks the flight attendant for a drink. She takes one sip and dumps the rest in my lap. I jump up, huffing and cringing from the cold.

"You fucking …" I say to her hardened glare.

"Did you have an accident? It's okay, but next time, just ask me to move so you can make it to the bathroom first." She smiles sweetly, and I match it as I open my Gatorade and dump it down her shirt.

"Oh no! And you wore a white shirt, too. Thank goodness you thought to wear a bra. Is that one French, too?"

"Shut up," she sneers, rubbing napkins over her shirt to dry.

"Hmmm rubbing your tits again? Sorry, that's not going to work on me this time. I'm sober now," I say laughing until she punches me. I nudge her sideways and into the person next to her. Dani pulls my hair, steals my fruit gummies, and then things go horribly wrong.

Chapter 3

Dillon

My father walks in, shaking his head at us. "When I said I was fine with picking you up at the airport, I didn't mean I was fine with picking you up from security. Some things never change. The only difference is Shane isn't sitting here with you two knuckleheads. You're lucky they aren't pressing charges. You're both a mess, like two children."

"She started it," I say, earning a pointed glare from my father.

"All these years and you can't just let the past be the past. Well this is going to stop right here, right now. From this point forward, you are both going to work together."

I jump up in shock, "What?!"

My father holds his hand up at me. "I will explain when we get home. Now, both of you get your bags and come on. I don't want to hear a word out of either of you the whole way there." My father follows us out while picking at my hair. "Is that a... fruit gummy?"

"Yep, it was in retaliation for announcing to the whole plane that she needed a tampon. Don't make me tell you where she put the others." I adjust my pants as he nods and then shakes his head with a deep sigh.

We both climb into my father's truck, still silent and refusing to look at each other. "So, how was your trip?" my father asks, glancing at our disgusted expressions. "Oh, yeah. Well, welcome back. We can get you both settled in and then head over to the factory and go through …"

"I have a question. Why is she here?" I ask, pointing to Dani.

"Dillon, she is here to help. I would think you could be a little more appreciative of what she is doing for us."

"What is she doing for us? What exactly is she supposed to be doing other than getting me into trouble?"

"For your information, I am here to help you and your father get the factory back on track. I am here to help with the other areas of the business that you can't such as accounting, negotiating of expenditures, and …"

"Why are *you* here? We couldn't find someone else to do that stuff? And how the hell did you even find her?" I ask, frustrated and quickly realizing I stumbled upon something neither of them is wanting to tell me. I sit back, thinking over everything I know so far. My father called and said the factory has been losing money and he is having trouble getting it back to where it needs to be. But … then he said he thinks he may have to sell our longtime family business for next to nothing … to a jackass who wants to burn it down and build condos. "Your father is trying to steal my family's business?"

"I didn't know what business it was until someone I know told me that he was working on a deal in Thomasville for him. I called your father, and he told me you were flying back to help him get it back on track, and I offered to help, too."

"Oh! I bet your father loves that! No way in hell. Go home

Dani!"

"Why?! I can help you, Dillon. Your dad said you can use my help."

"We don't need your kind of help. For all I know, you're here to help steal the business. What was your plan? Get me into bed, soften me up so you can weasel your way into the books and really mess things up for us? Make sure you really stick it to us good? Forget it. I might've been swayed a little by your womanly ways when I was drunk, but I am not that fooled by you now. So you can just book a flight right back home and tell your father to move on to some other suckers."

"You slept together?" my father asks. I wave him off.

"I am not here for my father. I quit working for my father actually, asshole. I am here completely on my own. If you would stop being so damn stubborn, maybe you would realize that I can be an asset to you. I know how my father works, and I can help you beat him to the punch before he attacks."

"Oh, he is going to attack us now? How wonderful. I can't wait to punch him in his fat head."

"Dillon!" she yells at me.

"Go home, Dani! Go back to your boyfriend, get married, move into your daddy's mansion, have your little bratty kids, enjoy your rich, snooty friends, and leave us normal people alone."

"Dillon, Dani is here as my guest, not yours, and she will remain our guest until I say so," my father says to me forcefully. "Now, I expect you two to get along and work together; otherwise, I will send you both back home and sell the factory to the vagrant on the corner for an empty can."

"Dad, you can't be serious? She was the one that …"

"I'm the one that what? I'm the one that left? That's right, Dillon. I was seventeen, and I left you all alone with your parents and your hundred friends and family members. I left you to be with my father and no friends in a country where I didn't know anyone and didn't have anyone to talk to but my father's assistant and a hired educator."

"Ahhh, poor little rich girl," I say with fake tears.

"I'm thinking of having pasta for dinner tonight." As soon as I open my mouth, my father quickly speaks up again. "Probably should pick up some bread. What do you think? A spinach salad or …" He looks us over after pulling into the local grocery. "…I'll just see what they have already made." My father leaves us in the truck alone so we can pretend we are more interested in the people walking around outside than each other. To keep the peace, I don't say a word, not the rest of the way home or even through dinner. "Well this was fun with all the excitement. I think we should save the factory introduction for tomorrow. I am going to go upstairs and read for a little bit. You two are welcome to do whatever you want to do for the night. Dani, I made up the spare room for you."

"She's staying here?" My father gives me a dirty look. "Of course she's staying here. Why not? This is the place of my hell now." My father shakes his head and announces again that he is going upstairs to read and for us to figure it out quietly. I silently, but with many huffs and rolls of my eyes, help Dani clean up the kitchen. "I'm going to watch the game. You can watch it, too, or, I don't know … go away."

"Are you watching my team or yours?" she asks oddly.

I turn back to her and look her up and down. "That's not even funny. Don't tell me that you now like … nope, I cannot even say that horrific team's name. It's your father. He's the one that has completely messed up your head and turned you into a disgrace to the state of North Carolina." I say with a straight face, but she laughs hysterically.

"Are you serious? I can't believe you are still so ridiculous about this. You know I was originally a fan of … oh stop looking at me that way. I won't say their name if it offends you so much, but I don't see how it could be such a disgrace to the state when both teams play in the same state."

"Both teams reside here, but they both do not represent the state in a way this great state so deserves," I say clearly before going to watch my game. She comes in shortly after with that other team's name written across the chest of her t-shirt. "Take that off."

"Make me," she says, crossing her arms and sticking her chin out like she is daring me to a battle.

"I am not going to make you," I huff. "Now, act like an adult and respect my home. Take that horrible thing off."

"You're right. We are adults now, and I will respect your father's home and take it off," she says, taking her shirt off and sitting next to me in her bra. *I refuse to look at her. This is a great game. Yep …great game.* She sits back comfortably, and I accidently glance at her and notice her breasts. "Is there a problem?"

"Don't you have a boyfriend? Why are you trying so hard to

get a piece of me? If you need me to, I will try to tone down the masculinity a bit for you. I can't make any promises though."

"I have no interest in you whatsoever," she says, crossing her arms and turning to face the game.

"Liar." *It is actually a little hot.* I pull off my shirt. "So, do you like my new tat?" I say, pointing at my chest. "I got it right after I got this one on my arm," I say, flexing my arm to give her a better view. She never looks my way, which is fine, but I do need to stretch. I move my arms out and accidently knock her in the head. "Ooops. My bad."

"You want to start this? If so, you know I can finish it," she says, squinting her eyes forward as if she doesn't see me.

"You're such a brute. No, I am not wrestling a girl."

"Pussy." *That's it!* I grab her and put her on the floor, holding her down while she smacks me around.

"Ow, damn it. No biting." *Damn, she is strong.* We wrestle around the floor, and she is somehow able to jerk my sweats down to my knees. She laughs hysterically. "Why are you always trying to undress me? I told you. I'm not attracted to you sober." A smack to my head and I tie up her arms behind her back, but I can't get control of her legs, so we roll on the floor, twisting each other's clothes around to try and get leverage. When her boob pops out of her bra, I get distracted, and she briefly gains an upper hand on me.

"I was thinking that we should eat breakfast at Millie's tomorrow," my Dad says as he walks into the room and suddenly catches sight of us entangled and half-naked on his living room floor. "OH-kay. I think I am going to go watch the game upstairs."

My father makes a beeline towards his bedroom, and we don't see him the rest of the night.

Dani and I quickly put our clothes back on, sit on opposite sides of the room, and watch the game without looking at each other for the rest of the night.

Chapter 4

Dillon

Dani and I have little to say to each other this morning which, for some reason, my father finds humorous. He keeps smiling at both of us, asking how we feel this morning.

As we load into the truck to go to the factory, my father is still smiling. "Dad, last night we were only … we were wrestling, to which I was winning."

"You were not! I was on top and clearly had you pinned," Dani points out while I shake my head.

"You cheated. I was distracted by your bare breast in my face, and as much I can't stand you, I am still a guy. Boobs are boobs, especially bare, perky, full ones with great lickable nipples," I say as my father mumbles a wish to be somewhere else.

"Can you ever just admit that I have athletic ability, too? That I have qualities you can't match?"

"Okay, you have great tits. I, however, do not." I inhale, proud of myself. "You're welcome."

Before she can say a word, my father starts waving at people as we drive down the road. "Oh … do you remember when that use to be a Hardee's? I have no idea how they got that law office in there." My father points out as Dani burns holes into the side of my head. "I should probably talk to you both about last night. If you are going to continue to …wrestle, please do it behind closed doors. I have known Dani since she was a little girl, and I feel like she is my own daughter. I can't bear to see you guys wrestle anymore."

I laugh and turn towards her, "Yeah, try and keep your hands off of me." I wink at her, and she punches me in the arm. *Ow! Fuck, she is strong.* "Did you hurt your hand?" I ask, flexing my muscular arm and waiting until she growls in the opposite direction before rubbing my stinging arm.

My father sighs, "This is going to be a fun day." As we drive up to the factory, I am in shock. The place looks like it is one step away from being condemned. I glance at Dani who seems to be as much in shock as I am. "I know what you're thinking, but when your mother got sick, I didn't have time to be around much and, I might have trusted the wrong people to handle things while I was gone." My mother was sick for a long time before she died; it nearly destroyed my father and apparently the family business too. "I should have listened to Warren, but I thought the younger guy had some great ideas and was better for the position. I am really still not sure that it was completely his fault. I'm not sure what happened, yet."

"Clark Owens? Oh Dad, please tell me you didn't?"

"He had a degree and a lot of fancy ideas that could put the factory on top and help me retire sooner. Unfortunately, the police think he was using our shipping numbers to transfer drugs across state lines."

I stare at him, waiting for more, but he avoids me. "Dad? Did the police arrest him?"

"No."

"Did you fire him?"

"No."

I look over at Dani who I know won't dare ask him, so I am forced to ask the next question. I cough and ready myself. "Dad, where is Clark now?"

"He, well, he was killed." My jaw drops, "I came in early one morning and found him and a friend beaten to death near their cars, but I never found any drugs and neither did the police, so as far as we know, it was nothing more than a robbery. Except for the other evidence."

"What other evidence?"

"The money that is missing from the company's accounts seems to be in Clark's account."

"Great. Then we can get it back, right?"

My father groans, "Not exactly. We can't have access to anything until it is proven that it is the company's, and Clark's accounts are all frozen, pending the investigation into his death." I sit back, numb and ready to run all the way back to New York. We walk into the building, and I become even more depressed. I wish he had called me sooner. I wish I had known. There are few workers left, half the machines are broken, the computer system is slightly younger than myself, and my father has no ability to do much more work than a couple of hours before he gets tired. He sits down and asks if we want to take a break for a snack, which I do, but not because I'm tired.

I grab some peanut butter and crackers along with a water

while I watch him carefully, wondering what all he isn't telling me. "So, what else is going on? Or rather, what is it that you don't want to tell me and are simply hoping a miracle will happen so that I never find out?"

"What are you talking about?"

"Dad, you're winded after only walking a few feet. There is something wrong, and I know it, so tell me."

My dad fidgets and looks everywhere but me until I huff. "Fine, I might have had a small heart attack a couple of months ago."

"A heart attack? Dad! Why didn't you tell me?" I say, shocked.

"I didn't want to worry you. I knew you would put your life on hold and try to come down here to help me."

"Which is what I am doing now, after you told me to come down here to help you," I remind him.

"Well, things change," he replies, getting up to look through the snack machine and act like our conversation has ended.

"What things change?" I ask as he turns and looks towards Dani, who is talking with another employee about the day-to-day job functions. "Dani? You brought me back here because of Dani?"

"She offered to help, and after hearing that Taylor dumped you for that piano guy, I thought maybe…." I stand back, annoyed by this whole thing. "She still loves you; I know it. You know, I think her father forced her to stay away from you. I think he threatened her somehow. I don't think she would have stayed away from you otherwise. As soon as she asked about you, I knew it, I heard it in her voice. So, I told her you were coming back, and look, she came back too. Of course, then I had to ask you to come down here, which wasn't easy to do, but it's for the best, I promise you."

I shake my head, not believing I got duped into this. "You heard what in her voice exactly?"

He pats me on the back with a big smile, "That sound when you know someone is in love."

"She has a boyfriend, Dad."

"Yeah I know. Thomas Monroe, he is the one that her father sent here to buy the land, or rather, do everything he can to force us to sell. He is a real piece of work. You know she quit working for her father and is going to break up with Tommy boy here soon?"

"Good for her," I say, sitting down trying to figure out how to repair the family business.

"You're still holding a grudge, aren't you? You need to let that go. She is here to help us."

"Are you sure? I mean as sure as you were about Clark Owens?" I say.

"I was not in the right state of mind then. You know how sick your mother was. I wanted to be there for her, but now …"

"But now you want so bad to believe that Dani is perfect for me because Mom loved her like her own. You need to trust me, Dad, and let the past be the past. Let's move on and try to figure this out between us and us only. Please Dad, let me handle this. If you want Dani here, she can do something to help, but let's not show all our cards until we know for sure whose side she is on?"

"Fine, but you be nice, and you try to be patient and not be so quick to believe she is out to hurt you." I roll my eyes and nod. "Alright, so where do you want to start?"

"From the beginning, before Mom got sick."

I rub my face, realizing the uphill battle we have in front of us. Although, my father doesn't seem to be concerned about any of it, which is even more bothersome. He hums a happy tune through most of our day and constantly tries to get me and Dani to work together. I really don't understand his happiness. His business is nearly gone, his wife died, and he can barely function for more than couple of hours before getting tired. This is not the same man I once knew. At the end of the day, I decide to stay behind and continue working through all the paperwork. Almost everyone has gone home when Dani comes walking in. "What are you doing here? I sent you home with my dad hours ago."

"What were you going to do, walk back? I brought back the truck and some dinner for you. You do have to eat," Dani says, setting up an arrangement of food and drink in front of me that suddenly reminds me I haven't eaten in hours.

"Thank you, but I can call a cab or take the bus. Hell, I will probably be sleeping here for days before I can get through all this. So, you can go back, and I will see you tomorrow."

"Dillon, don't be so stubborn. Let me help you. I am more

capable of …"

"Oh, here we go! Yes, I know you went to some big name fancy school, and I went to college on a football scholarship, which obviously means I am an idiot."

"Oh calm down, jackass, I was only going to say I am more organized than you."

"You are not! You're a slob. Organized? You have never been organized in your life." She acts offended until I take her purse from her, open it up, and dive in to pull out a half-eaten already brown apple. "Saving this for later, are you? And don't get me started on your packing skills. Oh, and the guest room is already a disaster. Organized? Please, you are not," I say, waving the rotten apple at her. She takes it from my hand and manages to toss it in the trash can across the room. "Oh look! Your first attempt at cleaning and it's a success." I fan myself and my fake tears. "I am so proud."

She shoves against my chest. "Shut up and let me help you."

"No. Now go home."

"Why?!" She yells at me. I ignore her and go back to working. She grabs some papers, and I jump up and take them back. "You don't trust me?"

"Nope." I sit down, and she sits down across from me and pulls out a magazine and begins to read. "What are you doing?"

"Reading. If you don't want my help, that's fine with me. I will simply wait here until you're ready to ask for my help." She is so aggravating, but I can wait her out.

There is a stiff feeling in my body and a crick in my neck when I wake up, but she is still here and reviewing the paperwork I was going through. "What are you doing?"

"Finishing up what you started so we can get moving on other things, like these patents your father has."

"What patents?"

"The ones I found while you were asleep. The ones that could bring in enough money to save the company." I take them from her and look them over. "If you sell these, then you could potentially …"

"I'm not selling these. Why would I do that? These are what make this company. To sell them would destroy us."

"You don't have to sell them all, just a few and then…"

"No, I'm not doing it. What, did your father send you to get these, to sex me into selling them to some attorney that is a front for you and your father?"

"Would you stop? I am not out to get you and your father. I love your father. I have since I was a kid. I would never hurt him or you. Why won't you believe that?" she yells at me.

"Because you show up here to help us when it's your father that has been trying to destroy us. The father that you defended until he was able to take you out of the country and leave everyone you supposedly loved behind. Now, suddenly you are here to help us and go against you father? Sorry if I am a bit suspicious of your intentions."

She looks up at me with hurt-filled eyes. "You wait. You want me to prove I am here to help you and not my father? Then tell me what you need from me to do that? Tell me what I can do to help that you don't find intrusive. Do you want me to work the line? Sweep the floors? Stock the vending machines? What do you want from me Dillon?"

"Any of those are fine. Do whichever job you want. Apparently we have openings in all those areas. Although, I hear the pay really sucks, but no worries because the benefits are even worse," I say, looking down on her hard and not flinching.

"Okay, sounds wonderful," she says, but I know damn well that the little rich girl will never do any of that.

Chapter 5

Dani

I wake up early today so I can leave with Dillon, who has been purposely going into work early to force me to have to take the bus since there is only one running car for us to share. He finds it fun to watch me walk up the hill with my backpack filled with my work clothes and an umbrella that keeps getting pulled inside out in the wind. One day, I caught him waving at me from his office window as I tried to pick the rats nest out of my hair. Most normal women would tell him to go fuck himself and leave him to do this on his own, but I am not most women, or apparently normal either. Although I may be a complete fool, I am definitely up and ready before he is this morning. To keep him from sneaking out of the house without me, I take my breakfast with me and wait in the truck for him. I watch him bite into an apple as he walks happily up to the truck and opens the door.

"Good morning!" I say, wiggling my happiness in my seat while he looks at me in disgust. "Well, let's get this day going." He sighs, glaring at me from the corner of his eyes, and drives us to work without a word.

I know him better than he knows himself; this isn't over for him. At the end of the day he goes to bed smiling, which means he thinks he will get up even earlier tomorrow to throw me. I sneak into his room late at night and change his alarm. The fun I have watching him rush out of his room the next morning to get a shower is more gratifying than I would have expected; it's almost as enjoyable as when he walks back out of the bathroom with the makeup I painted on his face right after I changed his alarm.

"That is a lovely shade of lipstick, Dillon. I really think it's your color."

"This shit better come off, Dani," he says, slamming the door behind him as he goes back into the bathroom. The ride to work is so pleasurable today, especially since he couldn't get all the mascara off.

As we walk in, Dillon continues to wear his sunglasses while I smile at him, "Have a great day, Sunshine."

"Shut up," he says, walking away.

"Oh, hey, Dillon." He turns around, and I toss him some makeup remover. "Try this. It's the only way to get that kind of waterproof mascara off." He catches it and rushes to his office. I make my way to my locker, change into my work gear, and tie up my hair. With a deep sigh, I feel Gina's piercing eyes on me. "Is there something you want, Gina?"

"Nope, just trying to figure out why Dillon would ever be interested in a freckled face freak like you?"

"I see you have matured since high school."

"Oh, don't get upset. I am only playing with ya. I don't mean any harm. I know you guys are not really together, right?"

I turn to the nuisance with her newly-added, oversized double D's hanging out of her shirt and sigh, "What Dillon and I are to each other, or do with each other, is none of your damn business."

She laughs with a large smile. "You know, we can be friends if you want? I know we never got along in high school, but that was really your fault. Things have changed. We are both adults now and can move on."

"It wasn't my fault we didn't get along. It was yours because you kept trying to screw my boyfriend."

"Dillon has always been irresistible. He is even more so now," she moans, smiling wide at me. "Yes, he is surely an incredibly fuckable man. I am sorry, but he doesn't seem to care for you anymore. Making you work as a cleanup girl. That's just… sad. Hauling all of our trash out must be horrible for you. That is quite a step down for you, rich girl." She steps to me with tense arms, readying herself for a fight.

"Dillon and I get along fine. I am here to help him and his father, and I will do whatever is needed. It doesn't matter to me what that means. That's how friends are, Gina, they do things for each other even when it means having to get dirty." I take a step towards her, meeting her toe to toe. "Now, if you have a problem with me being here, then you can get the fuck over it because I am not intimidated by you or any of your so-called friends," I say, glancing at the three women standing up behind her. I take hold of my broom handle, back her away from me, and walk out of the locker room to start my day. As if my day couldn't start off any rougher, my father calls me for the eighth time in two days. I have been avoiding him, trying to decide what to say to him. But I guess I am not going to be able to hide my whereabouts from him much longer. I answer my phone and brace myself for the expected yelling.

"Danielle! Where are you and why haven't you returned any of my calls?"

"I told you Daddy. I am taking a vacation."

"A vacation? Where? Thomas said he hasn't seen you in days, and you won't tell him where you are either."

"Thomas and I are not really …"

"Now Danielle, I don't want to hear any more about you and Thomas not being right for each other. He is a wonderful young man with a bright future. You couldn't do much better. Now, you get back here and work things out with him, and let's get this wedding back on track," he yells as I squeeze myself as far into a dark corner of the warehouse as possible, hoping no one can hear him. My father has never shied away from telling me what I should do with my life; at one time, I listened to every word. I never doubted that he has my best interest at heart, but I wonder if he is the right person to tell me who I should marry considering he never married any of the women he has been with, not even my own mother. Love is not his expertise, and surprisingly, this is a fact that I have only recently taken notice of. "Danielle? Are you listening to me?"

"No, Daddy, I am not. Not anymore. I am doing what I want, and what I think I need to do."

"Where are you?" he asks calmly.

"You know where I am. I am sure Thomas has already told you that I am here with Dillon and his father, trying to help them."

"Danielle, I swear! You get back here right now, or you will not have a job to return to."

"I quit, Daddy, remember? And I already have a new job. Nice talking to you, Daddy. I'll catch up with you again soon." I hang up and step out of my corner to go back to work and run right into Dillon's chest. He doesn't say a word, but he does look me over with suspicion. I cock my head and sigh until he steps aside and lets me go on about my day.

I put my headphones on and work through the horrible job with the best attitude I can muster, and daydream of better times, hoping for some even better ones in the future. The job is exhausting and as hard as I try to prove to Dillon that I am here to help, he still doesn't believe me. I walk into his office to take out the trash, but he grabs it back and checks through the papers before handing it back. When he calls me back into his office, I get a brief moment of excitement until he hands me some food packages and thanks me for my great effort in taking out the trash. At break, I walk into the break room with my lunch and get ready to sit down, only to have my chair pulled out from underneath me. I fall on my ass to the great joy of Gina and her friends.

"Sorry, we don't allow the cleanup crew to sit anywhere near us. You understand, with all the disgusting germs and dirt and all you have to deal with. It is too gross to be near," Gina's friend, Missy, says. I am pushed away to a table in the far corner by myself.

No one will talk to me or have anything to do with me, so I eat and quickly go back to work. The next day is the same as the day before. With each day, I retreat further into my headphones and put everything else behind me. At the end of the day, I wait for Dillon by the door, and I don't bother saying a word when he shows up, ready to go.

He glances my way. "Anything exciting happen in the janitorial department today?" he asks jokingly. I hate this job. I hate that Dillon doesn't trust me. I hate working with these horrible women, and I hate the disgusting things they leave for me to clean up. Dillon stops and looks over at me with concern. "Are you okay?"

His concern is all it takes for me to remember why I am doing this and not anyone or anything is going to stop me. I made a mistake giving up once before, and I am not going to give up and lose him again. "No, nothing at all exciting happened today," I say, sinking into my car seat and waiting to get home and into bed.

Today, I watch as Mitch Black sits in Dillon's office, shaking his head and looking as if his world came to an end. Dillon looks even worse. I know the business is struggling, but I have a feeling it is much worse off than I even realize. When Mitch stands up yelling at Dillon and then walks out, he looks at me and turns back to Dillon. "And what about her? You let me go, but keep your girlfriend here? How perfect is that for you and your little whore?!"

Dillon rushes out from behind his desk and pushes me behind himself. "She has nothing to do with me needing to let you go, and you know it. Now leave before I call the police and have you escorted out," he says, facing off with Mitch and waiting for him to make a move. The tension is so high that I expect fists to be thrown any second, but somehow, Dillon stares him down enough to get him to walk away. Dillon waits to move from in front of me until Mitch leaves the building, and then he walks into his office and shuts the door. I follow him in and look him over. His dropped shoulders and red eyes say a lot about the stress he is feeling. "What do you need Dani?"

"Are you okay?" I ask.

"Yeah, I'm fine."

I walk over to him as he sits in his chair and looks at the wall. "You're going to do great things here." He glances my way but doesn't say a word as he looks back at the wall. I lean over, wrap my arms around his neck, and kiss his cheek. "I know you can do it. You can make this place a success, Dillon. I believe in you, and you should, too." He grips my hand and let's go again. I walk away and smile at him when he looks my way with a smile, and suddenly, my knees go weak and my heart begins to beat rapidly.

Dillon Conrad: the boy that I have known since forever, it seems, and have been in love with just as long. He and Shane were my best friends from the first day I moved into this town and remained so until I left. Dillon, however, has been the one. My one, but not that he always felt the same about me. I was the freckled-face tomboy that he thought more of as his friend than ever as his girlfriend. That is, until Lucas Charles noticed me as more than just a girl he knew.

It was the summer before my junior year, and the boys had

been away at football camp. I was so lonely and bored without them that my mother decided to take me on a girls' weekend. I had my hair and nails done and even got some new clothes. In one weekend, I had become a girl, finally, at sixteen. With my boobs coming in and my body doing things I never thought possible, my mother decided it was time I looked more like the woman I was becoming. I returned home and was so anxious to see Dillon and Shane that I drove up to the school to wait for their buses to come in. There were many girlfriends there, most of them were actual girlfriends and not simply friends as I was:

When their buses pull in, I jump up out of my car and wait to see them, or rather wait to see Dillon get off of the bus before calling out to them. "Dillon! Shane!" I yell until they turn around and spot me.

Shane runs over and hugs me while Dillon's expression seems dazed. He walks behind Shane and looks me up and down before being able to say anything. The way he looks at me makes my whole body shiver and weak. "Hey Dani," he says, hugging me and seeming to breathe in my new perfume.

Before I can say a word, Amanda screams out and comes running over. "Dillon, my baby, I missed you," she says, jumping on him and kissing him.

"Hey, how are you?" he says back to her with a sweet smile and a glance my way. I didn't know they were back together. I thought they broke up at the last summer party. I glance at Shane who looks at me sympathetically.

"Conrad, you dope, you forgot to sign up for our charity event," Lucas Charles, the quarterback and captain of the football team, says, smacking Dillon in the head with a pad of paper. "We have to have everyone participate, you know that," he says before looking over at me. "Dani?" I smile at him, and he looks me over carefully. "Damn, the summer has done you well." Lucas

pushes past Dillon and Shane and takes hold of my hand. I have never been
that girl that guys push past to get to. I have never been the girlfriend type, but
when Lucas takes my hand, I gush like any other teenage girl. He is, after all,
the quarterback of the football team and just as dreamy as Dillon, but he is
standing in front of me, flirting, while Dillon has his arm around another girl.
"So, are you seeing anyone now?"

I shake my head. "No, why?" Lucas looks me over with a huge smile.
"Well then, do you want to go out with me?" Amanda begins oohing and
ahhing with laughter, which distracts me, until I see Dillon staring daggers at
Lucas. "Come on, please. I promise we will have a great time."

"Okay, I would love to," I say.

"Great, I'll call you later then, cutie," he says, winking at me before
grabbing the signup sheet back from Dillon. "I'll see you guys at practice,"
Lucas says, walking away.

"Wow, Lucas Charles, Mr. Quarterback. Nice catch, Dani," Shane
says, smacking my hand and making me feel good, for a minute. I look back at
Dillon, who now has Amanda all over him and her tongue down his throat.
Shane lets out a deep frustrated sigh as he puts his arm around my shoulders.
"Oh gross. Come on, Dillon is leaving with the leech, so we might as well go."
We leave Dillon with Amanda. It is really disgusting, so I have no problem
leaving that behind, but before we get too far Dillon quickly says goodbye to
Amanda and runs to catch up with us.

"Did you guys forget about me?"

"I thought you were leaving with Amanda? That was why she came
wasn't it?" Shane asks.

"I don't know. So, what is going on with Lucas?" Dillon asks, grabbing
my arm to get my attention.

"I don't know. He seems to like me, so I am going out with him."

"Why?" he asks, seemingly confused by the idea that a boy might actually be interested in me.

"What do you mean 'why'?"

"You don't date, Dani."

"Well, I do now, Dillon!" I yell at him before getting in the car and slamming my door. Shane gets into the back seat while Dillon slides into the seat next to me. No one says a word all the way home, and I don't feel like discussing it any further. My good mood was suddenly screwed up by his bad mood. Shane jumps out and waves goodbye as he dashes across the street to his house. I get out and try to ignore Dillon who continues to sit in my car. "Get out of my car, Dillon, and go home."

"No, I want to talk to you," he says. I ignore him and walk to my back door. "Dani! Get over here and talk to me," he yells.

"Don't yell at me. If you want to talk to me, you come to me and talk to me respectfully."

"Fine!" He slams the car door shut and curses under his breath before approaching me. "Dani, will you please talk to me?" I turn to him and cross my arms, which seems to piss him off even more. "You know, if you want to go out with dumbass Lucas, I don't care. I hope you two are very happy together and get married and have a ton of kids."

"Is that what you want with Amanda?"

"Who?" he says before realizing, "Oh, no, she and I are just …I don't know." He stomps around. "What happened to you? You're all … girly." I don't say a word as he bickers with himself walking in a circle between me and his own home. "You know what, I don't care, but if he makes you cry, I swear I will kick his ass!" he yells with assurance before going home and leaving me

with a huge smile.

Dillon and Lucas's friendship slowly changed after that day and only worsened when I broke up with Lucas to be with Dillon.

I walk out of the factory to take a call from Thomas, only to run into Thomas's chest. "Ah, so you are here. Is there a reason I have to play detective to track down my own girlfriend?" he asks me.

"I told you I needed a break and that I wanted some space," I say, surprised to see him. I was hoping I would have a little more time before he came searching for me here. I guess I shouldn't be surprised that my father's principal minion would be following me so closely.

"Oh, I heard you. I just didn't realize you meant that you were going to take a break and come down here and try and sabotage my work. Did I do something to make you hate me? Why are you purposely trying to demolish our relationship?"

"I don't hate you."

"Then why are you here, Danielle?"

"Don't call me that. You know I don't like it."

He throws up his arms. "I don't know what you want from me!" He takes hold of my arm and pulls me to him. "I want you to go get your things and come with me. Let's get whatever this is worked out for good. I'm tired of this, Dani. I don't know why you are doing this."

"Is everything okay here, Dani?" Dillon's father asks as he walks into work.

"Yes, sir. Ummm, Thomas, you know Matthew Conrad, don't you?"

"Yes, how are you?" Thomas says, shaking Matt's hand.

"Good, and yourself?"

"Great, I'm only trying to get my girlfriend to explain why she is here?" Matt looks over at me. "Dani, go get your things and let's go, please."

"I have work to do, Thomas. We can talk about it later," I say, which angers him greatly.

"How 'bout lunch?" Matt asks. "Let's all go to lunch. I bet we can get this figured out and have a nice discussion between us all. Okay, Tom?"

"Thomas."

"Right, okay. Well, we will see you at the restaurant down the street there, at around noon, what d'ya say?" Matt asks, guiding Thomas back out to the parking lot. Thomas nods, looking my way before leaving in a new Mercedes that I am sure my father helped him get.

"Thank you, Matt."

"No problem, Dear. Now, let's see what Dillon is up to for lunch. It's about time those two meet, don't you think?" I shake my head but realize he isn't going to listen when I see him turn to go straight to Dillon's office. *Oh no.*

Chapter 6

Dillon

I got the financials in order and though we barely have enough to keep going, we do have enough. Now we need to get the factory moving and get product out the door. I have been working with Warren, my father's right-hand man, closely and making sure my father has little to worry about. Hopefully, he can spend more time resting, not that he stays completely out of the way. He frequently stops by and tries to help out. I let him, of course, because it makes him happy, but I don't give him any information other than the good news. When I know he has come in for the day, I stand at the window of the office overlooking everything and watch him. Mr. Smooth, as always, likes to talk to everyone, especially Dani today. I assume he is up to something. He is so determined to get us back together. I finally had to tell her she needs to find someplace else to stay. It simply isn't comfortable having her in the house. She wasn't happy with my request, but she agreed to find a new place within two weeks.

My father walks into the office with a smile. "Things look very good today." I smile back at him before walking to my desk to start working again. "So, for lunch today, I was thinking something a little nicer. Maybe the nice French eatery down the street?"

"The French eatery? So Dani is going with us, huh? So glad you asked her before asking me. I think I will pass today, Dad."

"Okay, but I'm going to hate feeling like the third wheel. I am sure I will have fun messing with this Thomas guy, as he swoons over Dani, but not nearly as much without you."

I push my chair away from the desk and fold my hands in front of me. "Her boyfriend's here?"

"Yep, here and determined to convince her to go back to Chicago with him," he says, sitting down and putting his feet up on my desk. I roll my eyes. "Are you sure you don't want to come?"

I slide into my desk and start back where I left off. "Yep, I have a lot of work to get done." My father nods, smiling as if he doesn't believe me. Every time I look over at him, he looks up and smiles. It is irritating. "I told you I don't care what she does. Let her leave. I would prefer it." He nods with no words and goes back down to the floor to help out design. I really don't care, but I can't seem to get anything done since he told me. *So what if she leaves. I don't care if he is here, but she better not think, for one second, of inviting him to stay at our house. Oh, I bet she does. I bet she invites that loser to our house and then tries to sleep with him right in front of me. I'm not allowing it. I won't even allow him on our doorstep, and if he has a problem with it, then he can talk to me. He probably is some rich, tight-ass, dweeb her father approves of. I don't care. I'm just going to do my work and let her go on her way with dweeble. Haha! Dweeble.* I laugh to myself until I feel something odd, someone watching me. I turn slowly, and then I see it right in my face. "GEES … what the fuck!" Warren stands inches away, looking down at me with his beady eyes and stained beard. The man never smiles, and he looks like something they dragged out of Freddy's basement. He always wears a flannel shirt over a ratty t-shirt and Sears's jeans with work boots. He never, ever, smiles and barely speaks anything more than a grunt. "Hi Warren. I just love when you sneak up on me and scare the shit out of me like that. It's just loads of fun." His supposed happy snarl slowly turns to something less pleasing. "Is that a new flannel shirt? It looks great on you, the brown really brings out the color in your … teeth." He growls at me, forcing me to lean away. "I meant your eyes." *Your beady little eyes.*

He grunts and holds out reports from the factory floor for me. "Here," he says as if his voice is grinding out the words across a jagged saw.

I take them and wipe the dirt from his fingers off of the reports with as pleasing a smile as I can. "Thank you." He grunts back and walks out. "Heeerrrre," I mock him in private. I get up and look out at the factory window to make sure he is gone back to his area. Instead, I notice Dani getting shoved into a wall by Gina. I wait to see if she does anything back, but she continues on with cleaning and taking Gina's trash as the girls in the area laugh. "Why are you doing this to yourself, Dani?" I watch her continue with her work with her headphones on and her mind clearly somewhere other than on the women who are teasing her. Some things never change. When Dani sets her mind on something, there's no changing it.

My high school girlfriend, Amanda, was confident, captain of the cheerleaders, and a total bitch. Nonetheless, she was hot, or so I thought until I got back from football camp and Dani showed up looking like a dream. My perfect dream. I always thought she was beautiful, but she was my friend, and I would never think of looking at her any differently, but that day changed everything. The moment I saw her, my knees nearly gave out from underneath me, and I instantly stopped breathing. What made it worse was Lucas Charles being all over her the moment he saw her too. He barely had anything to do with her growing up, but suddenly, she wears a skirt, and he's all over her. Every time I saw them together, I wanted to jerk him off of her and punch him, and Amanda knew it. Every party and every place we went, Lucas and Dani were there together, and I paid more attention to them than I did to her. Amanda took it upon herself to do all she could to torment Dani. Dani never knew why until I finally confessed that I cared more for her than any other girl I knew.

As soon as Dani moved in, mine and Shane's little group grew to three. The three of us go everywhere together, we are always in the same classes and are always looking out for each other. The best of friends and nothing but friends. Dani is a girl, but she is our friend, and Shane and I don't see her as anything more than that. Our friendship remained the same for years. By the time we are sophomores in high school, I feel like my life is perfect. I am first string tight end, and I am dating the prettiest cheerleader in the school, Amanda Karl. She is so hot, when she isn't annoying me.

One day while I am joking around with the guys at lunch, Amanda approaches with her hands on her hips until I go sit with her at the couples table where we talk about all the couple things we are all going to do together. I barely pay attention or care when Dani comes in. I wave her over to come talk to me, so she sits next to me, eating her lunch and laughing about things that happened in class. I am so excited to have someone to talk to about normal things that I don't notice Amanda staring a hole into the back of my head. Dani looks over my shoulder and nudges me until I turn to see everyone at the table staring at me.

"You know, Dani, maybe you should find a boyfriend of your own," Amanda says to her.

"We are only talking," I say to her. Amanda huffs. "What is wrong with you? Dani is just my friend, not like anything would ever happen with her. She is, and always will be, just my friend," I say, but Dani leaves before anything else can be said. Amanda never quite warmed up to Dani, not that Dani ever cared for Amanda either. It took most of that school year before the two said more than two words to each other. Then Lucas came in and took my friend away, and I hated him for it. I couldn't think of anything other than him being with my friend, my Dani.

I cringe every second I see them together. They stayed together through the summer and on into our junior year. Still … it bothers me. I stopped dating Amanda and started dating Nicole, but Lucas and Dani stayed together. They go to every event together and spend their every birthday right next to each other, leaving no space for anyone else. The longevity of their relationship outlasts all of mine. I break up with one girl and start dating another, searching for someone that doesn't annoy me. Gina, Lucas's sister, has somehow made her way into my bedroom tonight.

Her parents never care what she does. I am waiting for her to be quiet, or preferably leave, so I can go to sleep, but when I see Lucas drop Dani off a little earlier than usual, I sit up, watching.

Gina climbs over my back and notices Dani coming home, too. "Oh, time for the exchange, huh?"

I turn towards her with a questioning expression, "What are you talking about?"

"Oh please. You must know? Everyone knows." I shake my head. "He's been doing it to her forever, not that I blame him. I mean, if she is going to be frigid, what else is he supposed to do?"

"Doing what to her?"

"Screwing around on her. He calls it 'the exchange'. He drops Dani off and then goes and meets up with another girl. It's usually one of the sophomores trying to get the popular quarterback's attention in hopes that he will dump Dani for them. Never happens, and they give it up too quickly." She laughs before noticing my expression. "What's wrong with you?"

"He's cheating on her. All this time he is supposed to be this perfect boyfriend and …"

"And he has developed the perfect, athletic, smart, beautifully rich girlfriend for all the papers and for his family to be proud of. If she would just screw him already, he might be more faithful. I know I would do anything you wanted me to, to keep you from getting away," she hums, kissing on my neck and trying to get me excited all over again, but something has me distracted.

I want to tell Dani what I know, but I know she won't believe me. She will only think I am saying it on purpose to prove that Lucas is the jackass I have always claimed him to be.

I spend my Saturday morning running, only to return to see Dani's mother leaving for what seems to be a long trip. I run up to her door and check to see if she is still home. She opens the door in shorts and a tank. I know she thinks it's relaxed and not much to talk about, but I think the outfit looks incredible. I have seen it many times from my window when she waves to me at night. She drives me crazy, so much so that I stumble over my words at first.

"Your mother ... she left ..."

"Good job, Dillon. Yes, that is the definition of leaving. Now, can you tell me what I am doing now?" she says, walking away but leaving her door open for me to come in.

I walk in and shut the door behind me. *"That's funny, real funny. I didn't see you running this morning."*

Dani crashes onto the couch with a box of cereal that she is eating dry. *"I know. I didn't feel like it this morning. I did enough at soccer practice anyway."*

I scoot in next to her and take some cereal too after she hands me the box to do so. *"Alright, so tell me what's wrong?"*

"What? Nothing's wrong," she replies.

"Don't lie to me. I know when something is bothering you," I say, hoping she realizes Lucas is cheating on her so I can bring up how good I have been about keeping quiet about it ... since last night when I first found out. Dani looks down and curls over herself with a huff. I lean over trying to look into her eyes, but she avoids me. *"Tell me what's wrong. It can't be that bad. You know I won't tell anyone."* I begin to think she does know and doesn't want to confess that I was right about Lucas all along, *"Tell me, and I promise I won't make any smartass comments, just straight your-friend-Dillon's best advice."* She glances my way. *"I promise."*

"Okay, but don't judge me." I cock my head and huff as she turns to face me. *"Well, it's not like you would understand. I mean after all with the new slut, and all the other sluts that have been in your life lately, I am sure you get laid what ...most every day now?"*

"No! Not every day, not with her anyway. The new slut has cheerleading practice that runs late sometimes, and I don't like to have to wait for her, so I

go find someone else to ..." I laugh.

"Oh, good for you. You know all those times you complained about Lucas to me and you turned into exactly what you accused him of being." I want to say something to her so badly right now. "Anyway, I don't care about all that right now. I want to know about the girls you have been with." I look at her oddly. "No, not because I am interested in them. I just want to know what they did that you liked and didn't like."

"What the hell are you talking about?" I ask, scooting to the edge of the couch.

Dani sits back and sighs. "I have never had sex, and Lucas really wants to. I thought, with my mother gone this weekend, that he and I ..."

"What?!"

"Don't make fun of me! There are a lot of girls that have never done it."

"That's not what I am talking about. I can't believe you want to know what to do so ...so ...so you can do it with him!"

"We have been together for a long time. He loves me."

"Bullshit!" I yell, receiving a hardened glare in return. "Get a clue, Dani. You really think Lucas has waited all this time for you?" Her expression plummets, and I instantly regret my words, but before I can apologize, she kicks me out of her house and won't return my calls. She spends the entire next day boarded up in her house, not even a light coming on when the sun goes down. I wait as long as I can before taking the key her mother gave us and letting myself in. "Dani? It's me... Dillon! I only want to make sure you are okay." I slowly move through the dark house and then up the stairs to her room where I have never been before, and it feels odd to do so now. I knock on her door. "Dani?"

"Go away, Dillon," she says with a sad voice.

"No. Not until you talk to me." I knock again, "Let me in, Dani. Listen. I'm sorry, but I was afraid you would make a huge mistake."

Dani swings the door open suddenly. "Don't worry about it. I decided to call Lucas anyway and just get it over with. Maybe if I start letting him, then he …" I look her over, realizing she is all done up and ready for this crazy idea.

"Are you stupid or something?" I grab hold of her and push her back into her room. "Call him back and tell him to forget it! He doesn't deserve you."

"But Dillon, he is the best thing that has ever happened to me and what will people say? I will never be able to get another boyfriend."

"Dani, you're beautiful. Any guy would love to be your boyfriend. I could barely speak when you opened the door. You're smart and fun and athletic and … hot." I look down into her eyes. "You are the perfect girlfriend. You are … simply… perfect." Dani leans into me and something in the moment causes me to gulp.

"You think I'm perfect?"

"I have always thought you were perfect," I say, feeling the need to take a deep breath.

"Then why haven't you ever asked me out?"

I look around the room, fidgeting, before looking back at her again. "Because you're too perfect for me, I guess. I don't know," I mumble. "Everything is so confusing when it comes to you, and I don't know why. It didn't use to be this way, and then … then you went and got breasts and stuff," I say, waving my hand up and down her body.

Dani nods with a girlish giggle, which confuses me more. "I'm sorry, Dillon. I didn't mean to become a girl on you."

"I guess ... it's alright. There's not much you can do about it now." She shakes her head. "Why do you want to have sex with Lucas? Even after everything you know?"

"Because I thought maybe, if I get it over with, then I would finally feel what I should for Lucas and stop thinking about..." She tears up and falls against my chest, allowing me to comfort her within my arms.

"Don't cry. You know I can't stand to see you cry. Don't worry about Lucas. I will take care of him. And, don't worry about what others will say either. I'll stand by you every minute you need me to." Her head turns slightly against mine, and I want so badly to kiss her, but she's my best friend. My whole body begins to feel oddly wonderful when I feel her lips right next to mine. I stroke her cheek and take hold of her waist, pulling her in closer to me as I pass my lips against hers. The feeling rushing through me weakens me all over, but it doesn't keep me from kissing her deep. She returns every motion I make with an equally wonderful touch of my body. I follow her into her bed, feeling her and kissing her until my mouth gets tired. And then, we hear the door. We both stop and stare at each other wide-eyed. "Oh shit, Lucas!"

"Oh no! I forgot. I need to talk to him, but you can't be here when I do."

"Where the hell do you want me to go?"

"Hide in my parent's room until I bring him into my room and then sneak back to your house."

I laugh, "I don't think so. I'm not leaving you here alone with him, especially not in your damn room. And put something on! You are not appropriately dressed for a young woman." She rolls her eyes and slides into some sweats. "That's better."

"Good, now stay here."

"What if your conversation takes a while, and I get hungry?" She turns back and huffs at me. *"I was only asking?"* I shrug.

As soon as she leaves, I cower at the corner of the stairs to listen to their conversation.

"Okay, Dani, what's going on? You got me over here thinking you wanted to do this and now you seem almost shocked to see me. I bought flowers and … well you know."

"I found out something today, and I thought, maybe if we had sex, it would change things between us, but I realized that it's not going to change anything except make me just as foolish as all those other girls you're sleeping with behind my back."

"Dani, I promise you …"

"Don't deny it, Lucas. I have known for a while. I just chose to ignore it. I see it in their eyes when they try to talk to you and you ignore them like they are nothing. I don't want that to happen to me."

"I would never do that to you. Dani I… I know it's going to sound ridiculous considering, but I do love you. Those girls, they corner me and say things and they leave dirty notes for me, and they make it so easy."

"They make it easy to cheat on me, which won't change if we have sex."

"Maybe not, but I will change."

"Why Lucas? Why? Because it won't be so easy to do anymore? It's not going to change. We both know that. This is not going to work out. I think we both need to move on while we can still be friends," Dani says. I peek around the corner to see him looking as if he is going to cry. She hugs him while he silently begs her to forgive him and give him another chance. He stays for two hours while she nurses his emotions to a manageable level. I fall asleep waiting for him to leave.

"Hey handsome, shouldn't you be home by now?"

I open one eye and look at her. "I would have, but I had to wait through the crying and begging. Gees, he was pathetic"

"He wasn't pathetic. He was genuine, and I feel horrible, which really pisses me off because he was cheating on me." She shakes her head, walking into her room, and I follow while taking off my shirt. "What are you doing?"

"I can't go home now and risk waking my parents up. They will ask where I have been. Mine aren't as lenient as Lucas's." She puts her hands on her hips. "Come on, Dani. I'm tired. I don't feel like trying to find some other place to go now." I smile, take hold of her waist, and drag her into her bed. "We can kiss until we fall asleep." I wrap the blankets around us so she will have no choice but to let me stay.

"Fine, you can stay, but you can't tell anyone about this. I just broke up with my boyfriend."

"No kidding! That's a coincidence, I'm single too." I pull her in close. "Maybe we could go out together? And be together?" She lays her head on my chest, and I wonder if her heart is beating as rapidly as mine is. "If you want to."

Dani leans up and kisses me with a blushing smile. "Okay."

I smile wide. "Yeah, I mean, someone needs to be there for you after your crushing breakup and who better than me?"

"I can't think of anyone better," she says.

We stayed up most of that night kissing and talking. I woke up the next morning with her in my arms, which I had never done with a girl before and never wanted to do with any other but her, from that point on. A promise I made to myself that hasn't always been easy to keep, so whenever I spent the night with any woman, I always turned away from her after she fell asleep, and then I fell asleep dreaming of Dani. No matter how much I liked any woman, no matter how hard I tried, none of them could erase the memory of her or the promise I made.

I smile fondly until I feel the breeze of my office door open. Dani walks in with a tall, suit-dressed man behind her. "Dillon, I want you to meet my boyfriend, Thomas Monroe." I promptly stand and look him over as he does me.

"Nice to meet you, Dillon," he says, holding his hand out to me.

I look at it and ignore it. "Yeah, aren't you the one that is trying to steal my father's business?"

"I assure you, it's nothing personal. I am only doing my job. In fact, I would love to get together and discuss the opportunities I could offer you for the land."

I step back from Tommy boy before I punch him. "It's nothing personal to you, but I promise you, it's all personal to me."

"Dillon, he's not here to argue. We simply wanted to invite you and your father to lunch," Dani says.

Tom puts his arm around Dani's shoulder. "Yes, I promise. I have no ill will towards you or your family. My girl here tells me so many great things about your father and …your family. I would love to get to know you more, and maybe I can help get you more of what you want for this place, if I understand your needs better."

I laugh. "Oh, you do? That's wonderful. No thanks." *Asshole. Damn, I want to kick you in your face so bad.*

"Your choice. I can't say I blame you, but I do plan on being here for as long as Dani plans on staying. I am actually looking for a place for us to live for the short time we plan to be here."

"You're moving in with him?" I ask her.

"Well, it's a temporary situation, but I do hope to make it permanent eventually. I prefer some place in the city where we can make a nice home together." I watch Dani as he speaks, but she never bothers to look at me.

"Good for you. Good for you both. Have a nice lunch."

They both nod and head out the door, but Tommy turns around and comes back in, shutting the door behind him. "Oh, and just so you know, I understand what happened between you and Dani, and I hope there are no hard feelings. I mean, I hope you're not shutting her and me out of helping you fully because of what happened?"

"Excuse me?" I ask.

"We broke up briefly when she first came down here, and I know she used you to try and get over me. I'm sorry about that, but we had a big argument and both said some things we regret. Nonetheless, in the end, we are meant to be, and she realizes who the better man is … for her, I mean. I am sure you understand. In fact, I am sure the right woman, or man, is out there somewhere for you, whichever you prefer. I don't judge." He laughs as if he is explaining something that should be easily understandable to anyone that hears his bullshit.

I look down, shaking my head. "She told you we had sex?" He nods. "She told you we fucked over and over? During which she never mentioned you once, but I did hear my name many times," I share happily.

"Yes, but then she came back to me." He smiles. "Better luck next time, Champ."

"Yeah, next time. You better believe I will for sure let you know the next time I have sex with Dani. But really, since she is still living with me and able to fuck me whenever she needs, then she is obviously not fucking you. So is that really her going back to you? If it is, then I am not feeling much of a loss here ... Champ," I laugh, mimicking his previous enjoyment. "Ah... I'm just kidding, Tommy. You know what? I think I will go to lunch with you guys." I close up and walk out with my new pal Tommy and his girl Dani with my father tagging along for his own amusement.

The French eatery seems nice, nicer than I have been to in a while. I watch as Tommy boy opens the door for Dani and pulls out her chair for her. The perfect gentleman also asked her to change her clothes and brush her out before leaving with him for lunch because he didn't want to be embarrassed by her appearance. *I think I am falling in love with him already.* We all sit down together, and I can't wait to get started. "So Tommy, why are you trying to steal my father's business?"

He sighs and leans in. "First off, it's Thomas. And secondly, I believe your father's business ... no disrespect ... has run its course. Mr. Portman has made countless reasonable offers. I think you should actually consider them and allow your father to retire so you can return to New York and do whatever it is you were doing or not doing. I don't know. Did you have a job?"

"The offers were bullshit, and we both know it, *Tommy*. You would force my father to live on social security for the rest of his life, and we both know how well that works for people," I say, sitting back and preparing to take on whatever this prick has in store for me.

"It is sometimes better to get out free and clear than worry about coming out ahead. You never know when you could end up coming out far behind and deep in debt," Tommy says, stopping to call the waitress over and give his order.

"I prefer to stay in and build something that will last a long time to come. Like my family before me."

"Your funeral, Champ," Tommy says, leaning back and putting his arm on the back of Dani's chair. Dani glances up at me, but she is doing her best to bury her head into her menu.

"We'll see, Tommy," I say, eyeing him and taking note of all his flaws for future reference. Dani changes the subject and engages my father into a talk about old times and explaining to Tommy about how he helped her when she fell off her bike once. "So, Tommy, ever play any sports?" Dani rolls her eyes.

"I have actually. I was captain of my university's badminton team," he says proudly.

"Badminton? No I said, 'sp…ort…sss'."

"I believe it is a sport. It is quite intense and requires as much skill and agility as football."

I laugh out loud. "It does? So you chase after that thing with your racket and then you have a 300-pound linebacker jump on you? Is that how it works? Because, otherwise, you're just running around after a little birdie."

"It's called a shuttlecock," Tommy smugly corrects me.

"Oh, well … that's much better," I laugh, straightening my posture with apologies. "I'm sorry. Seriously, I am. So, do you spend a lot of time chasing after cock?" I ask.

"I don't intend to indulge your disgusting attitude any longer. If you would like to talk like gentlemen, we can, but otherwise, I would prefer you not speak to me at all," he says.

"Okay, so Dani, is Tommy's dick really as small as you said it was?" I lean forward smiling. "I don't believe it myself. No one's penis can possibly be that small."

"Dillon, please, try and be nice. Thomas is here as a friend, not to start a war of words with you," Dani replies.

"Something I assure you that you could not win with me," Thomas retorts, crossing his legs with his chest out and his head sitting high above his shoulders. "However, if you would like to try, I am more than willing to go toe to toe with you."

"But I thought I wasn't allowed to speak to you anymore, Tommy?" I ask, receiving a frustrated sigh in response. "So, does that mean I win this battle? Wow that was easy! Must have been all that cock hitting you in the head and causing some brain damage." My father spits his drink across the table and has to hide his mouth to keep from laughing out loud.

Tommy stands up and leans over the table at me with flaring nostrils. "I will have you know I was a champion debater, and I also studied the art of Shotokan."

"Oh really, well I studied the art of …Fuck You!" I yell, standing and meeting him face to face.

My father quickly takes hold of my arm and pulls me back. "Okay, maybe this was a bad idea. Let's get our food to go and end this before it gets any worse. Nice to see you again…" Before my father extends his hand fully to shake Thomas's, he quickly pulls his hand back. "…oh forget it. I think you're a real prick, Tommy. Sorry I was never that good at proper manners. That was Dillon's mother, but thank you for lunch. I will see you later, Dani." Dani nods, seemingly pleading with me to calm down, but all I can see is red. My father grabs our food and leaves Tommy boy with the bill.

Lunch was fun, for me at least. By the time the day ends, I go home and enjoy walking around Dani with a smile. "What's your problem?"

"Nothing, but I did really enjoy meeting Tommy boy today. He's simply dreamy," I tremble, giggling.

"Thomas is a very successful attorney and negotiator. He has worked for my father ever since he passed the bar. He is also handsome, and he doesn't have a small penis either. And …" She stops, preparing her dinner and looks around for my father before leaning in towards me, "And he is very good in bed," she whispers to me.

I shake my head. "No he isn't," I say confidently.

"Yes he is!"

I move away from the counter with a handful of grapes and lean down to whisper in her ear, "No, he isn't. I bet he counts the number of times he hip thrusts into you …" I motion with my hips and she smacks me hard on the arm.

"Dillon!"

"What, he doesn't? Come on, don't lie …" She shakes her head with an angry stare. "1…2…3 ohhhhhh." She quickly hides her mouth and turns away from me. I walk back over to her, trying to get her to look at me. "He does, doesn't he? Oh shit! I was just kidding."

She turns back around, "No, he doesn't do that. He is perfectly normal."

"Sure he is, all 3 seconds of him." She shakes her head, biting her bottom lip to keep from laughing. "Not like me at all, right?" She turns away and goes back to making dinner. I lean over her shoulder, pressing my body against hers, feeling her tense and her breathing slow. I take hold of her arms and rub my hips against her ass as I lean down and then bump her, "1…2…3, ohh Dani."

"You son of a bitch!" she yells, chasing me through the house. We both laugh and enjoy the chase until she chases me into my room and jumps on top of me. I fall back into my bed, looking her over as she looks around the room, trying to figure out what to do next. I wrap my arm around her, turn her back to my bed, and breathe slowly up her body until I look into her eyes. My cock is getting hard and my desire for her is heating up. She touches my face with her hand, so I turn and kiss her palm. "Dillon," she sighs. I rub my face against her hand, enjoying her fingers touching my

Jennifer Loren

cheek, my eyes, and down to my lips. I lean down to get to her lips, and she stops me. "I can't Dillon. I am with Thomas now, and you're only doing this to get at him." She crawls out from under me and goes back to the kitchen to finish her dinner while I nurse my ego.

Chapter 7

Dillon

3:00 in the morning, and my cell is blaring. I frantically search for it while trying to rub my eyes open. The number on the phone is Warren's, so I answer it a little annoyed, "What? What is it?" I ask, not understanding why anyone would be calling me this early, especially him.

"You need to get down here now." Warren says in his usual, mundane, rugged voice, providing no clue as to the level of seriousness of what is going on.

I quickly get dressed and head out to the factory only to pull up to fire trucks and police cars. "Oh this is not good." I slowly walk inside and find Warren waiting for me with his arms crossed. "What happened?" He waves me to follow him and takes me to the back storage where I find a broken window and a charred area of the wall where we stacked our new inventory.

"They sent the fire ball through that window," Warren explains while pointing at the broken window.

"How did they know that we stacked the new inventory there? The windows are over fifteen feet above the floor. They couldn't possibly have looked inside. Most everyone had left already when I had a few guys help me bring it in and set it up today."

"They knew somehow. It's someone from here. I don't know who, but I have been smelling something rotten, so I have been sleeping here, waiting for them to act. As soon as I heard a car, I got up and watched them with my shotgun. Damn bastards got away before I could shoot one of 'em. If I hadn't had to take care of the fire, I swear to ya ...I ...I would of and you know it," he says, waving his finger in my face. I pat him on the back and move on.

"You sleep here?" He grunts with a nod. "Who would do this?"

"Those same damn bastards trying to buy this land for nothing, I bet'cha." He grabs his shotgun. "But I ain't about to let 'em destroy this factory. This has been my factory since I was seventeen. No way in hell am I gonna let some jackasses just turn it into rubble and build some highfalutin residential property, with its fancy pools and tennis courts," he says, spitting on the floor in disgust.

I quickly step out of the way of his liquid protest. "Okay. Well, we are not selling the factory. Don't worry. I appreciate your dedication, truly, and while I appreciate all that you do … except for the spitting thing, how about we set the deadly weapon down …" I ease the shotgun out of his hands and place it back in its corner. "Thank you. Now, something is going on that my father isn't telling me. What is it?"

"Bastards have been doin' everything they can to drive us out. Little at a time, they creep around and do just enough to not warrant too much heat from the cops but enough to scare the workers and cost us money we don't have. They are tryin' to take us down, penny by penny."

"Portman's people are doing this?" I ask him.

He nods. "Bastards."

"Did you get a good look at them? What about the security cameras? We can identify them with the video."

"Cameras don't work anymore, and I couldn't see them in the dark, but I am ready for 'em, next time. I won't miss again." I nod, trying to think as he spits again. "Bastards!"

"Okay! I got it! There are bastards trying to bankrupt us and …we just talked about the spitting thing. What is that? Do you have a glandular problem or something?"

He grunts at me before grabbing his gun and pointing it at me again. "You better get on it." I nod. "You know, your father loved this place. When he was running it, he was all heart. Blood, sweat, and tears he and I put into this company. You better take this seriously or you can just go right back to your fraternity brothers in the big city and leave the real men to fight it out."

"I'm taking it seriously. I'm here, aren't I?"

"You're here, but your heart isn't. You have only put one foot in, but you still have one foot out the door, ready to run. You better run now if you're going to, Sunshine, because it's not going to get any easier." He walks away and spits off to his side.

"Oh come on, really?" With my hands on my hips, I look around, trying to figure out who might have given up information to Portman's men. Then it hits me.

When Dani comes into work, I immediately pull her into my office. "Someone tried to set fire to the factory early this morning and nearly destroyed most of our new inventory. Do you want to tell me how anyone knew where we were storing it?"

"Are you excusing me of spying for my father?" she yells at me.

"Maybe not you. Maybe a guest of yours?"

"Thomas? No way! He would never do that. He knows how I feel about this and he would never do anything to jeopardize our relationship."

"I am sure he wouldn't. He picked you up last night and took you somewhere. Why?" I scoff.

"To keep me away from you as much as he can and remind me of his dedication to me." I roll my eyes away from her. "You know there were other people here when I left. Carl, Jack, Rafe, or even Gina. Why aren't you questioning them?"

"Because no one would give up information that might cost them their jobs. This factory is these peoples' only source of income. You don't give that up easily."

"Well, it wasn't me, and it wasn't Thomas. I promise you."

"He is no longer allowed on the premises. If he wants to pick you up, then you can walk to the edge of the drive and wait for him," I say to her fuming expression.

"Fine. Can I go back to work now, boss?" she asks as if she wants to say something else, but I wave her on before she decides to push me any further.

Someone is helping Portman, and if not her, then who? Many more attacks and Warren is right, people will begin to look for new jobs where they feel safe. I need to fix the cameras and get some new equipment and better security than Warren and his shotgun. I need to find some money and fast. The only thing I can think of is the patents Dani found. I dig into the safe, pull them all out, and go through them one by one, trying to find something we could stand to part with, when I come upon something I have never heard of or seen before. I read through it over and over, wondering why my father would even think of such a thing.

My father comes walking in with his usual upbeat smile. "You know we got attacked last night?" I say.

"I heard," he replies, souring some but not seeming to let the thought bother him too much.

"We need money, and we need it fast." He sits down with a large sigh. "I was thinking of selling one of the patents?" He simply nods with little assistance. "I was actually going through them to find something that might work, and I happened onto this strange idea that you patented." I hand it over to him and watch as he looks it over with a smile.

"Oh yeah, I worked this one out right before your mother got sick. I had almost forgotten about it."

"What is it exactly?" I ask, leaning forward making sure he understands my assured interest.

"It's a breathing sensor. The idea is to place it over a baby's crib and it would sound an alarm the instant a child would stop breathing. I designed it so it could be small enough to not be noticeable, but still be effective. You put a sensor here and there, and it will create a protective blanket of sorts that the child would breathe against. I thought maybe you could fit it onto one of those twirly things people put above their children's beds. You know what I mean? Those cutesy eye catchers that go round and round."

"A mobile?" He nods and laughs at me for knowing what he was talking about. Mom always used to finish his sentences, and now, here I am helping him. I guess it is kind of funny. I always thought I was like him, but I guess I am a little like her, too. I smile, remembering my mother as I am sure he is. "So what made you think of this, Dad?"

"Hmmm?" he says as if I startled him out of a dream. "Oh, I don't know, a news program I believe. I don't really remember the details. You think we should sell this?"

"No, I think we should make it."

"It's not furniture, Dillon. We don't make computer chips and mobiles."

"We could. The mobiles, I mean. And we could get the pieces of the sensor made and then put it all together ourselves." He stands up, pacing away from me to look out the window overlooking the factory floor. "This is an incredible design, Dad. This could really save the factory. Forget furniture. Let's do this and build something even more exciting."

"It's not furniture. We make furniture. We have always made furniture, Dillon."

"We make furniture and great quality furniture, but so do a

dozen other factories in this city and even more everywhere else in the world. With the internet, people will buy from anywhere. Hell, we could sell this online and in stores and make more money than you have ever seen. We could make ...."

"Could what? Make millions? Is that all you care about?" he snaps at me. "We make furniture. We have always made quality furniture here since my great-grandfather, and now you are ready to give all that up for money? You should be proud of your heritage, not dismiss it and ... be ashamed."

"Who said I was ashamed? I am proud, and I am doing everything possible to try and save this place. I quit my job. I moved down here to fix everything that isn't working."

"You mean to fix my mistakes, to fix everything I messed up by building furniture that no one wants? You disrupted your life to come down here and fix everything for your old man?" My father asks, standing up to me.

"No, you didn't mess up. It's not like it used to be, Dad. Technology changes constantly. If you turn your back for even a minute, you miss major changes in the world. An advancement of some kind that makes another company that much more capable to meet what people want and need and makes you irrelevant. They could advance something tomorrow to cause this whole place to disappear into the long forgotten businesses of the past. Mom was sick for two years. You were distracted for two years, and that was all it took for time to pass by this place. We make great furniture, but we need something new to put us back out in front again. The factory doesn't have to be about furniture anymore. We can still keep it going and even flourish if we make it about something more. We can keep this place open, hire more people, and hell… make a profit if we do something more than just furniture."

"Just furniture, huh? Yeah, that's all we make."

"Dad, that's not what I meant, and you know it! Why are you making this such a big deal?"

He stares back over the factory floor silently. "This factory has never been about just furniture. It is about the people here, the quality, and care we take in what we give our customers. It's a home away from home. It's not about a money making machine. If you make it only about money and fixing problems then … I have taught you nothing about owning a business."

"I don't know what the hell you are taking about! I am trying to make this place prosper and maybe help you retire the way you should. Maybe give us both a life we have never known before. We could hire more people, have benefits, and actually be some place people want to work because we can pay them what they are worth." My father shakes his head at me as if making a profit is the worst thing in the world. "Why are you so against growing and making money?"

"I'm not. I'm against forgetting what is important. Do whatever the hell you want to do, Dillon. The decisions concerning this place are all yours now."

"What? What are you saying?"

"I think it's time now for me to retire. I am handing it all over to you. This is all yours now, Son, so whatever you decide to do with it is fine with me." He looks me over and forces a smile. "You will do great, I'm sure. I am going to go socialize for a little bit and then I think I am going to go home and start working on that garden your mother always wanted."

"It's fall, Dad."

"Oh yeah." He begins walking out the door before turning back. "Maybe I can come around from time to time and say hi to everyone, at least until spring?" I am so dumbfounded that I can't form words, so all I do is nod at my clearly heartbroken father.

My day is completely ruined. My initial excitement about the patents has been destroyed by my father's obvious disappointment in me. I wish I knew why he felt that way. I don't understand what he wants from me. I'm doing everything I can. I'm killing myself trying to keep this place afloat, and all he cares about is some tradition, some *Conrad Furniture* tradition? It's a dumbass factory. What does it matter what we make as long as we make a profit?

Dani walks into my office an hour later, looking me over as my father did earlier. "What's happening?" she asks.

"My father is retiring, and now I have inherited all of this," I say, spreading my arms out wide. "All of this … crap." She instantly begins shaking her head at me. "Now, what is your problem?"

"You just don't get it. Everyone knows you don't want to be here, Dillon, so why are you?" Dani asks me with discontent in her voice.

"To help my father save his business."

"Well, it's not his anymore, so now what are you going to do?" I look up at her with every feeling possible rushing through my body and none of them giving me any answers.

"I don't know what to do, Dani. A smart man would sell it and move on with his life."

"You're smarter than the average, Dillon. I'm sure you can come up with a better option."

"I don't think I can. I don't think I want to. This is not my dream. I never wanted to come back here. I never wanted to be stuck in this shitty small town suffocating like a lab rat. All I am doing is running and spinning my wheels, trying to keep a company afloat. And for what? For a tradition? For pride? What pride is there in bankruptcy? I can't stand Thomas or your father, but every day that I have to come in here, the more I hate this place, the more I hate this town. I miss Shane. I miss our little apartment in the city. The parties and the pranks we would pull at work together, the women we would compete for, and the people we would get to meet. It was fun and exciting every day there. I felt young, with a real life ahead of me, but here, I feel old, with nothing but regret ahead of me." I sit back, exhausted, expecting some understanding from my old best friend, but when I look up at her, she shakes her head with pursing lips.

"You know, as long as I have known you, Dillon, this is the first time I am actually disappointed in you. Maybe I should go back to Chicago with Thomas. I thought I was here to fight for something. I can't do it alone, and I certainly can't do it without you, the owner." She turns to walk out, but I run out in front of her to force her to look at me.

"What do you want from me, Dani? You and my father look

to me as if I can perform miracles. I can't. I can't fix something without money, or without product that people want to buy. I don't know what to do, Dani. If you are so full of answers, then tell me … what do I do?"

"Fight."

"I'm too tired to fight and there are no more solutions left."

She cups my face within her hands. "You're missing the answers, Dillon, but only because you don't want to see them. There is no way to save something that you don't want to save in the first place. You don't want to be here? Fine. This is not what you wanted in your life? That's okay. There's nothing wrong with admitting this is not where you belong. If this is not what you want, Dillon, then you need to leave now and let somebody that does want to be here take over and do what needs to be done."

"Like who Dani? There is no one who wants this place as it is."

"Lucas Charles does. From what your father told me, he loves this place. He only quit to get away from you." A light kiss to my cheek and she walks out my office door without another word.

Fucking Lucas Charles? Ugh, that's the last name I want to hear right now.

Chapter 8

Dani

I shut the office door behind me and lean against it for support. I wanted so badly to believe that Dillon wanted to be here, that he wanted the same things I do. I think I have been forcing myself to believe that he belongs here, but maybe he really doesn't. Maybe he belongs in New York with all his new friends and girlfriends, while I belong here with my memories. The fears that build up inside of me are hard to grasp. I feel like I have lost him all over again. When my cell begins to ring, I check it to see Thomas calling to tell me that he is here to pick me up. I wipe away my tears and rush out to meet him before Dillon throws a fit that he is here again.

I jump in the car, and Thomas instantly holds his hand up to hush me. I sit quietly while he discusses business with someone on his cell. He drives me to a house, and I sit up and look at him, "Why are we here? What is this place?"

"Danielle please, I'm talking." I fall back into my seat, crossing my arms. Once he finishes his call, he gets out of the car and waves me to follow. "Come on, get out of the car."

"Why?"

"Because I have worked very hard to find this place, and out of respect for me, you should get out of the car and at least take a look at it." He opens my door and waits for me to get out. I do so, but with little interest in the place. "The agent gave me the key to look at it on our own. I think it works for us. Once the deal goes through, I will need to be here to oversee construction, negotiations, and …"

"You are still planning to build here?"

"Of course. Listen, I know you think a lot of the Conrads, but there is no way they are going to survive. That place is so heavily in debt that it has no way of surviving. In fact, I was just talking to my partner who said Dillon is ready to talk to us now. He wants our best offer. My people are drawing up the papers for me to take over within the hour," Thomas says.

"He said that?"

Thomas sighs. "Yes, I knew he wouldn't last long. He couldn't. That place is beyond done. Not even I could help bring it out of the pit it's in. Alright, now you look like I took your puppy away. I am not going to talk about it with you so you can pout about it all day. Now cheer up and take a look around, and make sure you can live with this place for a while."

"I don't like it."

"What? Why?"

"It's too big and cold, and well, I don't like it. I don't want to live here."

Thomas puts his hands in his pockets and takes in a deep breath. "I don't know what your problem is lately, but you better do something about your attitude." Thomas stares me down until I look away. "I am more than willing to let you do what you want with the place. I doubt I will be here that much anyway. Make sure you keep the bedroom the way I like, but otherwise, go crazy. You can even hire someone to come in and help you make it whatever you want it to be, but this is where we are going to live for a while. Sorry, but this is the best I could do in this city. If all goes well, we will back in Chicago or even L.A. ..." he nods with excitement, "before you know it. Your father has a lot of opportunities waiting after this works out."

"You have already signed a lease?"

"Yes, I assumed you would be reasonable and not act like a child."

"I told you I don't want to live with you, and I don't want to live here. Actually, I don't want to be with you at all." He laughs at me as if I am talking nonsense. "Take me back to work, Thomas."

"No, no you're not going back there. We are going to go to the Conrads' house and get your things and then you are going to be done with them. Your father is very disappointed in you, and so am I, frankly," he says, rushing me out the door and not allowing me to discuss anything else while he drives me to the Conrads'. "I have to go take care of this final piece of business so we can all get on with our lives. While I'm gone, I want you to pack so that, when I get back, we can load up and get you moved out of this hovel." I look over at him but don't say a word as I get out of the car and go inside to figure out what to do. Dillon may not belong here, but I do. I know it, and I will do whatever I can to save the family I grew up loving. After pacing and considering every possibility, I decide to make a call to an old friend.

"Hi, how are you?" I say, excited to hear his voice again.

"Dani? Holy shit! I'm good, how are you? Where are you?"

"Thomasville."

"What? With Dillon?"

"Yeah, but I don't think he wants to be here. I am not sure he belongs here. I think he would rather be up in New York with you and all of your friends and girlfriends."

"Is that what he said?"

"He didn't have to, Shane. I was wondering if you could tell me something. Was there someone he left to be here?"

"You mean a girl? No, there really hasn't been but one that he even showed much interest in. But she left for a singing career months ago. He might miss her, but I doubt it is bothering him that much. To be honest, there hasn't been anyone that broke his heart like you did. I would bet the reason he is so miserable there is because of you. You messed him up bad, Dani. And that place does nothing but bring back memories of what you did to him. Truthfully, I wouldn't say he was happy here either. There was just less here to remind him of you." I sink down into my seat, realizing that Dillon hasn't been the only one to be blind to the world around him. "So, how is everything else there?" he asks.

"Terrible. We are in real trouble, and I don't know if there is any way to fix it."

"Say no more. Shane will be there soon to help put everything back together." I laugh. "No, really. I am absolutely miserable here. I am having no fun at all. Hell… without my wingman, I can't get a decent date for anything. I actually had to go home alone the other night. I am way too cuddly to sleep alone, Dani."

"Then get your ass down here, boy, and let's get you back in the game."

"I'm on my way," Shane says with a smile that shines through his voice over the phone.

I jump up, go find Matt, and ask him to take me back to the factory. I need to talk to Dillon before he makes a big mistake.

I rush into the factory and up the stairs to Dillon's office to find Thomas and another one of my father's associates already there, talking to him.

"We can do this all for a 2% increase on the amount of money we offered your father originally, and we will even throw in first dibs on a condo," Thomas says arrogantly. Dillon looks defeated and broken as he sits across from him. "Don't dismiss it, Dillon. This is not the place for you. You know you don't want to be here. You're young, and I am sure you want to be out with your friends having fun and doing what you really enjoy doing. You know what? I will even let you make a choice of places. We also have a great complex in New York that I am sure you will love. I can get you in there for a great price and then you will have the perfect bachelor pad to invite all the women you want. Now, if you will just sign here and here, then we can get out of this place and you can be on your way back to a life without all the pressure."

Dillon shakes his head. "I don't think that I can do this."

"Of course you can. You have no choice. You can't pay your

bills; the city is going to turn off the power within a week. Unless, by some miracle, you sell all the product on the floor plus some. It's not your fault, Dillon. You came into the situation too late. No one could save this place, so don't take it as a failure. In fact, you are doing your father a favor. You're taking his stresses away and allowing him to live his final days out without worry," Thomas says, continuing to push the paperwork in front of him.

Dillon takes it, and begins reading it with a pen in hand.

"Dillon, stop!" I yell running in on them.

"Dani, what are you doing here? I told you to pack your things," Thomas says to me.

I ignore him and turn to Dillon. "You don't need to do this. I will help you if you will only let me."

"Dani, what are you going to do? What can you do?" Dillon asks me.

"Invest. I'm going to invest and be your partner," I say as he looks at me confused. "We will do this together, and we will succeed together."

"Are you insane, Dani? Get out of here and go take some Pamprin or something. You must be menstrual. Don't listen to her. You wouldn't believe the way she has been acting all day," Thomas says with a laugh between him and his co-hort.

I stay focused on Dillon, lean down to him, and look him directly in the eyes. "Fight, Dillon. Fight with me and let's build something your father and your mother would be proud of. You are never going to be happy if you keep running from your past and your pain. Neither of us are ever going to be happy unless we stop running. Please, let me help and work with you? Let me be your partner?" I take his hand as he looks at me hard.

"Seriously? This is ridiculous, Dillon. Sign and let's all go on with our lives. No one is running from anything. We are all simply trying to do what's best for everyone," Thomas says, pushing me away from Dillon.

Dillon abruptly stands up and steps in between me and Thomas before turning to him. "Get out."

"Oh, come on. I understand if you are put off by me being with Danielle, but if you could stop being so stubborn and really consider what would be best for everyone, then I think we can come to an agreement. If you don't like this offer, then counter. I am open to hearing it."

"Get out." Thomas starts to speak again, but Dillon stands a little taller and squares his shoulders with Thomas's. "Get out!" he yells again. The usual factory recluse, Warren, shows up out of nowhere with his shotgun.

"There is no need for violence. We'll leave, but this is the last chance for you to take this offer. Once I leave, we won't be back. We'll simply wait and buy it from the bank at the end of the month. Even with Dani, your business is barely surviving. One more setback and ..." Warren cocks his gun, and Thomas and his associate rush out the door.

Warren turns to us with an actual smile. "He ain't gettin' our factory." He nods and starts to spit, but instead, swallows with an odd twitch to his face before finally giving Dillon a quick nod and walking back out onto the floor.

Dillon laughs, looking back at me with a shake of his head. "Tommy boy is right. We are walking a fine line. One setback and we could be finished whether I or you want it or not."

I nod. "Well, let's sit down and figure out what steps we need to take ...together. Because we are in this together now, right?" I ask.

Dillon moves in front of me with his hand on his hips, looking me over before holding out his hand to me and waiting for me to shake on the new partnership. "Together. Partners until the bitter end and no running away."

"Deal." I smile wide, causing his sweet, crooked, mischievous smile to form. *Damn I love that smile.*

Chapter 9

Dillon

Dani wants so bad to dive in and get started together, but I am not real sure where to start. I am not even sure I want to tell her how bad it is. As I stand in front of her giddy, adorable excitement, I loathe myself on the inside. *What the hell was I thinking? She shouldn't be in the middle of this. It's going to end badly, and she is going to lose so much more than I am.*

"So, where should we start? I know I don't know much about this business, but I have been paying a lot of attention to things as I clean and take out the trash. I think we should move the inventory to the right side of the factory so we can have more room to build and get shipments out. Everything can start at one end and move through to the other… what do you think?" she says with a large smile.

"That sounds like an idea, but the drop-off trucks can't get through over there, so we will be stuck shuttling it from one end to the other."

She nods and then turns to me again, nearly bouncing into my arms. "Oh! Then the first thing we should do is have that drive widened. It will help with security too …" She babbles on and on about ideas, and now I really hate myself. She clearly doesn't understand what she is getting into, and she should before she hands over any money and gives up too much of her time. I sit on the edge of the desk, waiting for her to pause so I can explain in more detail. "What's wrong? Oh, am I talking too much? I'm sorry, I should probably wait until I hear your ideas first."

"They are great ideas, Dani, but we don't have the money to do any of that."

"Well, that's why I am investing," she says with a hopeful expression.

I reach out and take her hand to pull her in front of me. "We are really in debt, Dani." I grab a notice from my desk and hand it to her. "And that's just one of the bills we need to pay as soon as possible." She looks up at me and down at the bill, her shoulders sinking as if the world just fell onto her back. I take the bill back from her. "You know what? This was a bad idea. I will call the jackass back and tell him I changed my mind. I am sure we can still work something out."

"No, Dillon. We will figure this out. I promised, and you promised, and we are going to do this, together. Okay?" She grabs my hands and forces a smile. "I know we can do this. I believe in you and me. No two people are better suited to work together and get this place back to where it once was."

"You're nuts, do you know that?" I ask, shaking my head. Dani suddenly steps to me and takes hold of my face and kisses me.

"Try for me, please?" My head is spinning, and my heart is pounding as she sends a weak, but oh so effective bright-eyed plea my way.

I nod, wanting more and doing my best to get her to stay near me. "Your boyfriend isn't going to like us working together every day and most likely every night."

"He's not my boyfriend anymore. I don't have time for that. I have to help get our business running at full speed again." I lean in to take hold of her lips, but she steps away before I can, jabbering on and on about financials, negotiating this and that, and everything else not at all fun.

The night goes late, and I drive Dani and I home, completely exhausted. The only thing I want to do is finish up some work outside for my father, take a shower, and go to bed. After cutting up some firewood for my father, I begin stacking it until I hear Dani yelling. I rush to the front of the house and find Tommy dragging her out the front door. I throw down my work gloves and head straight for them.

"Stay out of this, Dillon!" Tommy yells at me with his finger in my face. I stop in my tracks, steaming, while Tommy turns back to Dani. "I am sick of this, Danielle. Now come with me and stop with this low class blue-collar lifestyle you are insistent on living right now. Your father and I are not about to let you lose everything you have worked for on … on this," he says, motioning towards me.

"No, I told you. This is important to me, and I am not changing my mind. This is what I want to do and there is nothing you or my father can do about it, Thomas!" Dani yells at him.

"That's not going to happen, and you know it. You know what a determined man your father is, and you may not know their exact financials, but I do. They don't have a chance in hell of surviving," Tommy says, looking my way. "They are not strong enough to overcome what's coming their way."

"You don't know a damn thing about me or my family!" I yell at him, edging forward until Dani pushes back on my chest. Our neighbors begin to come out of their homes to see what all the yelling is about.

"I don't have to know you to predict the disaster you're about to be a part of. I am tired of being understanding, Danielle. I told you, and I am not going to tell you again. Get your ass in that car. Now!" he says, grabbing Dani's arm and nearly pulling it out of the socket as he jerks her forward. I have had enough of this.

I meet him face to face with my fists ready and forcing him to release Dani. "Tommy boy, you better get your ass off my lawn and never come back here or to our factory again."

"I am not leaving without Dani."

"You wanna bet?" I say, edging him back on his heels.

He doesn't even consider challenging me. He takes a couple of steps back and curses me instead. "We're done, Dani. When everything goes wrong, don't bother to come crying back to me unless it's on your knees …with your mouth wide open." *That's it!*

My fist is quickly jammed into his jaw, and I take hold of his collar and drag him back to his Mercedes and toss him onto the hood. "I should call the cops on you and have you arrested for assault."

"This ain't Chicago, Tommy boy. You won't find any kindness here. Not amongst *my* small town," I say proudly as my neighbors begin to stand behind me with baseball bats and other miscellaneous weapons. He huffs, holding his jaw, but doesn't hesitate too long before getting back into his fancy car and driving away.

"Who's that jackass, Dillon?" Jeff Snider, one of our many longtime neighbors, asks.

"Oh, just some out-of-towner who doesn't belong here." I shake hands with my neighbors while taking Dani's hand. She doesn't say a word as I bring her inside and lock up the house for the night. Kissing her on her forehead, I take a moment to breathe before looking her over and rubbing my thumb gently over the red Tommy hand print on her arm. "You are welcome to go if you want, or you can continue to stay here. But no matter what you decide, you stay away from him. Do you hear me? There is something not right about him, Dani. He's going to hurt you one day, and then I am going to have to kill him." She looks up at me with wide eyes. "Actually don't ever bring him anywhere near me or my home again. I will knock him out before anyone has a chance to say a word." I take my coat off and go up to my room before stepping into a shower and releasing the stress of the day under the powerful force of the steaming water.

Suddenly, the shower door flies open. "Hey! Who do you think you are?" Dani snaps at me.

"What?"

"I can do what I want. Don't ever tell me what to do again," she says, looking as if she needs to relax too.

I look her over once before wrapping my arm around her waist and pulling her into the shower with me clothes and all.

Taking hold of her lips with mine, I work through the pounding water, letting her know what I want. "Take your clothes off." She looks at me in shock. "Take your clothes off, Dani, I know you want me."

"I most certainly do not. You're the one that pulled me in here. I have no desire for you whatsoever."

I laugh. "That's funny. Now take your damn clothes off and stop being so stubborn." I quickly help her pull her wet shirt off over her head. "You don't want to wear wet clothes; that's no way to shower." She leans against the wall while I move down to her pants, and, with one jerk, I strip her completely of the rest of her clothes and toss them out of the shower. "See, I knew you wanted me. Your pussy is hot and so incredibly wet." She opens her mouth to say something, but I swiftly shut her up with my mouth. Dani doesn't fight me for even a second longer before she is wrapping her arms around my neck and her legs around my waist. I put one hand on the wall and one on her ass, letting my protruding cock submerge inside of her. She makes a weak request and then crashes her lips against mine, sharing her tongue while I share mine. Squeezing her ass into my hips feels so damn good I can scarcely think. Dani kisses down my neck and back up again, licking the water off of my skin with each pass. A heavy breath passes from my lips, and I feel her tighten around me.

"Dillon," she breathes, leaning back and allowing me to look over her body. Her breasts, bouncing freely, are flushed with water dripping from her nipples and down to her stomach. I take hold of one breast, press it against my mouth, and kiss one of my many favorite hidden freckles on her body. The movement causes a shift, and I lean back and look down, in between her legs. I enjoy the sight even more as I slide out to my tip and shove it right back into the depths of her frenzy. Dani grasps my arms and shudders with pleasure as she clenches around my dick and provokes me to come right along with her. She slides back down to her feet while I hover around her. She closes her eyes and breathes out hard against my chest. I take a finger, remove the hair from her face, and kiss her on the head, regaining her attention back on me.

"Feel better? All that frustration and anger all worked out now?" I ask with a wink. "We should have all of our partner meetings in the shower, to save time in our busy schedules. Not to mention, it's warmer." I moan with satisfaction.

"Shut up," she says, smacking my chest. "You caught me off guard is all." Dani trails her fingers down my chest, glancing down. "I should go …" I nod, continuing to hover around her and blocking her from going anywhere. She presses her hands to my chest as if she is going to move me out of her way.

I push her hair off her shoulder and away from her neck, leaving it open for me to kiss. "Don't leave, surely you're not finished yet?"

She sighs, and I watch as she begins to bathe herself. She glances up at me through her eyelashes and fights a smile, knowing I am watching every move she makes. I love her freckles, the ones across her nose and the ones across her chest. I grip her ass, reminding myself of the ones she got the day she went skinny dipping with me at old man Rucker's place while he was out of town. Boy was he surprised to see us sleeping naked in his hammock when he came back early. I didn't think she would ever forgive me for talking her into that embarrassment, but she did. Dani is completely lathered up after I help wash her back so she turns and returns the favor. She rubs her hands down my arms and over my chest, but then she stops as she goes down. I spread my legs and wait with a smile. She looks up at me and feels down and inside my leg before grasping my suddenly awakened beast again. She seems shocked but continues stroking me clean with a sexy move of her tongue across her lips, making me crazy. I feel down her body, gripping her ass as my body tenses. My eyes close, and my mouth involuntarily gasps with heightened pleasure. "Better?" I smile wide and nod. "So glad I could make you happy."

I lean into her. "Sleep with me tonight, and I will make you very happy, again."

"I can't Dillon," Dani says, rinsing off and stepping out of the shower ahead of me. I quickly rinse off myself and follow her out to see her combing out her hair, naked.

"Not that I mind seeing you naked, but you used to be shy. You've changed quite a bit over the years, huh?"

"Don't worry, Dillon. I haven't changed that much. I'm only comfortable naked in front of you and maybe Thomas, but that was because I didn't care what he thought of me." She steps to me as I wrap a towel around my waist. "And I'm only comfortable in front of you because of that look in your eyes and the drool that is on the side of your mouth." She laughs, rubbing her finger across my mouth. "There. I do love knowing you adore me."

"Cut the shit. What the hell are you up to?"

"I'm not up to anything. We had sex, and now I am going to go read in my bed. Alone. Then tomorrow, I am going to go to work and do my job and act no different than I did today." She wraps a towel around her body. "I'm here as a friend, Dillon. I'm not here to start up something that will only distract you from doing what you need to do. Besides, you still don't trust me, and I can't be in a relationship with someone who doesn't trust me," she says before walking out.

"Who says I don't trust you? I did agree to being partners."

"You agreed, but some part of you still questions why I am here and whether I will leave again. So, until you believe I am here for the long haul, then we are only going to be friends and partners." She smiles and opens the door to leave.

"I trust you enough to be friends with benefits!" I yell after her.

Dani and I get together early and go through everything that has to do with the business in hopes of clearing up as much debt as possible so we can move on. Once we get that done, we have little money left and do our best to decide how best to spend it. She takes time to go analyze what inventory we have, what has been ordered, and what is expected for delivery. I stay behind, supposedly to gather our distributors' information, but instead, I stare through the office window overlooking the floor and watch her work. If she's not here for a relationship, then what's she doing working here? She is purposely working with those headphones in her ears so she doesn't have to talk about what she knows we should. Sitting across from me the way she was, with her hair up under that baseball cap, letting a few strands dangle around her face, knowing damn well that drives me crazy. I had to sit across from her, repositioning myself a dozen times while trying not to think about her or want her. *Trust her! Why should I?* Her father is trying to destroy us. I have no reason to believe she isn't here to help him, except that she did prevent me from selling to him and invested her own money to help. *Damn her for being completely baffling and desirable all at the same time!*

Someone walks into my office and stares over my shoulder, looking out onto the floor as I do. "Yes, what do you want?" I say, not bothering to look to see who it is.

"Yep, I should have known, spending your whole day watching Dani and not getting a damn thing done. I knew you needed my help," Shane says.

I turn around and smile, embracing my friend, "Shane! What are you doing here?"

"I quit my job."

"What? Why?"

"Because it's no fun without you there. All the day-to-day stuff that I used to enjoy wasn't so much fun anymore, the job became … a job. And if that's going to be the case, I can come here and get a job I hate, and at least then, I will be here with my best friend…," he looks over my shoulder, "both of them, and enjoy life a little."

"They fired you didn't they?" I ask him, analyzing him for any sign of deception.

"No, actually. Those assholes stopped threatening to fire me and even offered me a promotion." Shane shakes his head with his hands on his hips.

"No! How dare they?"

"I know! Being the obedient employee is boring. I tried to get into trouble, but somehow, it always turned out to be something good. I signed the boss up for a subscription to 'Big Boobs and More,' and he said it was a good place for the Hooters ads we have been working on. He said, 'Job well done, Shane. Keep up the good work'. I have never been more insulted in all my life."

I shake my head. "See, you always overthink it. You should have simply created an ad for his new assistant and handed it out at the strip club. *Assistance needed! $50 an hour! Professional job with optional benefits. All interested specialists please apply in person*," I say, like it should have occurred to him.

"See? Yeah, that would have been much better," he laughs. "So, other than the obvious, how's it going?"

I shake my head, sighing. "Well, Dad handed everything over to me and made me feel like shit for even suggesting to change it from furniture to anything else." I pull out the design for the mobiles and hand it to him. "He created this breathing sensor, and I drew up this to make it work." Shane looks it over, becoming more interested with his understanding of each detail.

"This is great! Dillon, you could make a fortune with this.

What's the problem?"

"The problem is that it isn't furniture. It isn't what my family's legacy is."

"Are you sure that's what he meant? To continue making custom benches and armoires forever?" Falling into my chair, I scratch my head, trying to figure out what would be best. "I see you have a lot of answers swirling in that head of yours, and I think you are going to need some help getting one to spit out. Ray's still have the best beer nuts in town?" I nod, laughing.

The moment Shane walks onto the floor with me, Dani looks up and tosses her headphones before running and jumping into his arms. I think she is the only girl I ever dated that actually approved of mine and Shane's friendship, and she is the only girl I dated that Shane really loved as much as I do. The three of us were always together growing up, until she ditched us and he was left picking up the pieces by himself. Don't know what I would have done without him.

Dani and I close out the day and meet up with Shane at Ray's for a few beers. There is nothing like talking about old times with the people you grew up with. "So, now that you two have had sex again, does that mean you are back together?"

Dani and I both look at him in shock. "What? We haven't …" Dani insists.

"Oh, please! I know you two better than you know

yourselves." He stops and points at us both, "Besides, it's written all over your faces. You're both awkward and all confused looking."

I stare at him hard, and then shake my head laughing. "You've been talking to my dad." I look over at Dani, "Apparently my father is not as clueless as he would lead us to believe." Dani smacks Shane on the arm with a roll of her eyes. "Nice try though."

"Nice try what? You have had sex, so I assume you're back together?"

"No. We are partners and concentrating on the business. We might have slipped up once …" I cough, and she sighs. "Fine, more than once. But we are determined and focused now."

Shane leans forward in his chair. "You had sex more than once?" Shane looks back at me, and I lean back proudly. Shane laughs, shaking his head. "Focused and determined …I bet." Shane leans back in his chair laughing until he sees someone walk in the door. "Uh-oh, I guess all good times must come to an end at some point."

I look over and see Lucas Charles walk in with a couple of mutual old friends. Lucas Charles, my old rival and Dani's high school boyfriend before I stole her away. The smile on his face disappears the moment he sees me, but it doesn't stop him from coming over to our table. "Dillon, I heard you were back, but I didn't know you brought back your whole crew of misfits," Lucas says. He looks over at Dani. "Hi Dani," he says sweetly to her.

Dani jumps up and hugs him; for some damn reason. "Hi

Lucas. You look good." She says.

"You look beautiful, even more so than I remember." Dani blushes, and I roll my eyes. "Love to catch up sometime if you get a chance."

"I would love to," Dani gushes.

"How 'bout tomorrow? Lunch maybe?"

"Sure." They exchange numbers, and I look at her as if she has lost her mind. Shane scoots his chair back from the table. "What?" she asks as if she doesn't know what my problem is.

"What? What was that?" I ask.

"I am having lunch with an old friend."

"He asked you out right in front of me, on purpose, and you're going knowing this?"

"I'm sorry, Dillon. Was I supposed to ask you before I go out with another man? I am not going to have sex with him, just lunch. Besides, we are not in a relationship. Remember?"

"Yeah, I remember. 'Cause I don't trust you, or some shit," I say, but she holds her hand up in my face and starts up a new conversation with Shane. I glance over at Lucas, who already has some hot women trying to get his attention. He's not all that good-looking. I look him over as he flirts and enjoys the admiration. *I don't get it.* I glance back at Dani and smile my sexy, irresistible smile, and she rolls her eyes before smacking me in the chest.

"You're so funny, Dillon." She laughs. *Funny?* I don't understand her. I don't know what she is up to, but I know she is up to something, and I am not falling for it.

Before I can get to the bottom of her mysterious ways,

Thomas and some new suits I have never seen before walk in with Dani's father. "Oh shit!" I slam my beer on the table, cursing under my breath.

Dani turns around, and, as soon as she spots her father, she sits up straight and faces away from him. Shane and I both scoot closer to the table and watch her back. The suits all sit together at a table as far away from us as possible. Dani´s father approaches us.

"Danielle, I didn't realize you would be here," Douglas Portman says, being sure to ignore Shane and me.

Dani stands up with a nervous smile and hugs her father. "Hello Daddy. I didn't know you were coming into town."

"Oh Dani, all that time and money spent trying to rid you of that damn accent and a few days back here and it is all for naught," he says, glancing my way. "I have missed you. Come sit with us and let's catch up. Thomas said you two had a fight."

"It was more than a fight and not at all repairable, Daddy. You can stop trying to fix something that isn't going to happen, no matter what you say. And I am here with Shane and Dillon; I can't leave them. That would be rude."

Good ole Doug looks Shane over and then glances my way. "How's it going, Doug?" I smile wide.

He sighs and turns back to Dani. "I am not sure the degenerates would know what rude is. They are not exactly decorous."

I turn to Shane as he looks at me in shock. "Is he talking about us, Shane?"

"Uhhh, I don't know," Shane laughs senselessly. "I don't

understand enough of what he is saying to be sure. I am just a simple country bumpkin; I don't understand all t'em big words he uses."

"Me neither, oh well. I guess we'll just sit here and drool on ourselves until we can remember how to get home," I say, acting foolishly with Shane.

"Funny. I really don't understand your fascination with these people, Danielle," Douglas says.

Dani kisses her father's cheek and walks him halfway back to his table. "I'm going to enjoy my night with my friends. I will set aside some time to have dinner with you before you leave, which is when?" Dani asks her father.

"I am actually renting a place here for a while. I have a lot of plans in process down here that I want to see to personally. It is a very nice place, with more than enough room for my daughter to move into. At least you will have a decent place to stay."

Dani sighs. "I'm fine where I am Daddy, but thank you."

Douglas tenses. "Nothing but trouble, Danielle. He has caused you so much pain, and he will only cause you more."

"It's my decision, and I am not discussing it with you any further." Dani kisses his cheek again with a hug before returning to our table to sit down. Her father walks away and sits down with his suit friends discussing matters. They don't order any food, and they scoff at the drinks that are brought to them, so I am sure they didn't come in here to be told *no*. Thomas looks over at us periodically and says something to make everyone laugh. It must be pretty bad since Lucas is sitting nearby and even he seems to look at me with sympathy.

"I think it's time to go," I say, tired of the whole mess. Dani and Shane both nod in agreement. We walk out together, and I make sure to lay a gentle hand on Dani's back with a sweet kiss to her head, just to piss them all off. Thankfully, she doesn't deny me the privilege and even lays her head against me, which makes me forget about everyone else and remember how great it is to have her in my arms.

Chapter 10

Dani

My father hates Dillon more than he hates losing money, which is about the worst thing in the world for him. He never approved of my mother getting involved with my stepfather and moving us here, but he was way too busy to be bothered with a child at the time. He simply paid my child support and allowed my mother to go wherever she wanted with me. My stepfather, Paul, treated me okay for a while, but he despised my father and wasn't always able to separate his frustrations for my father from his actions towards me. Paul dealt with my father constantly after he lost his job. My mother was always working, so he was in charge of taking care of me while she was gone. We rarely talked unless we had to. After Paul had a torrid conversation with my father about how inadequate the home was that my stepfather provided for me, he turned to me and instantly started yelling. I was only eleven at the time and scared to death of Paul.

"You spoiled little brat! Did you call him and complain about how small your room is?"

"No. I like my room."

"If you hate it so much here, then leave. Go live with your rich father in one of his many homes," he says backhanding me across the face and knocking me to the floor.

"I don't hate it here, and I don't want to leave," I say, quickly getting up

and backing away from him.

"You know what? Get out! Get your shit and get the hell out of my house," Paul says, grabbing me and pushing me towards the stairs. "You don't belong here. This is not a place for the Portman princess." I try to get around the large man and run out the door to what I believe is safety. "You want to go now? Okay." He opens the door and shoves me outside into the front yard as Matt Conrad comes home.

Matt runs and helps me up, "What's going on here?"

"Stay out of this, Matt!"

"I don't think I will. If you have a problem with this child, then you have a problem with me." The yelling intensifies until Nina Conrad comes out to see to her husband. "Nina, take Dani inside."

Nina puts her arm around me and hurries me inside. She sits me down on the sofa, hugging me tight, trying to drown out the sound of Paul and Matt fighting outside. I become hysterical, not knowing who to fear for more. Nina lies me down in the guest room and puts a cold cloth on my head while she holds my hand. "It's okay, Sweetie. Everything is going to be okay. I called Dillon's grandparents, and they are bringing him home early. You know he won't like seeing you sad."

"Paul hates me, and I don't know why."

"No, he doesn't Sweetie. He is angry about his life right now, and he is taking it out on you. None of this has anything to do with you. Don't you worry. Matt is going to make everything alright again and you can go home to your mom who is so very proud of you. She was just talking to me the other day about watching your game. She said …" Nina went on and on until I smiled and Matt came in with some scratches and a large smile.

"I talked to your mother, Dani. She is going to call you later, but she *wants you to stay with us for a couple of days. Your stepfather is moving out for a while."*

"Because of me?"

"No Honey, because your mother said she chooses you over him." Matt, who I think looks just like superman, hugs me. Everything always feels better when he hugs me. I fall asleep after Nina covers me up in bed and rubs my back, trying to get me to calm down. I wake up sometime in the middle of the night and find Dillon sleeping next to me and holding my hand, superman's son.

I trusted the wrong person when I ran away. I'm not about to make that mistake again; however, I fear if Dillon knows I am meeting my father for breakfast, he will freak out and assume I am sharing secrets that I shouldn't. My father hugs me as soon as I arrive, pretending he is okay with everything I am doing, but I know that is only because the waitress is standing by to take my order.

"You're late."

"I know. I had some business to take care of before I could leave," I say, looking over the menu quickly so I can give the impatient waitress my order. "I'll have the special."

The waitress smiles and leaves me alone with my father and open for attack. "So how are your disadvantaged friends today?" I ignore him by looking around at the décor of the restaurant, which isn't that great. "Alright, fine. I won't say another word about them. How about you? What are you doing cleaning out your accounts to help them? What if my investors find out that my own daughter is going up against me?"

"I am not against you, Daddy. We both know the only reason you picked the Conrads' factory to build those condos is because it's them. Otherwise, you would never think of building there."

"I don't know what you are talking about. It is a prime location to build. We could build a shopping center, condos, and open a public walkway with bike trails and everything. We could build an entire new town."

"This town doesn't want that. They like the old ways, the old buildings. They won't care for the new modern styles that you have selected for this endeavor. I want to do something of my own here, so please let it go."

"You want that boy in your life. I thought you were over him. You promised you hadn't given him a single thought in years."

"His name is Dillon, and he isn't a boy anymore."

"Oh, yes. He has clearly matured over the years from what I have seen."

"Daddy, I swear, my feelings for Dillon are mine, and there is nothing you can do to change them, so please stop trying. If we get back together, that will be our decision."

My father sits back, taking in a deep breath, his typical stretch to keep from losing it and yelling at the top of his lungs. "So does he know?" I glance up from my coffee with nothing to say. "You haven't told him? Well, that should make things interesting."

"He doesn't need to know. There is no reason for him to know and go through the hurt that I am sure he would feel."

"Oh, I am sure that's why you haven't told him."

"It doesn't matter why, but if you say one word to him about it, I will never speak to you again. I love him Daddy!" I say desperately and in a moment of panic. "There's nothing you can do about it. I have tried to forget him, but I can't. I wish you could try to understand my feelings rather than always being so combative about it. You should want to see me happy."

"I do want to see you happy, Danielle. That's all I want for you. However, I wish you would make better choices for your future and not worry only about the here and now. If this fails, I am not going to give you your job back, or am I going to help support you."

"Fine. I am good with that, but you also have to stay out of my personal business. No trying to get me and Thomas back together and no more degrading Dillon in every conversation we have. If you can't say anything nice about any of my friends, then we simply won't talk at all. This is my life now, and so this is what I have to talk about."

My father rolls his eyes with a sigh of disgust, "Alright. So, tell me how the factory business is these days," he says with another roll of his eyes.

"It's promising, very promising. Thanks for asking," I say, and he takes my hand with a more relaxed demeanor. "I love him, Daddy. I can't help it."

After breakfast with my father, I return back to the factory and to judging eyes. Dillon looks at me strangely until he can't stand it anymore. "So where did you go?"

"Who told you, Dillon?"

"Gina and one of the other girls saw you when they went to pick up some coffee."

"Of course they did. Yes, Dillon, I had breakfast with my father, and no, I didn't tell him anything that would help destroy the business," I say with an overly dramatic tone.

"Cute, yeah real cute. Don't worry … I trust you," he says.

I cock my head, looking at him as he tenses and tries to look me in the eyes with confidence. "You're ridiculous. Don't trust me. I don't care, but you would think you would understand that the large amount of money I put into this business, I am never going to get back unless we succeed." I look into his eyes and try not to smile when he does.

"You're so adorable when you're angry." He sits back in his chair, so happy with himself for making me crazy. I go to him and sit down in his lap, straddling him so I can look right into his eyes. "Oh, I like this much better. Let's work like this from now on."

"Oh, if you like this, then you're gonna love this …" I gently brush my lips across his and then twist his nipple.

"Ow! Son of a bitch!"

I jump out of his lap, "That's what you get!"

Shane walks in, looking at us both with a curious expression. "What's going on?"

"She touched my nipple," Dillon says, fighting a smile.

Shane looks back and forth between Dillon and me with scrunched eyebrows. "I don't want to know what you guys do in here all day. I assume it's work. Yep, nothing but hard work going on in here." Shane stops, and considers what he just said. "I didn't mean hard. I meant long? No. You guys are working, just working it. No, that isn't right either. You're pushing …errr …getting the job done? You're grinding …Wow, I didn't realize how many potential sexual terms there are in the workplace."

"Do you need something, Shane?" Dillon finally says, adjusting himself.

"Oh yeah, I wanted to let you know that the copier overheated, which caused the toner to explode everywhere." Dillon and I both sigh. Shane shrugs before smiling as he realizes what he said. "Ha, that seems sexual, too."

"Yeah, we got it. Now go." Dillon pushes him out the door and shuts it behind him. "We have got to find him a girl, and quick, before we find him humping some of the equipment." I nod.

Shane pokes his head back through the door, "Oh, and please don't have sex anywhere that I might walk in on, or sit near, or on, or eat on, or anywhere near where I work on my stuff. Just, stay away from my stuff. I know you two, and I beg you, no hanky-panky near my stuff. That's just gross. Really, really gross. Okay?" We both nod, and Shane seems happy with our acknowledgment of his concerns and shuts the door back, leaving us alone again.

I look at Dillon and smile. "So… do you want to have sex on his desk after he leaves tonight?"

"Absolutely," he says happily.

"Hi, I am so glad you could meet me today. I was afraid it was too last-minute," Lucas says, giving me a hug and a gentle kiss to my cheek.

"No, it's fine. I was anxious to get away from work for a little while anyway. So how are you?"

"I'm good, as good as I can be I guess, for a divorced, ex-high school quarterback that now works in a factory taking orders from a jackass all day," he says with an awkward smile.

"I'm really sorry. What happened to your knee, that was …"

"Don't worry about it. It was a long time ago, right? Besides, it wasn't your fault. You weren't the one that didn't block for me."

I reach over and take his hand. "I promise you, Dillon would have never asked anyone to do that for him. The play went wrong. Roberts was tripped and …"

"Yeah, he was tripped. I know. Let's not talk about that, let's talk about now, like, what are you doing back here? Please tell me it's not because of Conrad?"

"I'm here to help them get the business going strong again, that's it," I say with a shrug.

"Sure you are," he says, shaking his head. "I can't believe you are still in love with that fool." I would deny it, but what's the point. "I was really hoping that maybe you would see him and realize that there's nothing there anymore. Oh well, it wouldn't be the first time I was wrong, especially about you two."

"Lucas, you two used to be such good friends. What

happened?"

"The usual things that happen with competitive teenage boys, not to mention the girls we competed for. Then life goes on, and I am stuck here while he runs off to the big city, meeting celebrities, sleeping with models, and living the perfect life," Lucas says with a lot of bitterness in his voice.

"So, tell me about your new job?" I ask, hoping to change the subject.

"It's okay. I don't really care for it as much as the last one, or at least when Matt was in charge. I worked there for years, you know? I got worried when things started going south, and then I heard Dillon was coming back. I knew it was time to go. It really sucked because Matt treated me like I mattered, like my opinions mattered. I learned a lot from him, and he even paid for the extra classes I needed to get certified. I can fix any machine there is now. I hated to leave. I hated to do it to him, but he understood. I wish he would sell the place and retire happily. That place is such a waste of his time, and Dillon definitely shouldn't be in charge of it. He has no idea what he is doing. He never took an interest in it when we were growing up."

"He's learning, and so am I. I think we have a solid plan."

"Oh, really? Like what?" I shrug and take a bite of my food. "Secrets huh? You can't even tell me?" I shake my head. "Wow, okay. Good luck with that." Lucas stares at me delightfully. "By the way, I saw your stepdad the other day. He seems good."

"Paul?" He nods. "Hmm… I haven't seen him since my mother divorced him."

"Yeah, he kind of disappeared after that. Rehab, I imagine." I nod. "Sorry, I didn't mean to bring up a bad memory. Let's talk about something else, like that time we skipped study hall to make out in Coach Jack's office. He never did find out what happened to his broken chair." I laugh, enjoying his stories, while admiring his still-handsome good looks and incredible physique. I thought he was the one that would get me over Dillon, and now I wonder how he was never able to.

It has been one busy week already with the men in my life. I wish they would all get along; it would make my life so much easier. After sneaking out to meet my father for breakfast yesterday, and Lucas for lunch today, I am ready to get back and pretend I am not hopelessly in love with Dillon Conrad. As I leave the restaurant, I drop my keys while trying to hold lunches for Shane and Dillon. I set the food containers on the truck hood and grab my keys. As I bend to retrieve them, I swear I see someone out of the corner out of my eye. "Hello?" No one responds, or do I see anyone. I shake it off and open the car door before reaching over to get the lunches. I gather them carefully and hear a low groan echo down the alleyway around me.

"Dani …" Is whispered within the wind with no one in sight. I don't take another breath before I jump into the truck and lock the doors, waiting to see if anyone comes out. After a few minutes with no sign of anything, I dismiss the creepy feeling due to my stress and lack of sleep.

When I return to work, Dillon waits for me, still on the same spreadsheet he was on when I left. "So did you get a lot done while

I was gone?"

"Yeah a lot. Probably would have been a lot more if my partner had stuck around to help rather than worrying about her dating life," he says, watching me from the corners of his eyes. *Damn Gina and her gossipy friends. I can't have any secrets in this town.* "Oh, and you might want to stay clear of Shane for a few more hours. He is on the war path. He swears there were butt prints on his desk when he got in today."

I laugh, "I told you all we had to do was create those."

"Yeah, but I would have preferred to do the real thing, not moon Shane's desk." He turns, looking me over with a crooked smile. "Anyway, he's sanitizing his entire area and computer and demanding a new chair because he swears some questionable, disgusting substance was found on it."

"My lotion isn't disgusting. Questionable? Maybe. But certainly not disgusting." I pull it out. "It's milk and honey, the best," I say, causing Dillon to laugh.

He gets up to fist bump me, but pauses unusually and gently rubs his finger over my nose. "It's the cute freckles that make you dangerous. No one would ever believe you're as much trouble as you are. I am on to you though. I know you're trouble. Lucky for you, you're worth every bit of the trouble you cause," he says, reminding me why I love him.

Chapter 11

Dillon

Executive decisions are hard, especially when you are making them for a long history of relatives that built a business for you. We have hardly anything left over after everything is paid; we can barely make payroll. I have had to let several people go I didn't want to, although letting Gina go is not nearly as hard as some of the others.

"I was wondering how long it would take for you to call me to your office. I will honestly tell you that I prefer sexual harassment in the work place, especially if it is from you," Gina says, completely oblivious to why she is actually here. "So, did I do something wrong? Are you going to spank me for it?"

I look her over as she squirms and fidgets her clothes halfway off her body. I have to speak up quick before her breasts actually pop out of her work shirt. "Um, no, you didn't do anything wrong, but I am going to have to let you go." Her relaxed posture quickly changes. "Sorry, I don't want to, but money is tight, and we are going to be making some changes to the work style here, which means we no longer need your expertise."

"My expertise? You haven't seen my expertise. You never come down there to see anything to know what my expertise is," she says angrily.

"We hope to be back to running at full speed soon, and once

we are, we'd love for you to come back."

"We? Who the hell is we?" she asks as Dani comes in from behind her. Gina turns to eye Dani with revulsion. "Oh, I see, back in bed together are you? I can't believe you would let her fuck you into a bad decision, Dillon. I thought you were smarter than that."

"Dani is now a partner of the company, Gina, so yes, she has every right to make decisions right along with me, but never for me. I'm sorry, and like I said, we hope to be able to increase sales and increase staff again very soon."

"Oh really? And how do you plan on doing that? Are you planning on building your own product and selling your slut on the street as an extra giveaway to the beds you make?"

I glance towards Dani who is doing her best to stay seated and keep her mouth closed, but I can read every word she wants to say right on her face. "Have a nice day, Gina. I would go before you say something that you might regret." I stand and help block her from Dani as she walks out.

"Well that went well," Dani says.

"I hate doing that to anyone, even her, but a few more to go, and we are down to a skeleton crew. I hope we can do this," I say to her with a hard exhale.

"We can do it, and we selected the right people to help us." I sit down groaning at her. "We had to do this, and you know it. We can't close down for two weeks and still be able to pay everyone. It is going to take some time to ramp up too. Besides, if we try and make changes with all the people here, the word would get out that we have lost our minds."

"Are you sure we haven't?" I say to her, and she simply smiles. I shake my head and groan. "I think I am going to run away from home." I crash my head onto my desk, face forward.

"What's going on in here?" Shane asks as he comes in and plops down on the sofa.

"Dillon is running away from home," Dani says with an annoying tone of optimism in her voice.

"Oh, okay. Send me a postcard. I like the ones with the funny sayings on them. You know the ones," Shane says.

"I like the one with the two old ladies talking about sex on the beach, but one was talking about the drink and the other thought she was referring to the hot guy in the water," Dani laughs.

"Oh yeah, I do love that one. Or how 'bout the one with the two old men who decide to wear their shorts below their butts like all the kids are doing, only their underwear keeps slipping down too, because they have no ass to hold anything up." Shane starts laughing along with Dani. "Their asses are all hanging out. It's so gross."

I lift my head off the desk and look at them both. "Ha ha. Shut up. We are in real trouble here, and you two are making jokes?"

"Technically, they are not our jokes, they are …" Shane tries to point out.

"I don't care whose they are. Just shut up and help me. Help me!"

"Okay, calm down before you blow one of those blood vessels in your head," Dani says, standing up and coming to my side to rub my head like I'm a child.

"Is that better?"

"Go, please. Both of you. Just go." *They drive me insane.* I am under severe stress and they are laughing? A sudden knocking on the door and Shane jumps up to talk to the unfamiliar man.

"Uh Dillon, you have a visitor," Shane says, stepping to the side to let an older gentleman step through my door. I stand up looking the man over, who stands tall in his expensive suit and questionable approach.

"Can I help you?" I ask.

"Yes, my name is Johnathan Skelton. You can call me John," he says, holding out his hand to me.

I take it glancing at the bodyguards standing behind the man as if he is a walking Fort Knox. "Hi John, my name is …"

"Dillon Conrad, I know. I have heard a lot of good things about you and your family." I cock my head and start to question him, but before I can, he finds a suitable chair and sits down as if he plans to stay awhile. "I am going to get straight to the point Mr. Conrad. I want to buy your factory." Dani stiffens at my side with a sharp gasp.

"Well, I'm sorry … John, the factory isn't for sale."

"Oh, no? I heard it was near bankruptcy and that other offers were already being considered."

"You heard wrong. We have found a new life and plan on making some changes. We are rebuilding and coming back better than ever."

"Oh really? How is that?"

"We have a plan underway, a plan that isn't available to the public right now."

"Well it must be a good one." I nod. He takes out a piece of paper from his pocket and borrows a pen to scratch something off of it and write something new. "Well, I had a number in mind, but since you seem so sure this place is going to be more valuable, then here, this is my new offer." He hands me the piece of paper, and I glance at him once before glancing at the number and handing it to Dani. "I'm sorry, my dear. I don't believe we have been properly introduced," he says standing to greet her more formally.

"Dani Portman. I am a new partner in the company."

"Portman? Oh yes, you are Douglas Portman's daughter?" Dani nods. "I thought he was one of the bidders on this place?"

"He was, but I am not associated with my father. I am here on my own," Dani says, looking at the number and trying to hold onto her poker face, but she has to gulp, which gives us away.

John smiles, knowing instantly he offered way more than we are worth. "That offer comes with jobs. Unlike Mr. Portman, I don't plan to tear the factory down, but help it flourish. I have an interest in building up the community and providing jobs, not tearing down and destroying history. I would, of course, like all your best employees to stay on and hope to be able to hire even more over time. And, from what I have heard, you are the man to head up this place, so I would like for you to stay on and run it for me. I would be a financial support mostly."

"Mostly?" I question, unsure if I really want to know.

"Well I don't let anyone have complete say over my money."

"I don't understand your motives, John. Excuse me if I am a little skeptical."

"Sure you are. You are an intelligent man. You would be foolish to believe that I am offering this with no catches."

"And the catch is?" I ask as Shane stands behind the men mimicking us being strangled to death. *Well at least I know his opinion without having to ask.*

"I want to run a side business out of the factory too. I have a man that will be running that part of it with his people, but it will be run in conjunction with the furniture you are already making. I find it to be a lucrative place … *way* to handle my prime business interests," he says with a demonic greed about him.

I sit back as Dani stands next to me, sighing. She places a hand on my shoulder, and without even looking at her, I know she is nervous and anxious to get this man out of here as quickly as possible. "Well we will discuss your offer, and if we decide it is of interest to us, then we will be in touch," I say, standing and showing the man and his guards to the door.

"Mr. Conrad, don't take too long to make your decision. Otherwise, I might have to resort to less preferred tactics to get what I want," Skelton says, nodding towards both Dani and I before walking out.

Once they leave, I feel an overwhelming pressure weigh me down like never before.

"Oh Dillon, what are we going to do?"

"We are going to keep going and hope we find a way to make this place more valuable for what it can build, rather than what criminal activity it can hide. We need an indestructible plan and fast."

No matter what my father wants, I only have two choices: close down forever or start up a new and fresh idea. At this point, I decide it better to make a big move rather than throw it all away. Now that Shane is here, I have someone that I can trust to help me with design and marketing. We are going to go from casual living furniture to baby furniture with our new technology leading the way. Creatively designed cribs and dressers, changing tables, and anything else we can match up and sell as a set, including a mobile that fits nicely with our new beds. The change is going to be a shock, but our existing machinery should be good enough to build the furniture pieces we need, and we are partnering with a technology manufacturer to help make our sensors. I am even having a new mobile build center put in, which we don't have the money for, so I cleaned out my retirement fund and put everything I had into this insane plan. Now, all we have to do is … *make it work*.

I worked out the final details of my ideas with Dani, and then we brought in Warren to confirm that it could work. He was a step higher than unenthusiastic, which we took to be a good thing. With the help of the few people left at the factory, Shane, Dani, my father, and I rearrange a few machinery pieces in the factory to help make my idea work seamlessly. Shane and I have already figured out a sales campaign, and Dani has been negotiating contracts with our suppliers for days. We only have so much money to make this work, so it has to work the first time. Once we begin to get supplies in, we go to work. We have Warren, Rafe, Carl, Jack, and Colleen in addition to Shane, Dani, myself, and sometimes my father when he can't stand being left out any longer. It's tough to get it all done with the small crew, but we can't afford to hire any help until we sell product, and we can't sell product until we have product to sell. This vicious circle is killing us all. Everyone is working way past their limits to help out where they can and being good enough not to ask too many questions. I am keeping the main idea behind all of this change, the mobiles and sensors, between Shane, Dani, and myself. Security hasn't been the best for this place, and I would prefer to let our enemies think we are on our last leg and leave us alone than give them any reason to strike a final blow against us. The rest of the staff is curious as to why we are doing this, and I am sure they're already looking for new jobs. Soon after the furniture building staff leave, my mobile crew stays and works on our secret project. It's stressful, and we are all exhausted. We're taking shifts to sleep and shower when it becomes too much for the others to handle. Tonight, Dani and I are left alone when one of the machines malfunctions. "Damn it!" Dani yells as sparks fly around her. I rush to her and pull her out of the way before trying to calm the sparking beast down. "Dillon, be careful!" Dani yells at me when one of the live wires flies up and nearly hits me. I wait for the right moment, grab the live wire with my gloved hand, and pull the key to cut the power.

"Get the tools and let me patch this thing again," I say, cursing it.

"That's the third time this week. I am not sure a patch is going to hold anymore. We need to fix it, Dillon."

"That takes time Dani, and it's already …" I look at her face and realize she's right. Someone is going to get really hurt next time. "Alright, I'll try to fix it." I crawl underneath the damn machine, look at the belts and wires, and wonder where to start first.

"How's it look?" Dani asks me. "You don't know, do you?" I try to say something smart, but for some reason, I can't think of anything that won't instantly tip her off that I don't know what the hell I am doing. "Dillon?"

"I'm thinking!" I yell back at her.

"We should call someone that knows what they are doing."

I think for a few minutes. "Okay, call Rafe. He's good with electronics. He can probably figure this out."

"Rafe?! He's a computer junkie; he doesn't fix large machinery. Your Dad told you who knew how to take care of all these machines and keep this place working," Dani says, peeking her head under to give me her attitude eyes.

I crawl back out and meet her face to face. "I'm not calling him, Dani. Besides, he would never even consider coming to help me."

"He wouldn't be only helping you," she says with a smile. I look her over with a snarl. "Don't look at me that way. Lucas and I had a nice lunch the other day, and he has really matured since high school. I'll talk to him and ask him to come back. We can add him to the payroll; it's only another week before we go live."

"Let's try Rafe first," I say, and she huffs in my face.

"Ugh! You are so stubborn! You are part of the problem, you know. If you would grow up and learn to let things go then you might be less frustrated in life."

"I am just fine with my life," I say, slamming my work gloves down on a nearby table.

"Oh! You are …" I smile in her face, waiting for her to finish. "I'm going to do what I want; I am a partner, so I can make decisions too." I watch her stick her chin up at me in defiance and walk away.

"Where are you going?" She ignores me and continues to the office, "Dani, don't you dare!" I yell after her. She continues on, so I run after her, and then she starts running. *Damn it.* I chase her around the factory, trying to catch her until we both start laughing. "Come here!"

"Make me." She dashes away to her bag and grabs her cell. "I'm going to call him right now." I shake my head and dive across the floor and grab her. Dani falls into my arms, and I am able to roll her over and pin her arms above her head. "What are you going to do Dillon? Hold me here forever?" I try to grab her phone, but she slides it across the floor and I have to let her go to get to it. Dani takes advantage of her freedom and slides in under me, grabbing it first. I have to hold her down from behind with her ass pressed against my cock. At first, I think I am the only one distracted by the position, but when she wiggles her ass against me, I quickly realize the temptress knows exactly what she's doing.

"Keep rubbing my dick with your ass and I am going to fuck you right here. Now give me that phone." She looks over her shoulder at me and winks … *oh what's that?* Dani suddenly scrambles forward and gets away from me. "Oh no you don't." I chase after her again, grab her, and throw her down on a table, holding her down with my own body. "Oh yeah, you're mine. Now give it to me! Give it to me, Dani!"

The sudden footsteps near us cause us both to look up and see my father and Shane watching us with our dinner in their hands and both shaking their heads. "Um, I don't think that's how that machine works," Shane says. I help Dani off the table with our spectators judging our every move.

"They told me it's called *wrestling*," My father says.

"Oh," Shane replies, smiling wide. "Oh yeah, 'wrestling'. I use to wrestle, but since I have been here, I haven't had any time to wrestle. I would very much like to get back to wrestling… before I die. So, can we please get back to work and finish this project?"

I roll my eyes, "She was trying to call Lucas to fix this stupid machine, but I tried to explain to her that Rafe could fix it just as easily."

"Lucas? Oh, I hate Lucas," Shane says. "I vote Rafe. Sure, he smells like road-kill sometimes, and he's really creepy, but who isn't these days?"

"Dani is right. Lucas is the best one for the job. Rafe would be able to patch at best, and you have already patched too much already," My father says, looking over the machine.

"Well considering I am the controlling partner, I say Rafe it is," I announce proudly with a high five from Shane. Then, I see Dani cross her arms and push her chin up in the air at me. *I swear, women!*

Chapter 12

Dani

"Thank you for coming out, Lucas. I know it is risky for you to be leaving your current job to come here, but once I explain what we are planning to do, I think you will be as excited as the rest of us."

"You know I would do anything for you Dani, but I am not sure about Dillon. Did he really suggest this idea?" I stand back, trying to think of the right words to say. "That's what I thought. He doesn't want me here anymore than I want to be around him."

"Okay no, he actually said don't call you, but like you, he is stubborn and is not considering what is best for the future of this place. I promise you, Lucas, if you come in now and help us get going, you won't regret it. We will remember who was there for us. Besides, you really owe Matt to help give this place one last try. He would do it for you."

"What exactly is this big idea? I can't imagine it being so great that it can save this place."

"Are you going to help?" I ask with a look of determination.

He sighs, "You know I have a hard time resisting you. If I do this, then can I get another chance too? Go out with me one night, dinner and a movie, no hand holding or anything else unnecessary. Just two old friends having a night out, I promise." I consider it while looking him over. Lucas seems sweet as ever so...

"Just two friends having a fun night out together?" He nods with a sexy smile. "Deal." I hold out my hand and end up hugging the tall hunk, wondering if I made the right decision. "How in the world are you divorced?"

"I was an immature idiot, and she was smart enough to get out before I messed up her life any more than I already did," he says honestly.

I motion for him to follow me, and we end up on the floor with Rafe who is looking things over with a screwdriver in one hand and a hammer in the other. Not exactly reassuring. I pat Dillon on the back as he and Shane watch Rafe in horror.

"Okay, now are you ready to do it my way?" I ask.

Dillon turns and sighs the instant he sees Lucas. "Oh great, Lucas Charles is here. Fine. You can stay, but don't start following me around and asking if you can be my friend, and no need changing yourself to try and match me. You're not that ugly Lucas." Dillon smiles and pats him on the arm. "You just be the best Lucas you can be, and that will be good enough. I'll take care of being the good looking one in the company."

"Hey?!" Shane pipes up suddenly.

"Oh, sorry Shane, of course you're totally hot too," Dillon says, smiling once Shane nods happily.

Lucas rolls his eyes as do I. "Dillon, don't you and your hot girlfriend have something else to do for a little while?" I ask. "And take Rafe somewhere before he breaks something."

"Go clock out, Rafe. Get some sleep and come back later. Shane and I are going to go talk beauty secrets. Don't try and listen in," Dillon says, looking Lucas and I over suspiciously before walking up towards his office with Shane happily following behind him.

"I see not much has changed with those two. Why again did you ever choose him over me? Over anyone for that matter?" Lucas asks.

"I know he seems immature at times, but he is really smart. Once he gets in that office and starts working, he is all business. He won't let this place fall, I guarantee you." I look up at the office window as Lucas does and notice two bare asses pressed firmly against the glass. *Oh wonderful timing, Dillon.*

"Ah, yeah, all business," Lucas laughs. "I'll trust you and try to believe the jackass has some potential, other than being able to moon an entire factory at one time."

"Thank you," I say as Lucas nods and gets to work. I quickly begin to explain what we need done and why.

It's been another long, hard day, and with still more to go, I decide to take a shower at the factory and then take a quick nap on the sofa in Dillon's office. It is not the nicest of places to shower, but anything at this point would be refreshing. As I wash off, I hear a noise and look to see if I see anyone.

"Hello? Hello, is anyone there?" No one says anything, yet I still feel like someone is watching me. "Dillon? Dillon is that you? It's not funny. You're creeping me out. Stop it!" Still no answer, so

I quickly finish up and grab a towel to investigate, but I find nothing. I get dressed faster than ever before, and leaving the locker room, I walk up on Shane and Dillon, laughing hysterically. *Jackasses, it was them.* "It's not funny. You scared the shit out of me!" I snap at them. They both turn to me, looking confused and unsure what to say. "You weren't spying on me in the shower room a few minutes ago?" They both shake their heads slowly.

"Are you okay?" Dillon asks. He stands up and takes hold of me. "You are shaking like a leaf. Neither of us was in there, and I don't think anyone else could have been either. Lucas is the only other one here, and we have been busy watching him this whole time. Well, watching him and trying to hit him with spit wads."

My shoulders sink. "Can you please try to be mature for a few minutes when he is around?" I ask. They look at each other as if they are trying really hard to consider the idea. "Oh you know what? Forget it. Just please stop messing with me at least."

"I swear, Dani. We weren't in there. I think you are overly tired is all. Go upstairs and get some sleep. I promise we will leave you alone so you can rest," Dillon says, kissing my forehead and scooting me along.

I don't hesitate to take him up on his offer. I head upstairs, turn out the lights in Dillon's office, and crawl onto the sofa with a blanket and a pillow. I am so tired that I begin drifting off almost immediately.

"Dani!" I'm hearing someone screaming my name, but I am so tired I just want them to be quiet and leave me alone. When I feel my body aggressively picked up, I open my eyes slightly to see a raging fire surrounding me as I lie against Lucas's chest. I hold onto him, shielding my eyes from the fire and trying to comprehend what's happening. Shane and Dillon fight the fire with extinguishers as sirens begin to blare outside.

Lucas sets me down outside, and falls down next to me. He quickly begins looking me over for injury. "Are you okay?"

"Yeah, I think so. Are you okay?" I ask while looking him over. He smiles and nods before hugging me tight. "What happened?"

"I don't know. I looked up at the window and saw a glow, and by the time I got up there, the fire had spread throughout most of the office." Lucas sits back and curses. "The fucking alarms never went off, and how the hell did that fire start? Fuck."

Dillon and Shane stumble towards us and sit down, huffing and puffing, trying to clear their lungs while the firefighters take over. I look over at Dillon, and he's an absolute mess, but I don't care. The moment he opens his arms up to me, I fall in. He kisses the top of my head, "Oh Dillon, I am so sorry. I don't know what happened."

"As long as you're okay, I don't care about anything else. You scared the shit out of me. I was screaming your name. When you didn't answer, I swear I …" He holds me a little tighter. "Luckily Lucas was able to see clearer and figure out where you were. Did you move the sofa to the other side of the room?" I shake my head, and he sighs. "I guess someone was watching you." I lay my head on his shoulder with a new fear creeping up my spine. I fell asleep so heavily. If Lucas hadn't of seen the fire, I can't imagine I would have ever woken up.

The fire destroyed most of the office interior, but thanks to the boys' quick work, it was contained long enough for firefighters to extinguish it before it spread to anywhere else. Someone broke the rickety latch on the back door, snuck into the office while I was in there, and tossed a match to the desk full of paperwork. The computer was destroyed, as were a lot of files, but thankfully, Dillon and I had saved everything to an offsite server two days ago. The place needs to be aired out and inspected before anyone can work in that area, but the rest of the building is free to use. Dillon moves the office to the break room and sections it off with an inventive arrangement of the vending machines. We use the home computer to get back online and back to work. The only problem is, someone is determined to break us, and we can't leave the factory vulnerable anymore. If anyone gets to our machines or our stock of product, we could be finished for good. Warren is ready to stand and block as much as he can, but he needs help, so Dillon steps in and begins sleeping at the factory too. As does Shane. As do I. The dedication and desperation seem to impress Lucas, Rafe, and a few others that we have kept on, and they, as well, begin sleeping at the factory, helping to take shifts to protect what little we have. The exhaustion is beginning to become too much though.

"I said move to the right of it!" Rafe yells at Colleen as she tries to help him.

"But you said left before, Dumbass!"

"You're a fucking idiot! Why would I say left when I clearly need you to go right?" Rafe yells.

Dillon steps in immediately and calms Colleen. "Rafe go take a break, and I'll finish up here."

"I can do it!" he snaps back.

"You're tired, and you're making simple mistakes." Dillon stands his ground with Rafe until Rafe throws his gloves and stomps off to the break room.

I watch everyone go back to work before going to talk to Rafe. I walk in on him kicking a vending machine and cursing under his breath. "You should go lie down and take a break. I will clear it with Dillon," I say, walking towards him with a sympathetic tone. "It's been a long day, and we really appreciate all the effort you have put into helping us."

Rafe turns towards me and looks me over from my head to my toes. He twirls his tongue in his mouth with a twisted smile that sends chills down my spine. "You appreciate my effort huh, all my efforts? How much do you appreciate my efforts? As much as you do Dillon's?"

"Excuse me?" I ask, stepping away from him disgusted.

I watch him as he glares at me for a few seconds and then wipes his expression clean and stands back with a smile. "My bad. I promise I don't mean any harm. I guess I really am tired. I'm sorry." He grabs his drink and chips and goes off to the locker room to sleep while I walk back out to my workstation.

"Are you okay?" Lucas asks. "You look pale." I smile up at

him with a quick nod. "Maybe you should go take a break and get some rest too," he says, trying to guide me away from my station and towards the locker room, which is the last place I want to be right now. "You are really shaking."

"I'm fine, I …" I say before a fire bottle is thrown through one of our windows and lights up my workstation.

Lucas shields me while Dillon grabs an extinguisher and puts it out before it gets out of hand. "Fuck! What is happening here?" Lucas says.

Dillon looks over at me, "Well I guess it's a good thing we invested in non-flammable fabric," he says, fisting the fabric on my station and tossing it into the trash. "I am so sick of this shit!" Dillon kicks some trash cans and slams his fists into some nearby sorting shelves. His animated frustration mirrors all of our frustrations. Someone is trying to break us, and I hope like hell it's not my father.

Another day, and we are all barely able to look at each other. Every little noise we hear we all jump and wait to see what direction we should run. Our nerves are shot, and we all look like hell, but we are still moving and trying to meet our goals. The sounds of the machines and slow motions of our bodies working is all we really hear lately, but as we work, we begin to hear car horns going off and pulling in around the factory. I stand up, and Dillon grabs my arm and pulls me back. "You and Colleen stay here." The men head out the door, and after a few minutes Dillon walks in with a giant smile on his face. He waves for me to come outside. I walk outside to see an entire community drive up to the doors and begin parking around the factory; standing guard with a wall of shotguns and baseball bats. With three days left to meet our goals, Matthew Conrad comes up big, calls in every favor owed to him, and creates an army of neighbors to keep our hopes alive. I lean against Dillon's chest and smile up at his incredible, crooked smile. "We are going to do this."

"Yes, we are!" I shout, jumping into his arms. He spins me around, screaming for joy, as does everyone else.

"Alright let's get back to work!" Dillon yells out. He looks down at me. "You especially, partner," he says, smacking my ass forward.

"Yes, sir."

Chapter 13

Dillon

Early Monday morning at the Conrad factory, everyone looks about the way I feel: half dazed and the other half still asleep. We brought back quite a few people for our big day, hoping for the best and planning for even better. We have everything ready and opened up to begin taking orders. It's a packed house this morning, and the factory is bright. My old office is somewhat back together after some much needed help from my father and friends. Neighbors came in to help wherever they could and repaired our doors, got our broken windows covered and set up some temporary, and fairly cheap, security cameras to help deter as much criminal activity as possible. I never thought we would make it to this point and to make sure everyone feels as good about our future as I do, I walk around and greet everyone, but when I notice my father come in, I cut my new, morning routine short.

"Decide to come out of retirement?" I ask him.

"No, I thought I would stop by and see if you wanted to go to lunch?"

"It's 8 o'clock in the morning, Dad. It's a little early for lunch."

"Oh, well I guess it is. I must have gotten through my errands faster than I thought. Then, maybe I will hang out here for a little while until lunch," he says, but it sounds more like he is searching for permission.

He's curious, and rightfully so. He hasn't been here to see everything finally together. "Actually, I am glad you're here. It gives me a chance to give you a tour." He turns with a brightness in his eyes that makes me smile. I was afraid of my father's opinion on things, not that he would ever tell me he dislikes it or would ever show an ounce of disappointment in me, especially not at this point. But as we walk along the freshly cleaned floors, he seems happy. He greets his old friends and workers like he always did, and he does it all with his old Conrad Furniture cap on his head.

"This is nice," he says, looking over a new crib we just finished.

"Yeah, that's one of my favorites. too. Do you want to see the rest of the set?" He nods with anxious anticipation as he follows me. I show him everything, explaining in excited detail how it all works and waiting to see if he approves. When he turns to me with tears in his eyes and a bright smile, I know I have done well according to him.

"This is wonderful, Dillon. You have made it your own, and it is truly wonderful." I pat him on the back and look away so as not to embarrass the teary-eyed man any further. "I have to get back to work, but feel free to help out. We can use all the extra bodies we can get." My father happily agrees and gets started almost immediately. I go on about my day and leave the old man to enjoy his retirement the way he wants to.

Numbers are beginning to move in the right direction, and for a brief moment, I feel optimistic about this place. Then, there is a cacophony of disturbances from the factory floor. I run down to see everyone standing around, staring into the storage area. I move in and find Dani hovering over my father who is laid out on the floor. "Dad! What happened?" I say, noticing the collapse of some of our heavy storage shelves.

"He was helping Maggie get some supplies, and next thing you know, the whole thing came down on top of him," Dani says, holding his head and keeping him calm.

I look over my father who clearly has a broken leg and no telling what else. When his breathing becomes forced and jagged, I know something else is very wrong. I stay with my father until the ambulance arrives and leave with him. Dani shows up at the hospital soon after we do, sits down right next to me, and takes my hand. We don't need to speak to know what the other one is thinking. Hours later, she is curled up against my chest while I lay my head on hers. When the nurse comes out, we both jump up to greet her.

"Your father had a heart attack, in addition to several broken bones. We had to perform emergency surgery and put a stent in to help his blood flow properly again. He's going to need to stay here for observation for a while."

"Is he going to be alright?"

"He should be fine, but it is going be a long healing process.

He is going to need some rehabilitation and lot of care, even after he gets out of the hospital. He either will need in-house care or he needs to be admitted into a long term care facility, depending on what you can afford." I stand in front of her completely dumbfounded, unable to think of anything else other than my father. *Afford? The vagrant near the factory gave me back change this morning.* "There are a number of government assistance programs that could help you if you need?" I look at her with my stomach churning. She seems to understand my turmoil and lays a gentle hand on me. "Well no need to tell me now, just let me know what you would like to do before he is released. I will gather all the information you need to make a decision and get it to you as soon as I can. If you would like to see him, come with me, and I will show you to his room," the nurse says, showing us into his room. He looks terrible and so feeble it makes me queasy. "He is pretty heavily sedated right now, so I wouldn't expect too much out of him," the nurse says before leaving us alone with him.

I near the side of his bed and take his hand, causing him to open his eyes and look my way. "How are you feeling?" He nods, trying to speak. "No need to answer that. Just rest." He grips my hand tight to keep me from leaving. "I'm not going to leave, Dad."

"I'm sorry," he says roughly. I shake my head and try to calm him back down. "I'm sorry about the baby," he gulps. "You will have another chance." He looks over at Dani and grabs her hand. "You both have another chance … together." I assume he is delusional until I look up at Dani, whose expression tells me more than I could have ever expected.

I calm my father back down, nodding in agreement and saving my questions for later. After visiting hours are over, I drive Dani and I back home without a word spoken between us. She is waiting for me to be the first one to speak; only I have no idea of what to say. We reach home and walk inside, and I am shocked that she doesn't rush out of sight. Instead, she stands in place with her back to me, taking deep breaths.

Then she turns. "His name was Evan, and he died of SIDS a few weeks after his birth. He was why I left when I did." I stare hard at her, afraid of letting anything out that might release something I can't handle. "Say something. I know how you must feel right now, but ..."

"Oh you do? You know how I must feel? Not only is my father in serious condition, but I also find out that my son died, a son I didn't even know I had!" I yell as my whole body begins to tremble with emotion and understanding of the loss of my own child.

"Dillon, it was a very confusing time for me. I loved you so much, and I thought it would ruin everything for you. I didn't know what to do... My father convinced me ..."

"Your father? I'm sorry, Dani. As much as I despise your father, I know you well enough to know that even he can't make you do something you don't want to do." I fist my hair, wanting to scream at her every damn thing that is coming into my mind.

"True, and I would have never left except... that night, after he found us, it was awful, Dillon. I had been arguing so much with him and my mother. He wouldn't even let me stay at the house. He threatened to sue for full custody of me and label my mother as unfit. My mother was crying, my father kept yelling at her, and things only got worse from there. I couldn't sleep, and then I started getting sick. My father forced me to see this doctor he knew, and that's when I found out. I was in shock, but mostly, I was scared. The initial plan was to get away to clear my head for a while, but the longer I stayed away, the more trouble I had being able to tell you. I became so depressed that I didn't want to see anyone. We were both so young, and we had only been together for a few months. You never stayed with anyone longer than that. I was sure you were done with me, or soon would be, anyway. I just couldn't stand the thought of you turning your back on me."

"Did you ever think that the reason my relationships never lasted was because none of those girls measured up to you? I loved you! You were all I cared about, Dani! And you left me and then took something even more from me. At least you got to hold him." She gulps with the most heartbroken look I have ever seen, and at once, she begins to cloud my anger towards her. "I need to take a drive alone, so I can think. Don't call me or try to talk to me at all. I mean it, Dani. I don't want anything to do with you right now." She nods, holding herself within her own arms."

"I'm so sorry, Dillon," she cries.

I start to look at her, but I am so angry and hurt that I'm afraid of what I might say, so I walk out, without another word spoken between us. I shake my head realizing, *that's why my dad designed that sensor.* I am not sure where I am going or if I am even going anywhere in particular. Memories of when she left have haunted me. Nothing made sense, but now, it all makes sense. Even the smallest of peculiar details now fit:

Dani's Dad is in town this weekend, and she wants me to have dinner with them. He has never been a fan of mine, so I insist on Shane coming too. Maybe he can distract the man's sharp eyes off of me some. Douglas Portman is a wealthy businessman who believes you should never let your life interrupt business, which is why he has never been married and why his only child lives with her mother full time. He seems to love Dani and care for her when it's convenient to him. He never liked the idea that her new friends were both boys, and now that we are dating, he is even less thrilled. I don't know why Dani insisted on me coming with them. The moment I show up at the door, he looks me over with disgust, and I even wore a suit like my mother said to. Shane walks in behind me and immediately tries to walk back out. I grab him by his dorky sweater and pull him back in. "Don't you dare leave me."

"I changed my mind. A free steak dinner isn't worth this. Tell Dani …"

"You are going. You owe me. I got you that date with Jessi, didn't I?"

Shane rolls his eyes into a gentlemanly smile. "Mr. Portman, so nice to see you again," Shane says, shaking his hand and ignoring the man's grumbling about Shane's dumb looking sweater.

I step in with my hand out. "Mr. Portman, how are you?"

"I've been better. The fucks in Washington are trying to steal my company piece by piece, and they think I am going to just sit back and let it happen. I am preparing to go to war. I am prepared to battle every single day and night if I have to. I will crawl through the muddy swamps and fight alligators to prove I won't give up. In the end, they will know I am not to be messed with."

"Oh-kay. Good to hear?" I say, looking back at Shane who is just as confused as I am.

Dani comes down in a sweet dress, and I smile all over myself when I see her until I catch site of Mr. Portman eyeing me down with an intent to kill. "Daddy, you look handsome," Dani says, distracting him away from my throat.

I want to kiss her so bad, but I hold off until I can sneak in a kiss when he isn't looking. She holds both of our hands throughout the night. I am not sure she was able to eat much since she was trying so hard to appease us both. Shane never said a word. He smiled a few times whenever someone asked him a question, but would never do more than nod or shake his head and continue to stuff food into his mouth.

Needless to say, I got bombarded with questions about my studies and education, career plans, life plans, and, "Do you really think football is the career path for you, Dillon? It's fun for now, but where can it possibly take you long term?"

I try to stay quiet and ignore him, but no matter what I do or don't do, the man jumps all over it to make me feel as bad about myself as possible. Dani tries to defend me, but it only encourages the rudeness more. The best I can do is endure the horrible man. When we return from dinner, the man seems surprised that Dani's mother decided to take a trip out of town while he is here. He is so distracted by her, "lack of parenting skills", that Shane and I are excused so he can call her privately and let her know.

As soon as I step out of the house, I jerk my tie off and sigh as Shane simply tries to shake off the bad from himself. "What is that man's problem?" I say, throwing my hands up in the air.

"Well, he clearly has stepped up his game on hating you. I guess dating

Dani has not helped him warm up to you any. If you ever marry Dani, I suggest running away … far, far away and never coming back," Shane says, getting ready to walk away before turning back to me. "Let me know before you do that though so I can run away too and hide. Don't leave me here to be questioned to death by him." I laugh as he heads across the street home. I go up to my room, change, and wait for the jackass to leave so I can be with Dani alone.

Mr. Portman takes his sweet time leaving Dani behind. After an hour, I creep over to the back door and get ready to knock, but she has the door open and is pulling me in before I can even say hello. Dani is all over me, and I am starting to not care about any of my previous issues. "So, what did I do to deserve all this?"

"You put up with it and didn't try to fight with my dad at all. He baited you over and over, but you stayed quiet and let it go. I think you're maturing, Mr. Conrad."

"Yeah, I must be because I really wanted to kick him in his big fat head," I say, picking her up and carrying her to the sofa in the other room and boldly going underneath her dress. She pulls my shirt off over my head and wraps her legs around my waist. I don't waste any more time and remove her dress. The moment gets away from me before I realize we are screwing openly in her living room. "Are you sure your mother isn't coming back tonight?"

"Are you kidding? With my dad in town? I am surprised she is still in the country," she says, pulling me back to her lips.

"Good point."

Dani and I take advantage of the empty house. Wrapped up naked under blankets, we spend all night talking and watching movies before waking up to her father bearing down on us.

"Danielle!" he yells, startling both of us.

Dani quickly covers herself while staying at my side. "Daddy, what are you doing here?"

"I was worried about you being here by yourself, and rightfully so." Mr. Portman grabs me by the throat and picks me up off the floor. "You get up and get your ass away from my daughter before I kill you!" The argument only intensifies when Dani runs in between us and cries to save me, telling him that she loves me. I am forced to go home after he calls my parents to come get me, before he has me arrested.

I spend the whole next day waiting to speak to her, waiting to find her at my door or something. I show up at school early, thinking surely I will see her there, but a week passes, and another, and she never shows up. The best I can get is a brief appearance she makes at her window crying. She tries to tell me something, but before I can get my window open, her father walks in and pulls down her window shade. I can't take it anymore, so despite my father's wishes, I go to her door and knock, begging to see her, but she has already gone.

Her mother answers the door with swollen eyes and a clearly broken heart herself. "I'm sorry, Dillon. She's not here. She left with her father, and I don't know when she will be back or if she will ever be."

I went home dazed and inconsolable. I didn't care about anything for a long while, and then I hated everything and everyone. I couldn't wait to get out of this city and never come back. I blamed everyone for my troubles except her, but the longer I went without hearing from her, the more I told myself I didn't need her, and that, in fact, I hated her. The only trouble was, it was never true. I could never stop loving her.

I decide to sleep at the hospital and wait for my father to wake so I can talk to him. He has always been my idol and the one I go to when I have a problem, and I need him now more than ever.

As he wakes up, he looks over at me, groaning, "Whoa, did I get hit by a semi?" He sits up some, looking around the room. "Why aren't you at work? You know I will be fine, right?"

"You're not fine at all, Dad."

"I'll manage."

"Not by yourself, you won't. From what the doctor told me, you are going to need some constant help for a while."

"I wish they hadn't told you that crap, about needing special care," he says, dismissing it as nothing important. "Anything else happen while I was out of it?"

"Yeah, actually. I found out quite a bit while you were drugged up." He looks at me with wide eyes. "You told me you were sorry about my son." My father's eyes focus hard on me. "How long did you know, Dad, and why would you keep that from me?"

He doesn't answer me right away. He takes several breaths while he closes his eyes tight. I wait patiently, and he finally grabs my hand. "Dani's mother told your mother about the baby. The woman was so excited and crazy, trying to rush out of her house with a suitcase and in her house shoes. We thought something was wrong, but in her excitement, she said the baby was coming and she had to get to Dani. Once we knew, she confided in us about everything after that. We wanted to see him so bad, and even planned a trip, but before we could get there, we got a call, and she told us what happened. The woman was a mess, and your mother was always a good shoulder to cry on." I shake my head, clenching my fists and trying to understand why they would keep this from me. "We didn't tell you because we didn't want to cause you anymore pain. Dani wasn't coming back. She was hospitalized; she was so distraught." I look up at him. "Yeah, she was not good. She left because she didn't want you to see her pregnant. Her father told her you would leave her as soon as she started gaining weight. I am sure not something a vulnerable teenage girl wants to hear." I cringe, sitting back in my chair, hating that man even more. "She thought, after the baby was born, she would come back and find you, but when Evan died, she fell apart, and she wouldn't see anyone. Oh I don't know. Maybe we should have told you, but we weren't sure what was best for either of you at that point. We only wanted to protect you Son, especially after the baby died. What good would it have done to tell you then?"

"She should have told me."

"Maybe, but until you understand what it is like to be a young, scared, pregnant girl, I don't think you can make a judgment call on what she should have done."

"So why is she back now?"

"Because I talked her into it. You still love her, and she still loves you. Sometimes you have to forgive in order to keep the right person in your life. Her coming back here should be a sure sign she is here for you; she is by your side every step of the way, just like when you were kids. You need to stop being so stubborn and try looking at it from her point of view. Try a little understanding, Dillon." He sits back exhausted, and I give him some time to rest.

When the doctors come in to check on my father, I say my goodbye and promise to be back to check on him.

I head home to take a shower, but Dani has already taken the bus into work, to be a factory worker. The girl who graduated from the top of her class in college, an ex-successful attorney, now helps run a rundown factory. For me. When I show up to work, I let everyone know about my father's condition and thank them for their concerns and well wishes. I don't talk to Dani as much as she seems to want me to, but this is not the place, and I am still trying to process everything. How can I simply let what she did go? She took something I can never get back. She took my son away. I want so blame her, hate her and her father, but then, I would lose more than just a son. I would lose her too. Forgiveness is not something I have ever been good at; however, I think it's about time I learned. Towards the end of the day, I make a point to tell her I will see her at home later, and she nods with a nervous smile.

As soon as I walk in the door, she has a huge dinner ready and cleaned the house to an immaculate condition. I look around, not sure if I am in the right place. When Dani walks into the room, I ask, "You only left an hour before me didn't you?"

"I was nervous, and when I am nervous, I need to work on something to take my mind off of things. Um, I made dinner. Actually, that's a lie. I ordered it and put in nice dishes. I did try to make spaghetti, but that didn't work out too well. This is from that new place though, and I hear it's really good."

I laugh, imagining her trying to cook. "It smells good."

"Do you want to sit down and eat …with me?"

"Not right now. I want to talk first." I pause steadying myself to ask the question I have long wanted to ask her. "Why did you leave Dani? I would have never left you, especially not pregnant."

"I tried to tell you. I did. When I saw you through the window, I had just found out that day, and I wanted so bad to run to you. You looked so happy and perfect, and I felt like I was a complete mess. I didn't want to do that to you. I wanted you to stay happy. I didn't know that I hurt you as bad as I did, and I am very sorry for that Dillon. I am so sorry. If I had known then when I know now ... I loved you so much, and I still do. The moment I saw you again, I wanted to run into your arms and never let go," she cries, looking up at me with her weepy sad eyes.

"Yeah, if we had known then what we know now, I imagine we both would have done things differently. Like, I would have stayed by your side no matter what. I would have never let you leave, no matter how much you thought it was best. Or maybe, I just wouldn't have had been so selfish and had sex with you in the middle of your living room while your father was still in town." I clear the tears from her cheek. "I'm sorry, Dani. I'm sorry I didn't know how to love you properly then. I promise that's not going to happen again." I lean down, taking her face into my hands and pressing my lips to hers with a slow motion that brings her into my arms. "I love you," I whisper against her cheek. Dani suddenly leaves my grasp and rushes out of the room. Before I have a chance to yell after her, she runs back in with something in her hand. She cautiously walks towards me and hands it to me. I look down at a picture of a baby. "This is him?" She nods. I sit down, feeling as if the wind was knocked out of me. "He's adorable."

"Yeah. Mom said he looks just like you, like he's nothing, but trouble. Sweet trouble. I wish I could tell you more, but I didn't get much of a chance to know him." Dani crashes in next to me, and with a slow inhale, I put an arm around her and sit back to enjoy the silent comfort that we both apparently need.

Chapter 14

Dillon

While concentrating on my work, I suddenly feel like someone is watching me. I slowly turn my head to see Warren. "Son of a bitch …Gees! Wow, what is with you? Say something."

"I thought you were busy, so I was waiting until you were done."

"Okay, thank you, but next time, please, the moment you walk through that door, actually no, before you walk through that door, announce yourself in some way so that I know you're here before you cause me to attach myself to the ceiling. Okay?"

"Okay. How would you like me to announce myself?" he asks dryly.

"I don't know, surprise me. No! On second thought, don't surprise me. Walk really hard and whistle so I hear you coming."

"Whistle?" I nod. "Whistle what?"

"Don't care. Now, what is it you need?"

"I was cleaning up the collapse of the storage shelving so I could restructure them," he says plainly.

I wait a little bit longer to see if there is any more to his important information. "Okay, great. Is that it?"

"No, I found something."

"Are you going to share it with me or am I supposed to guess?"

"I can't tell you. I have to show you." Okay. I get up and wave my hand for him to lead the way. When we get to the storage, he picks up some broken pieces and shows them to me. "See?" I look it over not understanding. "It didn't break. It was cut cleanly three-quarters of the way so that if anyone touched it, it would collapse and cause everything below it to collapse from the added weight. Now do you see?"

I take the piece and look at the smooth edge from where it was clearly cut, and suck in a breath, understanding. "Who did it?" He shrugs his shoulders. "Great, someone here is trying to sabotage us?"

"They are trying to intimidate you, intimidate our employees. This morning, I found people selling drugs in the parking lot. The other day, I found needles in the bathroom, and before that, I had to run off some hooligans harassing some of the women employees while they were outside on break, and before that …"

"Okay. I get it, but why am I just now hearing this?"

"Beause I thought it better to handle it and let you deal with getting the factory back on track, but now, we need more security. We need better cameras. We need some night watchmen, and we need proper fencing around the facility. There is a rumor around town that this place isn't safe."

"We don't have the money for any of that right now."

"Then we won't have employees much longer, no matter if we can pay them or not."

"Okay, I'll figure it out; just do your best to keep everyone calm." He nods and starts to spit, but holds off when I stare hard at him.

"Until you do, I think we should lock up our inventory. Only key-holders can get in, no one else. We need to keep a better eye on the product before someone comes in and really does damage."

I don't know how I am going to find the money to keep materials coming in to build with, get the new marketing ads made, and put in all this new security. When Dani walks into my office, I have my face buried in my hands. "That bad huh?" I nod. "Then I guess it is a bad time to talk about what you are going to do with your father. I went to see him on my lunch break, and the hospital is releasing him tomorrow. You know he can't stay in that house by himself."

"I can't afford to hire anyone, Dani. I am not even paying myself right now, and I certainly can't afford a full time care facility."

"I can do it." I look up at her. "If you can trust me, I can take care of your father, and handle business from home in between. I can help your father until he is back on his feet and then come back here full time."

"Dani, you have done enough already. This is purely a family matter. I need to figure this out on my own, but thank you for the offer," I say, believing I am making it better for her, but she growls and throws something at my head before rushing out and refusing to speak to me for the rest of the day. Every time I approach her at work, she walks in the opposite direction. "Dani, come on. I need to talk to you." I yell at her back. I kick a trash can and anything else within my path before noticing Shane and Warren watching me.

"Rough day?" Shane asks.

"She is impossible!" I yell, returning to my office to pace and try and figure out what her problem is now. I drive home alone and walk in the door to find her sitting alone in the dark. "Are you meditating?" I ask her.

"No."

"So you're talking to me now?"

"I am moving out," she says.

I sit on the coffee table across from her and wait for her to look up at me. "What do you want from me Dani? Forgiveness? Trust? What are you really doing here?"

"I love him too, you know. I loved your mother, and you, I am just as much a part of this family as you are," she says with her arms crossed and her lips pursed.

I laugh, realizing the mistake I made. "Oh, wow, I am an idiot."

"Yes, you are," she snaps back.

"I said that I was. If you want to help out …*our* family …then that would be great, Danielle."

"Don't smile like that at me. I'm mad at you." I stop smiling and look at her seriously, but she starts laughing. "Stop it. I am really mad."

"As mad as you were when you attacked me in the shower because that turned out well for me?" She jumps on me and starts hitting me as we both laugh. She finally settles down into my lap and begins playing with my shirt, "Forgive me?"

"If you do what I want," she says, unbuttoning my shirt and pushing it off my shoulders.

"And what is it you want?" I ask, enjoying her wandering hands and eager lips on my chest.

"Take your pants off, Conrad. I want to wrestle." I laugh and stand to unzip my pants for her. Stripping down to nothing while she feels up my legs and cradles my rapidly hardening erection into her mouth. She takes a long exhaling breath, and I watch my cock slide past her lips and against her tongue. My head spins, and I reach a maximum level of horniness I can't control.

I pull her up and look her over. "You need help with that zipper, Baby?" She turns her back to me as she pulls her hair over to one side. Kissing her neck, I drag the zipper down her back and just past the blue lace of the panties underneath. "Oooh my favorite color. Did you wear these for me?" She slips her dress off her shoulders, and I release the clasp on her bra, pushing it away as I feel around her body, take hold of her breasts, and rub them free. Pushing my hand down, under her panties, I rub my fingers against her wet softness. I can't contain myself any longer. There is one thing she has never let me do to her before. I turn her around and look into her eyes begging. "Dani please?" She doesn't speak while I fist her panties and pull them down to the floor with me. "Please, Dani?" I say, kissing her thigh. She steps back, sitting down on the sofa, and I smile. Taking hold of her ass, I pull her closer to the edge of the sofa and push her legs out far to the side. She watches me so intently that she stops breathing. I play and fondle, familiarizing myself with every freckle and every pink, succulent part of her. A kiss here, a touch there, and a deep force of my tongue dead center and she grips the cushion behind her head. I dive in, savoring. Her pussy is all mine, and I'm not letting it go until I taste what I want.

"Dillon!" she screams out until I lick my lips clean.

She's an easily controlled doll now; I take hold of her and turn her ass to me. Dani holds her bouncing breasts still as she backs up into me with a moan, feeling my erection drift in between her perfectly round cheeks and letting me play with a firm touch. Feeling my way in and sliding back out with a kiss to her neck and a grip of her hair, I tightly grasp her hips, and she whimpers my name again. She suddenly jerks away from me, pulling me into the floor and on top of her. I slide my hands up her arms, above her head, and push my fingers in between hers, holding her hands tight as my erection penetrates with ease into a rich, heated tightness that collapses against my dick. I can hardly breathe. Slowly, I drive in and draw out my cock while she arches her back, forcing her breasts into my face and allowing me to take each one into my mouth. I look down into Dani's eyes as she cries out in pleasure, and I quickly take hold of her lips with mine and embrace her warmly until we both erupt into a blissful release. We kiss, both smiling wide. "Did you like that? Me between your legs I mean?" Her bright eyes cause me to laugh. "Oh, that much huh? Well then, I must do that again, because I loved it, too." She hides her blushing face against my cheek. "Alright, my adorable girl, go upstairs, and I will make us dinner, in bed." I smack her bare ass as she runs away from me. Taking a moment, I grab my pants and put them on before suddenly having an odd feeling. I look around, feeling as if someone is watching me. Warren doesn't live here, so I start to dismiss it until I see a strange glimmer of light outside. *What the fuck is that?* I grab my shoes and open the front door to look around.

"What is it?" Dani asks from behind me with a blanket wrapped around her.

"I don't know, go back upstairs." I grab my coat and a baseball bat.

"Where are you going?"

"I'm going to go look around outside. I saw something out the window." She looks at me nervously. "Don't worry. I'll be right back. Go upstairs and warm up the bed for me." I kiss her quickly and head out the door, shutting it behind me. The wind is rough, and I begin to think what I saw had something to do with the weather. I wander around the house, reviewing the area and finding not much of anything. I push the trash cans against the house and shut the garage the door that is, for some reason, flapping in the wind. I turn around to a dark figure and jump several feet backwards with a firm grip on my bat. "Who the fuck are you?"

"I don't mean any harm. I only wanted to see Dani," the strange man says as he backs away from me.

I step forward, realizing. "Paul?" He nods, forcing his hands deep into his coat pockets. "What the hell are you doing here?"

"I heard you took over for your father at the factory, so I was wondering if maybe you had a job I could do? I'm good with my hands, and I'm willing to do anything." This man was horrible to

Dani and her mother. I remember him beating on our front door when I was younger, threatening us after my father gave him a beat down for striking Dani. You could always smell the alcohol on him. Once he lost his job, he became a nightmare to deal with. Thankfully, Dani's mother didn't wait around too long before she kicked him to the curb. "I swear, Dillon. I am sober, I haven't had a drink in …" I watch as he raises one hand out of his pocket but quickly pushes it back in when he can't control the craving that is vibrating through his veins.

"In how long Paul? A few hours? Don't ever come back here again."

"Let me talk to Dani!"

I get in his face and stare his temper back down. "If you ever come near her, I will make sure you disappear for good. Stay away from me, and most definitely stay away from Dani," I say through my teeth.

He runs off, and I go inside to make sure the doors and windows are securely locked.

"Dillon? What was it?"

"Some man, looking for his cat."

"If it was nothing then why are you locking everything up?"

"You should always make sure you keep the doors locked. It's not as safe as when we were kids, you know?" She nods with a worried look about her. I quickly take her into my arms. "There is no reason to worry. I am sure I am being paranoid from the lack of sleep." *I hope.*

"Dillon, I was thinking," Dani says to me as I try to get in one cup of coffee before work.

"Oh no, it's too early for that. My brain can't take it. Let me have my coffee first at least," I say, laughing as she crosses her arms unamused. I wrap my arms around her stiff stance. "Okay Baby, what is your brilliant idea that I am sure I am going to love?"

"Never mind." I kiss her cheek and her neck, whispering sweet things in her ear until she laughs. "I was only going to say that I could run some errands and pick up something for dinner and cook for us all tonight. I was thinking of making this pasta recipe I found."

"You're going to cook?" I ask, hiding my face against her neck.

"Yeah, Shane's Mom loaned me this cookbook for healthy eating. I think it would be really good for your Dad." She pulls away and looks at me. "What?"

"Nothing, except that you don't really know how to cook." She looks at me in shock. "Don't look at me that way. The other day I watched you play around with the stove for twenty minutes before you finally turned it on, and then you put a frozen pizza in there, still on the cardboard." She shrugs. "Yeah, it wasn't a big deal because you turned on the burner and not the oven, Honey."

"I never got to cook growing up because either my mom did it for me or my father hired a chef to come in."

"I know. So sad. Your rough upbringing was an absolute

tragic story that I am sure Lifetime is anxious to do a movie on." I smile wide as she glares at me. She leans back, thinking and looking pitiful. "But hey, if you read the instructions …carefully, very carefully, I am sure it will be great." *Hopefully at least edible.* She smiles and hugs me with joy while I think about what I can sneak home to eat without her knowing.

I leave the house in a great mood and actually don't dread creepy Warren today. I take a deep breath as I get out of the truck and head into the factory. The only thing to break my daydreaming is the sound of a revving engine. I turn my head just as a car comes racing towards me. I take off running, trying to get out of the way, but it quickly becomes clear that it is aiming for me. I dive behind one car, and it chases me around another. I race towards the front door of the factory, but I can only outrun a car for so long. The moment I feel the heat of the engine at my heels, I feel the breeze of another car slamming into it and sending it spinning in another direction. I fall backwards, watching the chaos as Warren drives his truck further into the asshole until he spins backwards and squeals his tires out of the parking lot.

Warren gets out of his truck and spits on the ground, cursing under his breath. "Damn, sons of bitches!" He continues to curse and spit as I get up and dust myself off. "Did they get ya?"

"No, I'm fine. Thank you. I'm sorry about your truck."

He groans. "My brother does body repair. It'll be fine; not the first time."

"You chase down crazy people in your truck often, huh?" He nods, and I worry about his sanity.

"Ex-wife, she was half-Cuban and half-Irish. She was a great lover, but she wouldn't hesitate to cut your balls off with a sledge hammer or chase down your new girlfriend with her Caddy."

"She sounds lovely."

"I told ya. I told ya they are not going to be happy until they shut you down. We have to get that fencing up and those security cameras updated."

"We should call the police," I say, taking out my phone.

"Wrong."

"Wrong? The guy just tried to kill me!"

"Call the police and you alert the entire place to our security issues. People will stop showing up to work, and next thing you know, we are shutting down. It's their plan. Did you see the guy?"

"No, all I saw were headlights aiming at my head," I say to him. "You were the one aiming at him. Didn't you see something?"

"Nope, didn't have my glasses on."

I look him over trying to understand. "Glasses? I have never seen you wear glasses."

"I never do. I hate them."

"Wait, how bad is your vision? Could you see me?"

"Sort of. It is still kind of dark this morning, so everything kind of blended together. Don't worry. I figured one way or another I was going to stop 'em."

"Oh, well that's wonderful. You saved my life accidentally. I feel so much better. I'm going to go to my office and throw-up now. If you need me, wait until tomorrow to talk to me about it." I rush up to my office and shut the door. I have a bottle of bourbon from my father's drawer and an ibuprofen bottle sitting on my desk as I squeeze my head between my hands. "You look awful," Shane says, walking in on me. "Rough morning?"

"You could say that. Someone tried to kill me."

"Did you piss Dani off again?"

"What? No! Someone ran me down with their car. If not for Warren's blind ass running into their car *accidentally*, they would have succeeded."

He nods, seeming to consider my issue. "Are you sure it wasn't Dani?"

"Shut up! No. Dani and I are good. We had sex last night. She sleeps in my bed every night now." He looks at me with a questioning expression. "The sex was great. She loved it! I promise you."

"Just trying to eliminate the obvious suspects. What about Lucas?"

"No, Lucas doesn't care enough about me to dislike me that much. It has to be Dani's father or someone that works for him."

"Or the drug kingpin that said you would be wise to sell the business to him."

"Oh yeah. I have to get our security issues resolved and quick. We are so backed up on debt, any profit we are making right now is going to that so I can get into the good graces of our distributors. I need a bigger investor."

Shane nods, thinking as I do, "We don't know anyone with that kind of money except ...." he laughs until I realize just the person I need to see. Shane sits up, shaking his head at me. "Dillon no. Don't you even think about it! Sean doesn't like you. Why would he ever consider investing in something you're in charge of?"

"What? I don't know what you are talking about. Sean loves me! I am like the brother he never had."

"You mean like Ethan, his brother, and you're nothing like Ethan, who also does not like you."

"Why do you keep saying that?"

"Because they said, 'Dillon we don't like you, don't come back here'."

"That's how they tease. They don't mean it." Shane shakes his head at me. "Everyone loves me! I am like the most loveable guy there is."

"This coming from the man that was nearly rundown by a car this morning."

"Don't you have work to do? Have you figured out that campaign? I am going to need something to sell Sean on this idea?"

"You're going to need a miracle to sell Sean on this idea." I throw a wad of paper at him as he leaves, but he quickly pokes his head back in. "You might want to take that bourbon with you, too."

"Good idea. If I get him drunk, he might be persuaded easier."

"Not for him, for you, to ease the pain after Sean beats you senseless for showing up at his door."

"Get out!" I'm not listening to that. I know better. *Or maybe I will talk to Ava first. Can't hurt to be safe.*

Chapter 15

Dillon

Before I leave for Atlanta, I check on my father and make sure Shane stays with him and Dani while Warren does what Warren does and looks after our factory. I have everything I need to help sell my idea. I just need to be able to get in the door, and the only way I can do that is by a surprise visit. I did my research, and Sean is not doing any movies anywhere and should be home, at least according to Randy, who seemed more than happy to tell me when Sean would be home. I was surprised at how helpful he was. I didn't realize we had made such a great connection. Randy is so excited; he even offers to help me get into the house so I can wait for Sean inside and surprise him. I show up at the gate, and he happily lets me in. When I get inside, he greets me with a big smile and introduces me to Sean's mother, who is apparently watching the kids until Sean and Ava return.

"Now, Dillon, please, please, tell Sean I did this for him, in appreciation for what he did to me the other day," Randy says, proud of himself. He shakes my hand and walks out laughing. I turn towards Sean's mother, confused as she cradles the baby and shakes her head.

"Sometimes you boys never grow up. Come sit down, Dillon, and tell me how you are doing." Sean's mother is easy to talk to and clearly is a mother of two boys. She isn't the least bit surprised about the trouble I used to get into.

As I sit waiting, I notice their little girl, Lillah, staring at me. She comes near me and lays her hands on my legs as she smiles up at me. "Hi, how are you?" She holds out her hand to me with a ring in it. "What's this?"

"My ring. You're supposed to give it to me so we can be married," Lillah says as if I should have known that already.

"Oh, well let's do this right away, before your father gets home and hurts me." She giggles, letting me put the ring on her finger, and kisses me on the cheek.

"She is such a flirt; she is more like her father than he cares to admit." Sean's mother says. "So, are you just visiting or are you going to be in Atlanta for a while, Dillon?" I respond with more words than necessary, to the point she is more confused than before she asked the question. I try to clarify, only to babble on and on about nonsense. I am so anxious and nervous about trying to sell something to Sean when I know he doesn't endorse any product. I don't know what I was thinking. This is a really bad idea. I should leave before it's too late.

"Oh, there they are now," she says, as I start to get up and make my apologies to leave.

I sit quietly as Sean and Ava come in and greet their children. I catch sight of Sean as he picks up Lillah and swings her around in his arms. I sit back and breathe and continue snacking on some food I found in their kitchen, all the while trying to look relaxed.

"What are you doing here?" Sean asks with something less than a smile.

"Hey Sean, how's it going?" I say with my patent too-cute-to-refuse smile.

"Dillon, so good to see you again," Ava says, rushing up on me with a warm hug. I look over her shoulder at Sean and continue to smile, but I think I actually hear him growl.

"I'm good, thank you. I thought I would come see the new addition, and I must say, he is one good looking boy. Obviously gets his looks from his mother," I say, winking at Sean who is not amused.

"Thanks for stopping by, Dillon. It will save us the time in sending you an announcement, but I am sure you have a flight to catch?" Sean says, trying to rush me out the door.

"Nope, I'm good," I say, sitting down and taking hold of my snacks again.

"Well then, you must stay for dinner," Ava says sweetly.

"I would love to," I say, feeling better about things. Thank goodness for Ava.

"Wonderful. Now, if you will excuse me, I need to go feed my son before he leaves with his grandmother." Ava says.

"Sure," I say, watching Ava walk away until I meet Sean's eyes. I try smiling, but he growls at me again.

"Sean, let me go get Lillah ready to go while you spend time with your friend," his mother says as she takes Lillah from him.

"He's not my friend," he says. "Did you tell her we are friends, is that how you got in here?" I put my hand over my heart, shocked that he would say such things. "Don't play that game with me."

"Damn Sean, I make an effort to stop by and see you, and this is how you treat me? You really need to work on your friendship skills," I say, continuing to munch and relax.

"*We* are not friends!"

"Sure we are, with everything we have been through together. You like me. Don't lie. I know you do." He cringes, rubbing his head. "So, does Ava breastfeed? That's hot," I nod, smiling.

"Do you want me to hurt you?" he asks suddenly.

"I'm just saying. And damn, Ava got her body back quick, well except the," I motion around my chest area. "They seem a lot bigger. That's got to be a plus, huh?"

"Are you suicidal Dillon?"

"No, why?" I say, enjoying this game we play. I forgot how much fun it was to aggravate him.

"Don't you have a girlfriend or something in New York to annoy? Why are you here bothering me?"

"I don't know."

"You don't know?" He sits up, looking at me as if I am insane.

"No, I mean I …" I sigh, searching for the right words. *Do it Dillon, ask, you need to do this.* The moment I look up at him, I can't do it. I feel like a jerk asking someone that has no reason to help me whatsoever. We aren't related, and as much as I like hanging out with him, it's really only because he is fun to drive nuts and cause that vein in his head to pop out. I lean forward, ready to say something, but I can't. I drop my head and think there has to be a way I can do this on my own. But this isn't about my pride, it's about my father and all his workers, and Dani, and … "Sean, I …"

"What?" he asks impatiently.

"Damn you're worse than a girl. Just spit it out already," Sean says, checking behind himself, for Ava I imagine. He is so whipped.

"I need your help Sean," I say with every muscle in my body tightening.

"What did you do? Do you need a lawyer? Because you can't afford the ones I know," he says.

I roll my eyes. "No, I don't need a lawyer."

"You got Taylor pregnant, didn't you?"

"Who? Oh, no. I just…" I stand up, pacing around the room, gripping my head trying to say what I need to, but all I can do is breathe out with no words. "Hell, I don't even know why I am here. This was a stupid idea. I'm sorry Sean. I don't know what I was thinking." I grab my coat and start out the door.

"You already told Ava you would stay for dinner. If you leave now, she's going to think it's my fault. So, at least stay until after that so you don't get me into trouble," he says, motioning for me to come back with some cursing under his breath. I nod and sit back down, feeling like a complete failure.

Sean's mother gathers the kids and says goodbye to Sean and Ava before fussing over me and hugging me with a motherly kiss to the forehead. "I enjoyed talking to you, Dillon. I just adore you. I can see why you are such a close friend to Sean. Now come back to see us anytime." I smile, but when I look over at Sean, he is shaking his head at his mother. Her reassurances only helps me so much. If anything, they make me feel worse. I don't want it to seem like I am taking advantage of my friend Sean or his family.

I have few words throughout dinner, and I do my best to answer as politely as I can, but all I really want to do is go home.

"Well, how about I clean up so you boys can go and talk in the living room?" Ava says.

"Thank you, but I really should probably get out of your way here. Thank you for dinner. Are you sure you don't need any help cleaning up?" I ask, trying not to look at her too long since Sean is within punching distance.

"No, I'm good, but Dillon, if you don't have a flight out tonight, you are more than welcome to stay here."

"Thank you, but I really need to go."

"If you need to," Sean says, rushing me out of my chair.

"At least let me wrap up some food for you to take with you," Ava insists.

"Okay." I will never turn down food, especially good food.

Ava jumps up smiling as I walk into the next room to grab my coat and wait for my care package.

Suddenly, Sean walks up behind me and grabs hold of the back of my neck. "Come with me," he says harshly.

"Hey, what the hell?" I say, trying to release his grip on me while he pushes me into his office.

"Sit down!" he yells, pointing at some chairs in front of the desk. I sit down like a child being scolded. "Now talk."

"What do you want me to talk about?" I ask, seeming unaware of his concerns.

"Dillon, I am not going to play games with you. Now tell me why you are here or I will kick you out and deal with the wrath of my wife later."

Fine, might as well do this now. I sit up and take a deep breath and go for it. "My father is real sick. I had to move back to North Carolina to take care of him and his business." *There, that wasn't so bad, now …oh just say it already!* "I came up with this really great product, Sean. I think you will love it, and with your new son, it would be wonderful if you could … well, if you could endorse it for me. I have a sample in the car. I can leave it with you and Ava and you guys can try it out. I know she will love it, too."

"You know I don't endorse products, Dillon. No matter how great it might be. I don't want to get into that business."

I sit back, letting my shoulders sink, *I knew it.* "Sean please, I am begging you to consider it, just consider it. You are my only hope right now; otherwise, I will lose everything to a man I hate." I fist my hands, trying to work up the courage to fight for what I believe in. "My whole world depends on this product succeeding, Sean. Please."

"You obviously want me to help you with something Dillon, but I'm not even going to consider helping you until I know everything."

I can't imagine telling him about all the issues that will surely convince him not to help. "It is really a long story, Sean," he huffs, letting me know he's not budging until I talk. Fine, probably won't say yes anyway. Maybe it will be good to at least talk it out with someone. "Do you remember that girl? The one I told you about

… Dani?"

Sean sits forward, seeming interested suddenly in what I have to say. "She is the girlfriend you never saw again, the one whose father took her away in the middle of the night?"

"Yes, her … I found her again, or rather, *she* found me. And now, I need your help … *we* need your help."

"How exactly?"

"Dani's father wants the land that my family's factory sits on, so he is doing everything possible to ruin the business. When my mother got sick, my father left the factory day-to-day details to two guys who nearly cleaned him out. Now, I am trying to get it back in the black, but we are dealing with a lot of security issues. Someone keeps trying to scare our employees away. They nearly ran over me with a car the other day."

"They what?" He starts to smile, but then straightens back up. "Are you sure it wasn't Dani? You don't always say the right things you know," he laughs.

"Why does everyone keep saying that? No, it wasn't Dani. We're fine. It had to be someone that works for her father."

He nods, considering the possibility. "I could see a father wanting to do that to you," he says, and I nod before looking up at him and his sinister smile.

"Your daughter approached me to get married. I was simply minding my own business, Sean." He scrunches his eyebrows, and I smile. "Check the ring on her finger. Think about it, I could be your son-in-law one day if you don't help me."

"Or I could just kill you now and feed your body to my dogs."

"Oh." I glance over at the two big beasts' picture on the desk and decide it's best to flash my innocent smile. "Point made." I say, sitting back thinking. "There is one more thing that we are dealing with. There is a drug kingpin wanting to buy the place too, so he can use our shipping abilities overseas to sell his drugs. A Johnathan Skelton. He is very persistent, and he actually could be the one trying to kill me, too."

"Drug dealers? How the hell do you get involved with drug dealers building furniture?"

"It wasn't me. The guy that my father hired to oversee things while my mother was sick started that shit. He was trying to make money on the side, and after he was killed, my father found some evidence of it and we have since ..."

"Wait! He was killed? You mean murdered?"

"Uh-huh. We assume something went bad with the side business." Sean nods before rubbing his hand over his face and head. "I talked to the guy and told him no."

"Yeah, and because drug kingpins are good with rejections, I am sure he said *okie-dokie* and left you alone."

"Well, he hasn't approached me since."

"No, he wouldn't. He would simply hire someone to run you over with a car." I sit back into my seat with a sigh. "Is that it, or is there someone else trying to get into the furniture business?" I shake my head. "Okay, so then tell me about your brilliant idea."

"Well, in an effort to get things back on track, I decided to change our everyday living furniture to baby furniture with the lead item being mobiles."

"Mobiles?" he asks, confused.

"Yes, but not just any mobiles. They incorporate a breathing sensor that will alert parents the moment their baby has any kind of breathing issues."

"SIDS?"

"Yeah, that was the main reasoning behind it." Sean sits back in his chair thinking. "Do you want to see it?"

He doesn't speak at first but looks me over. "You own the patent?" I nod. "Who did the design?"

"My father created the initial technology design, but then Shane and I added a temperature gauge and a way to connect to it through an app so you can hook it up to any mobile device you own. We even added a camera, so if you are in New York, you can see your baby and get his temp and breathing levels all at the same time. You would always be connected to him."

"As long as he is under this mobile?" he asks, watching as I nod excitedly. "Can the mobile or technology be added to other pieces? Can it be taken with you when you travel?"

"Yeah I suppose, but it works best with our furniture, with our specially designed baby furniture pieces. We have the patents and everything Sean. The possibilities are endless! Just like you said, we could figure out a way so people can travel easier with them."

"I understand the possibilities, but does it work?" he asks, and I jump up, ready to run to my car for everything. "Hold up …" He looks me over, arguing with himself under his breath. "Fine. Go get it."

I nearly run over Ava as I run out to get all I need to prove that the technology works. I run back in and begin setting up in their living room. Sean watches with a skeptical eye while Ava stands next to him, curious and looking to him for some answers. Once I have everything setup, I turn to them.

"What now? Did you bring a small child with you in that suitcase?" Sean says smartly.

"No, but I have a demonstration doll that will work." I get the doll out, whose arms and legs are slightly twisted from the abrupt packing. *Damn it, Dani. I'm never letting her help me pack again.* The doll's twisted limbs are hard to turn back around, so I turn away to force them back into shape. "There, see?"

"I see that I am never going to let you touch my child," he laughs.

"Sean!" Ava yells at him.

"What? It was funny."

"Ha ha. Now watch. I place the baby here, turn the mobile on here, and then I can see it instantly start to get readings here on my laptop. See?" I say, excited to see everything working perfectly. *Phew!*

They both look over it and check the fake baby over and over while they look at the readings. "Now watch." I turn the baby off, and instantly, alarms start going off on my laptop and my phone. "I preloaded the app to my phone so I would be sure not to miss a single breath. See?" I feel good when they both look speechless and enthusiastic about what they are seeing. "And like I said, this is just the start. If you want to come in and invest …"

"Invest? I thought you wanted me to endorse it?" Sean asks.

"Either, or both, would be fine," I say, backing off my excitement some.

"I love it Dillon. What made you think of such a thing?" Ava asks, eagerly inspecting the bed until she looks at me. I pushed all those feelings about Evan to the back of my mind until now. I am so grateful to have Dani back in my life. I have been trying to concentrate on that and not on the son I never got a chance to know. I don't know why I am letting it bother me now. *This is not the right time, Dillon.* I choke a little, trying to push my emotions back again. "Oh no?" Ava says, seemingly reading my every thought.

"Oh no what?" Sean asks.

"My dad thought of most of it because of …" I fidget, suddenly feeling awkward and lonely. I pull out my wallet, take out the picture Dani gave me, and hand it to her. "His name was Evan. He was my son, but I never got to actually meet him or … Anyway, so you like it?" Ava hands me my picture back and kisses me on the cheek before hugging me tight. Sean sits down, staring up at me with no clear sign of what he is thinking.

"I love it, Dillon. It's wonderful, it really is." She leans over Sean, and he kisses her, grasping her hand. "Well, it's late, and it's been a long day for us, so I am going to have to say goodnight. Please feel free to make yourself at home in the guesthouse, Dillon. Sean can show you around." Ava hugs me again before Sean stands up and follows her out of the room and embraces her again.

I hear them whispering to each other, and I assume I just made a big mess of things with the sad story. Good job, dumbass.

Bring up the sad baby story to a still grieving couple. Sean comes back into the room and helps me pack up. "Get your bags. I will show you to the guesthouse."

"I can stay here?" I ask, and he nods with a deep groan. He shows me into the guesthouse and where I can find anything I could ever want, including snacks. I quickly grab an apple and bite into it.

"You just ate. How can you be hungry?" I shrug, and he looks me over. "You must have one hell of a metabolism."

"I workout, Sean. Trying to keep up with you," I say, showing him my guns and abs. "Impressive right? I even got the tats, too. Maybe I could play in one of your movies?" He rolls his eyes, ignoring me.

"You can find extra blankets there, towels there, and you know where the food is. There is wine, but stay away from the stuff on the top three shelves, or else."

"Oooh wine, I'm going to have to call Randy and thank him."

"For what?"

"He's the one that let me in and said you would be excited to see me. Oh, he said it was a special gift for what you did for him earlier in the week."

"Asshole," Sean says. "Well then, Randy's specially imported beer is still in the fridge if you want to help yourself. Please help yourself; he loves to share his beer." Sean smiles wide, patting me on the back.

As Sean starts to walk out, I feel the need to say something. "Thanks Sean. Don't worry, I won't come bother you guys in the morning. I will sneak out and leave Ava a note of thanks so you guys can enjoy your time away from the kids. I know it's been awhile since you got any. I can tell by how antsy you are," I laugh.

"Thanks," he sighs with his hands out. "You know, it is a really good idea, Dillon. I was impressed. I was shocked that I was impressed, but it is an interesting investment. I'll have Ethan contact you and setup a time to come tour the facility, and we can talk more about what is needed to get this idea going."

"Really? That's great!"

"Don't get too excited yet. If I find that it is too disorganized or in any way a bad investment, I won't even consider it," Sean says. "But, if it looks good, then we will work something out."

"And we will be partners!" I say, so excited that I try to hug him only to realize that was a mistake.

"Oh no. Don't hug me, never hug me," he says, leaving me to celebrate on my own. I have to dance until I see him looking at me through the window, shaking his head. I stop quickly and wave, hoping to disguise my oddness, but he rolls his eyes, shaking his head, and walks away mumbling something.

Chapter 16

Dani

With Dillon away, I try to help out with the factory and with his father at the same time. It's tough, knowing no one is going to easily follow any orders that I give since most of them think I'm only here because I'm screwing Dillon. No matter what they say behind my back, I am able to ignore it, but what they say to my face is a whole other matter.

"Rafe, I need you to clean up your space and shift product to the next person before you continue on. You know you should already be doing this," I say, making eye contact with him briefly before moving on.

"Bitch," I hear him whisper when I turn to someone else.

I make my rounds ignoring him and his snide comments, which he makes just loud enough for me to hear whenever I am near. When I return to Rafe, he still has not done as I asked him to do. "Rafe, go clock out. Jake, come take over for Rafe," I say, causing a hush around us.

"Why the fuck should I clock out?" Rafe yells at me.

"Because you obviously are not capable of listening, so instead, go home and we will try this one more time tomorrow." I stare into his bloodshot eyes, not wavering. His nostrils flare, and I feel his muscles tighten as his sour breath releases into my face. I wait for him to challenge me, daring him to take another step towards me. Lucas comes running to my side, as does Shane. Warren, spotting the trouble, decides to open his mouth to me for the first time since I have been here.

"What are you doing?! This is my floor!" Warren yells at me, taking a stance in front of his son.

"This is my company. Now get him out of here before I fire him," I yell back at him.

"I don't know what's worse, the city boy or his …"

"Finish that statement and you can find yourself a new job too, Warren." Rafe stands behind him, smiling with glee, assuming his father will win this battle for him. After learning more about this place, I have come to find out that Rafe isn't nearly as valuable as we believed. His father cleans up all his work for him, or has someone clean it up. The estranged father and son are only civil to each other when it suits Rafe. Warren spits off to the side of me before taking his son and talking to him privately. Rafe throws his fists around while Warren talks him down and finally convinces him to clock out and leave. I nod towards Lucas and Shane, relieving them of their protective duties. As soon as I shut the door to the office, I release my tension with a deep exhale, but I don't get long to breathe freely.

Colleen comes in, shutting the door behind her. "Now that was a confrontation. Are you alright?"

"Yeah, I'm fine. I had to do what I had to do. Dillon would have done the same."

"Of course he would have, and he wouldn't have caught half the flack you got. You know, you are a lot tougher than anyone thought. Gina said you would never stay here, that you were only here to get a piece of Dillon and steal this place for your father. But I think she was wrong. I think you are here to prove you can create something on your own, build something without your father's help." Colleen says, patting me on the back with a large smile. "You know, a few of us girls are getting together at my place this Saturday night, if you're interested?"

Her posture shifts from one leg to the next. Her hand twitches, counting a well-timed rhythm against her thigh, seemingly counting the seconds she has to be around me. Her forced smile seems sweet enough, but her eyes never stay focused on my face. They wander over my figure as if they are searching for flaws. "Thank you, that sounds like fun."

"Great, so we will see you on Saturday?"

"I wish I could, but Dillon will be back by then, and well …" I bite my bottom lip with an anticipating moan, "well, we have a lot of catching up to do," I say, watching her tense and her sweet smile press tightly against her teeth like she is holding back a roaring challenge. "Dillon is so hard to let go of, I couldn't possibly say yes, knowing I would only end up canceling so I can stay in bed with him."

She fakes a laugh, "Okay, I understand. You be sure to let me know if you change your mind, now," she says sweetly, stepping out of the office as Shane walks in.

"I will," I say, rolling my eyes at Shane.

"What did she want?"

"To invite me to a girls get together on Saturday."

"No way!" I nod. "You're not going, are you? Dani, please tell me you didn't fall for her sweet as pie bullshit. She and Gina have been tight since grade school. No way in hell she friends you while Gina is still alive. They are probably planning a way to kill you and hide your body in their backyard."

"Don't worry. I know better than to trust her or any of the rest of them."

"Well that's good to hear. Now about Rafe and Warren, you know damn well they are going to talk to Dillon as soon as he gets back and ask for his pay he lost today." I shrug and he nods. "Of course, he doesn't bother you because you're Dani Portman, the toughest chick I know."

"Damn right." I smile wickedly.

Shane and I have been friends as long as Dillon and I. They were best friends, and they allowed me to join them, be the third musketeer as they called us. If one was away, I usually had the other I could depend on, except Shane was always my friend and sometimes the shoulder I needed to get over my broken heart.

I remember watching Dillon trying to explain to Amanda that I was *just* his friend and I was nothing for her to worry about, ever. He didn't see me as anything more than his friend for a while, no matter how much I wanted him to. Her pretty face, long blond hair, and perfectly tanned skin were like magnets to the boys at our school, Dillon especially. I loved that we were best friends and that he was always around me, until his penis woke up and started doing half his thinking for him. Then, I was only good enough until a pretty girl walked by, and then he was gone. Shane wasn't much better, but he was the one to notice my love for Dillon first.

He doesn't even realize what he said. I run out of the school and hide in a corner before falling against the wall. I just couldn't take it any longer, watching him act like I am not even there and she is all that. I have known him forever; she doesn't even care what he likes or doesn't like. I shouldn't even care about him. He is nothing but a stupid boy that won't even matter when I leave here one day. That's right, one day he is going to be sorry, He is going to look around, and I am not going to be here anymore. Then, all he will have are those stupid fake girls that he thinks are so awesome. It will serve him right for …

"Hey, what are you doing hiding over here?" Shane says, rounding the corner and squinting at me as I try to quickly hide my tears.

"Nothing, I simply needed some fresh air is all. What are you doing out here? Go back to your girlfriend, Shane."

"No, I want to see if you are okay. You ran out of there so fast I thought your ass might be on fire or something."

"Ha ha. No, I'm fine."

He nods, leaning against the wall next to me. "You know, he doesn't even know how you feel."

"Who?"

"You know who. Dillon. He doesn't think anything of it when flirting with other girls because he sees you as his friend, Dani. He doesn't want to look at you any differently; he loves you so much. He doesn't ever want to mess that up."

"He doesn't love me. He barely notices me," I pout.

"He notices you, just not how you want him to, but I promise you that's going to change at some point." I look up at him, wondering what he knows *that I don't. "Yeah, you see, you're like the swan that is waiting for the right opportunity to bloom in front of him, and then you won't be just any other girl he notices, you will be Dani, the last and only girl he notices."*

"You think so?"

"Oh, hell yeah. I mean, look at ya. You're beautiful, but you aren't ready to be noticed yet. When you are though, everybody better look out 'cause you will be the hottest, toughest chick alive."

"Definitely the toughest," I say as he nods with a smile. "And you know I have a skirt like Amanda's, but I choose not to wear it 'cause it's not practical for school. It's not that comfortable, especially when you have a bottom locker."

"I know. Whenever I wear mine, I can never keep my Shane Goodies all covered up when I have to lean down to get my books out of my locker. It's a real problem," he says, fidgeting like a girl. I laugh, smacking his arm until he laughs back.

"Your Shane Goodies?"

"Yeah, you know, the girls all like sweet treats, and I got all the goodies they need," he says with a cocky nod.

"You're not right at all. I don't know who is worse… you or Dillon?"

"Dillon, by far. Have you heard what he calls his penis? Never mind. You don't want to hear that. It may ruin your view of him," he says, guiding me back to school and laughing with me.

I love Shane like a brother, and if I didn't know better, I would think his sister and I were switched at birth. Actually, knowing Shane's sister, he would probably prefer that.

While taking care of some last minute paperwork, a timid man comes walking up to the open door of the office and looks in at me, but turns back to the edge of the doorframe. "Hello?" I say, standing and stretching to see him. He steps in, removing his baseball cap, and I realize. "Paul?"

"Hi, Dani. I hope I'm not bothering you, but I was in the neighborhood and heard you were here," my ex-stepfather says.

I haven't seen him since he moved out. "What do you want?"

"I was wondering if you might be able to give me a job?" I look him over for any signs of alcohol, noticing his swollen lip and black eye. It doesn't seem like he has changed at all. "I swear I'm sober. Have been for nearly a year now."

"I'm sorry, Paul. We aren't hiring right now. Maybe try again in a couple of months."

"Okay, I understand," he says. "Actually, you know what, all the things I did for you and you can't give me another chance. I told you I quit drinking!"

"It has nothing to do with you, Paul. We aren't able to hire right now."

"I should have known better. Dillon said he couldn't hire me because of you and you say it's because you aren't hiring."

"You talked to Dillon?"

"I tried, but the moment I came near him, he threatened me. I thought, maybe if I spoke to you, then you would change his mind. I guess I was wrong about you both. You're still two, over-

privileged children who don't care about anyone but themselves."
He stomps away, and I quickly call Dillon.

"Hey, Paul just came into see me. Did you threaten him?"

"That son of a bitch. Yes, he was the one that came by the house. He asked to see you, and I told him to stay away from you."

"He came to the house to look for me?"

"Yeah, that's why I made sure Shane was there with you. Call the cops on him Dani, and let them deal with him."

"He says he has quit drinking."

"Dani! No! We are not hiring him. Don't you dare go near him."

"We can talk about it when you get back. Have a safe trip," I say, hanging up as he swears at me. I rush out the door and take the truck, looking for Paul. I find him walking down the road alone. I pull over and roll down my window. "Paul!" He turns and looks me over. "Have you really quit drinking? If you have, then come back in another week, we will need people then." I step out of the truck and walk over to him to hand him some money and a business card to call us.

He knocks the money out of my hand and grabs me by the coat with both fists, jerking me off my feet. "I don't want your damn money! I want a job, Princess!" he yells in my face.

I smack him and push him away from me. "You could have had one if you hadn't of just proven that you're still a jackass. Dillon was right about you. You don't deserve another chance." I walk away from the fuming man to jump back into the truck and drive past him without a second thought.

A long day at work and then coming home to help Matt with his medicine and rehabilitation is tiring. If not for Shane's help while Dillon's gone, I am not sure how I would get everything done. "Thank you for your help today, at work and here."

"Thank you for letting me move in and away from the Putnam crazy house. I don't know who's worse, my mother or my sister. I don't think my father is tolerant. I think he has purposely gone deaf so he can't hear them any longer. They're insane." I laugh as he grabs a beer from the fridge. "No, seriously, you laugh, but they are. For instance, my sister announced the other day that she is starting a new career."

"Oh, well that's great, right?" I ask as he shakes his head, taking a drink of his beer.

"What? No, she has only decided to start one; she hasn't decided what it is yet." He walks into the room with his arms stretched out from his side and a huge smile, prancing around the living room like a girl, "I am here to announce, that I ..." He glances all around the room batting his eyelashes before taking a deep breath, "Brandi Putnam, have decided that I am going to embark on a new career." His smile disappears as he crashes onto the chair. "Idiot then got pissed off when I said, *'Great... and what career might that be?' 'Shut up Shane! I am trying to improve myself as a person. Stop pushing me to make a quick decision on a life changing opportunity.'*" I laugh until I cry as he rolls his eyes and mocks his lunatic sister. "What an amazing opportunity for you, Bran. You have decided to get off your ass, and … do nothing, way better than sitting around all day and doing nothing. Don't let those big, life-changing steps change you, Sweetheart."

"Oh, Shane you poor thing. How are you two related?" He shakes his head with a shrug. "Well, at least she stopped selling puppet socks outside the Walmart."

"She didn't stop. Walmart called the police on her. Do you know how embarrassing it is to pick your sister up at the police station and have to ask for her box of socks back? *Oh no sir, the other box filled with socks only, the ones with drawn-in faces on them.* Uh, that's right, she didn't even bother to sew anything. My talented sister, drew faces on with a permanent marker." I hold my hand over my mouth as I fight my laughter. "Don't laugh, the first year Dillon and I lived in New York I had to wear those socks, because I didn't have enough money to buy any. My mother swore they were good socks that shouldn't go to waste, she wouldn't let it go until I took them. I didn't have any at the time without holes or I would have never worn those crazy things." He shakes his head seeming to recall a bad memory. "The first time I brought a girl back and took my shoes off …I swear those little freaky eyes on my toes looked right up at her, as she laughed and ran out the door." Shane sighs heavily as he leans back in his seat. "Next week, I will probably have to pick her up after she gets arrested for wearing her underwear on her head. *But Shane I was only trying to start a new fashion trend.*"

"I wouldn't know what that's like, having a sibling to worry about and love like that."

Shane snaps his head in my direction. "Don't rub it in. I didn't ask for this. You and Dillon both know I asked for a puppy, not Dopey."

As I clear the tears from my eyes from laughing at the big goof, his phone rings. I watch as he glances at the name and smiles. *It's a girl.* He gets up and walks into another room to talk. *I wonder why I have never been attracted to Shane.* He is a good-looking guy, funny, smart, caring, and has always been a great friend. Maybe that's why. Shane was always at my side while we both looked ahead to follow Dillon. Shane and I have been Dillon's followers, and we were both good with that, even when he got us into trouble. Dillon is, and always has been, that guy you want to follow. His charisma and handsome smile has had girls swooning for him since he was a kid. Then, he developed a great body. Oh wow. One look at him in the shower, and I become stupid girl, wanting nothing more than for him to touch me, kiss me, do anything he wants to me, so I can feel his body next to mine. I love looking into his eyes and watching that crooked, *I am up to something really good,* smile form.

Oh wow ... I suddenly feel someone watching me, and I turn and look up at Shane who is laughing at me, "What?"

"Calm down, girl. He will be back tomorrow."

"What are you talking about?"

"You and your I-love-Dillon-so-much eyes ...ohhh, I miss him, ohhh I want him to do dirty, disgusting things to me." Shane dances around, making kissing faces and rubbing his chest.

I get up and shove him. "Shut up!"

He laughs, "Don't worry, I am going to leave you to fantasize alone for a little while. I am going to go see about a girl I met the other day." I sit up on my knees on the sofa as he walks behind, anxiously waiting for more information. "No, I am not talking about it… yet. I like this girl. She's got potential."

"Huge boobs, huh?"

"Yeah. Wait. What? No, I mean yes, but no, it's not like that. She's smart, too, and funny. She makes me laugh."

"Does she make your Shane Goodies all tingly?" I laugh as he sighs at me.

"Ha ha. You're never going to let that go are you?" he says, kissing my forehead. "I will be back later. If you need me, call me."

Shane leaves me in the overly quiet house by myself with nothing more to do than to watch old movies on television and wait for Dillon to call with any news. A few hours by myself and the creepy old movies begin to mess with my mind. The little bumps and odd noises in the dark night become louder and more hair raising until I am sure I see a shadow cross by the kitchen window. I get up slowly and grab the fireplace poker before stepping quietly into the kitchen and looking through the windows. I edge to the corner of the big bay window, watching the trees blow and the glistening sparkle of the rain against the light of the distant street light. There is a sudden roaring of the wind passing strong through the clouds and storming down deep into the darkness, sending chills up my spine. My breathing halts as I lean in closer and watch an odd shadow against the glass. The movement is subtle, and the curious shape is beyond reasoning. *A cat in the bushes maybe? No, too tall. A bend in the light?* A closer look and the shadow moves and breathes… my heart stops as a veil of mist forms against the glass in front of me. My shaky hand reaches up, hovering over the foggy form before touching its edge and tracing it with my finger. *It's a cat. I'm sure.* When the shadow breathes again, forming an even bigger misty cloud and moving in for a closer look at me. I step back and breathe in as I feel it watching me, studying me, and waiting for me to form a breath to scream my fear of the cursed shadow. A larger blanket of breath forms, and I close my eyes to try and get a hold of my dread and open them to a message written in the foggy haze: *Die.* I stumble backwards, away from the jagged words as they are blasted over by another heated breath. Scrambling quickly, I try to reach the phone and fall to the floor to get to the home line, only to find it dead. My cell sits mockingly in the middle of the room, on the kitchen counter with the dim nightlight highlighting its edges. I glance over at the big bay window and see nothing. I run for the phone and grab it as a text comes in, *Die Bitch!*

I scream, and as I quickly try to dial for help, I turn to the glass and see the bright wide eyes of my shadow feeding on my fear and growing stronger by it. I can see nothing more than his wicked eyes penetrating through the glass and straight to my heart. *Run. Run! All I can think is run, I scream inside … RUN.* The back door begins to shake, the knob begins to turn this way and that, trying to break through. *Run damn you!* I run. I run from his sight and try to get a signal to call for help. The sudden knocking on the door causes me to scream and scramble, crouching under a desk as I frantically try to dial and redial.

"Dani?"

"Thomas?" I come out from my hiding place and rush to the door, looking through the peephole. It is him. I open the door and fall into his arms, crying.

"Oh, my sweet Dani, what happened? Did he hurt you?"

"No, someone is outside the house in the back. They are trying to get in. The phone lines are dead, and I can't get a signal to call for help." I quickly try to tell him, pointing to the kitchen while dragging him inside and locking the door behind him.

Thomas looks back behind me. "Stay here. I'll go take a look."

"No, don't go back there," I try to hold onto him, but he hushes me and calms me back down before leaving to walk through the house and into the kitchen. He looks around, and then I hear him open the door. "Oh no!" I rush to the back door with the poker in hand, ready to strike before going out the door.

"Thomas?" I whisper into the wind. "Thomas?" I look around, walking further out into the darkness when Thomas walks out in front of me.

"Whoa, Sweetheart, gees! You are going to hurt someone with that," Thomas says, taking it from my hand. "It's okay. There is no one out here. If there was, they are gone now. I promise there is no one here. Wow… you are shaking like a leaf. Come here." He puts his arms around me. "Come on, let's go back in." We walk in and find the front door open. I look up at Thomas as he looks puzzled. He pushes me behind him, takes my poker, and quickly shuts the door before looking around the house carefully. He returns, shaking his head. "No one's here other than Dillon's father who is out cold, so I doubt it was him. It must have been the breeze." He looks sympathetically at me and holds his arms out for me to fall into, "It's okay now. You're safe, I promise you."

I take a deep breath and step back, feeling a little better before realizing a strange coincidence. "Why are you here?" I ask.

"I heard Dillon was out of town, and I wanted a chance to talk to you alone. I wanted to apologize for my actions and see if we can't work this out?" I sigh, feeling my head spinning in pain. I walk back into the living room and sit down. "Is this what you were watching? No wonder you are freaked out. You really have to stop watching these horror movies, Dani. They always scare the hell out of you."

"There was someone out there. I saw them."

"Then who was it?"

"I don't know. All I could see were these eyes."

"Floating eyes… yeah that happens."

I look up at him harshly, "They weren't floating. It was dark, and that was all I could clearly see." I look down, as my phone finally gets a signal. "And the phone line was cut. My cell phone wasn't working at all."

Thomas walks over and picks up the phone and listens. "The phone's fine, Dani." I jump up to listen and hear a dial tone and stand back in confusion. *Maybe I am being influenced by the scary movie?* Thomas walks over and picks up my cell. "You said you couldn't get a signal?" I nod as he goes through my phone, checking it. "It seems fine now; signal is coming in strong."

"I know. I don't understand … wait! I got a text too!" I grab my phone scrolling through and finding nothing. "It was here … I swear, I saw it."

"How much sleep are you getting?" he asks, making me question my own sanity at this point.

"Not much, but there is a lot to do and not a lot of people to do it."

Thomas sits down next to me. "Dani, this is ridiculous. I understand why you want to do this, and I am willing to support you in this if you will only give me another chance to prove it to you. I could help. You don't even have to tell Dillon. It doesn't have to be anything that involves whatever secret he may have, unless you think I can help with it. I am willing to help however I can. Maybe I can hire someone to help take care of his father so you don't have to?"

"I want to help him. I don't want some stranger doing it."

"It's not some stranger; it's a professional." I shake my head, sitting back in the sofa and not knowing what else I can say to him. "Give me another chance, Dani. I love you, and I want to marry you. I want to have kids with you and build a life together. We belong together," he says, taking my hand and pulling me into him quickly and kissing me. I jump away from him.

"Thomas, no!"

His true nature breaks free instantly. "This doesn't have anything to do with, *feeling independent and wanting to help a good family from your childhood out.* This is about *him.* Are you fucking him?" I don't respond, and he forces me to turn towards him. "The least you could do is be honest with me."

"Yes, I am sleeping in his bed with him every night, and nothing has ever felt more right to me. I love him, Thomas. I have always loved him. I'm sorry that you were hurt in the process."

"You're sorry?" He grabs my arms and shakes me. "You are the dumbest woman I have ever met. You are going to choose a degenerate over me?!"

"Let go of me, Thomas, and leave, please."

"You stupid fucking …"

"Let her go now!" Shane says, walking into the house. "Let her go before I call the police and have you arrested. That is, of course, after I beat the shit out of you and claim breaking and entering." Thomas lets me go and glares towards Shane who doesn't seem to be bothered by it at all. He makes sure Thomas walks out the door before locking it behind him. "What the hell was he doing here?"

"He wanted to talk and see if I would come back to him. I had to tell him that I am in love with Dillon."

"Oh, I'm sorry I missed that. I would have loved to have seen the expression on his face when you told him that. Wait till Dillon hears about this."

"Don't tell Dillon! It's not worth him getting upset about. He has enough to deal with. Please, Shane?"

"Okay, but you know he doesn't like us hiding things from him. I guess you're right though. There is enough for us all to worry about, right now. But you need to not let him in here again, and if he comes around, you need to let one of us know. That guy is a loose cannon, and he is going to really hurt you if you're not careful." I take Shane's hand and smile with a nod. "Did he hurt you?"

"No, I'm fine," I say as I rub my rapidly bruising arms. "I don't know how I can hide these from Dillon, but I certainly can't tell him Thomas kissed me."

"He kissed you?" I nod. "Oh yeah, we definitely can't tell him that." Shane crashes on the sofa, shaking his head. "Dillon is going to be pissed at us both if he ever finds out." I know he's right, but I don't want to think about it.

Chapter 17

Dillon

I walk into the house with a huge smile, and Dani instantly greets me with open arms. "Hi, how are you?" I ask with a kiss.

"I'm fine. Your dad is fine, too. He is doing much better. He's a fighter," she says.

Shane leans in between us. "I'm fine, too, if you were at all curious?" Dani and I separate, but stay holding hands as we sit together. "Alright, you seem good, but how did it really go?"

"Great, really great. We need to make sure everything is ready and working perfectly, Sean wants to do a walk through."

"Really? Oh wow, Dillon, you really did it! After talking to Shane, I assumed Sean wouldn't even let you in his home," Dani says with surprise in her voice.

"You really did it?" Shane yells.

"Of course I did. I told you, Sean loves me. I'm like the little brother he always wanted. He even hugged me, but I'm not that kind of guy, so I told him to try and get a hold of himself. I mean, we can be friends, but no point in making his wife jealous, you know?" I sit listening to them both laugh. "It's not that funny, and it really did happen." I pause, waiting for them to stop laughing. "Okay, you both are hilarious. I'm going to bed. I have an early day tomorrow." I start to go upstairs, but then I reconsider. "Although, maybe I should call Ava and invite her to come too. She is so hot. I wouldn't mind spending a little more time with her. Maybe I can convince Sean by convincing her. Or maybe I will simply tell Sean about the naked pictures Shane has of his wife, which should get him down here fast, because we all know how calm and understanding Sean is when it comes to his wife." They both stop laughing. "Yeah it's all funny when it's at my expense, but when I turn the tables, it's not so much fun now, is it?"

"It will be even funnier when you have to sleep with Shane in the guest room," Dani says smartly.

"That's not funny. I won't sleep with Dillon; he likes to spoon. And don't ask how I know that." Dani looks at him with curiosity. "We had both been drinking pretty heavily, and that's all I am saying. I can't go back to my parents' house. My mother drives me nuts talking about *hot* women she thinks I should hook up with. She has her friends bring their daughters over and then she nudges me and says, *'You should hit that Shane.'* And that is just not right at all. She calls herself my wingman. I can't go back there. I won't go back there," Shane pleads while Dani laughs.

"Don't worry, Shane. She's all talk; she won't kick me out of my own bed. She likes to be spooned by me and for me to do other things." I give her a look while she fights the smile she wants to give me.

"Okay, well… that's gross, so I am going to go to bed. By myself, and you two can work out whatever sleeping arrangements you need to." Shane goes halfway up the stairs before yelling back at us. "Now you two kids be good, and there better be no foolishness going on down here," Shane says, waving his finger at us before leaving us alone for the night..

"There won't be any foolishness going on down here," I say to Dani.

She turns and looks up at me. "There won't?"

I shake my head. "Nope, not down here." I chase after her and throw her over my shoulder. "Now, there will be a whole hell of a lot of foolishness going on upstairs in bed though."

The moment we reach the room, I shove the door shut with my foot and throw her into bed.

"Now, Dillon."

"Now Dillon what?" I strip my clothes off all while she watches, biting her bottom lip and trying to hide under the covers of the bed. I dive in under the blankets at the foot of the bed and pop my head up between her legs, yanking off her pants and underwear and tossing them in the floor. I give her a sweet kiss along her inner thigh and squeeze her ass, dragging her down to me. Once her lips meet mine, I fist the edges of her sweater and push it over her head. She relinquishes her bra and tosses it as she wraps her naked body around me, and I am able to feel my way inside of her. Every touch of her skin sends electricity vibrating through my body. Every sweep of her lips against my skin makes me want more from her. Spinning her around, I sit her up on me and encourage her to lean back and let her breasts heave into the air. I twist my tongue around her flushed pink nipples as she raises up along my cock and slides back down with a pleasing whimper of my name. A light stroke of my thumb against her clit and she clenches her tits with a heightened plea for me not to stop. Dani unleashes her final, pleasure-filled cry, provoking me to lift her up and back onto her back, thrusting my hips into her until my erection fills and bursts.

The surprising thing in the paper today - Johnathan Skelton's home and other properties were all raided today. A Senator for our great state decided, all of a sudden, to make it his personal mission to take Skelton and his empire down. When Ethan calls to set up a day and time for Sean to do a walkthrough of the factory, I let him know about the sudden misfortune of Mr. Skelton, but he doesn't seem to be surprised by it at all. "Did you or Sean have something to do with that?"

"I don't know what you are talking about, Dillon. He or I might have happened to mention something at a fundraising dinner, but who knows who actually pays attention to what we say. Besides, you know how senators are; they will do anything to get good press on themselves. I am sure Skelton happened to make himself too known to be ignored," Ethan says with little concern.

"You guys are really scary."

"Never hurts to maintain certain friendships, Dillon. Sean will see you in three days. Be ready." *Okay. Now I really feel sorry for the guy who falls in love with Sean's daughter.*

I have everyone on their toes, making sure every T is crossed and I is dotted. Shane is bouncing around like a nervous expectant father, while I am not doing a whole lot better.

I keep thinking about that bottle of bourbon in my drawer when Shane comes running in, "Dillon, he's here. Are you sure you know what to say?"

"Yes, now go away. You are making me nervous," I say as Sean walks through the door with Randy right behind him. *I guess I don't have time to drink now.* I straighten my tie and hold my hand out to him, which he takes with a smartass expression about him.

"You look all sweaty and nervous, Conrad. Don't worry. I didn't tell Randy it was you that drank all of his beer." Sean smiles looking back at Randy. The big bear of a man lets out a deep growl that makes me think it best not to shake his hand.

"I have some nicely aged Kentucky Bourbon in my drawer if you would like a drink?" I take it out and he holds out his hand, so I hand the whole bottle to him and realize I'm not getting it back. "Sure, you should definitely have the whole bottle."

"Thank you," he growls.

"Okay, so let's get started. What do ya say?" I head out with Sean following, and the first person we come upon is Warren, who I begged to be on his best behavior. "This is our top man. He pretty much runs this whole place."

Sean nods to him, "I've seen some of your movies," Warren says.

"Oh yeah, you like my movies?"

"Nope," Warren says bluntly.

I look at Sean and laugh, "He's such a kidder. That's our Warren, always joking around." I eye Warren and mouth to him to go away. I move on, showing Sean all the processes and equipment and introducing him to a few people, the few that aren't gushing and taking pictures of him. "I told them not to take pictures, I swear."

"It's alright. They all seem like good people," Sean says, smiling and waving as he walks through the factory with me.

"They are very good people. Hardworking and loyal, too."

"This is the only shift?" I nod. "You don't have a lot of people here Conrad. How are you meeting needs or going to meet needs? Have you rolled out product yet?"

"Yeah. Sales are good. We are already looking to hire more, and we will add shifts as we need," I say as Sean walks down the long hall towards the break room that holds all the old pictures of the factory through the generations of Conrads. "Is this your father?" I nod. "I would like to meet him. Can we do that now?"

"Sure, but he isn't here. He's at the house recovering," I say, hoping to keep him from stalling and tell me already what he wants to do.

"So… invite me to dinner. You have eaten enough of my food. About time I eat some of yours."

"Oh-kay, would you like to come to my house for dinner, Sean?"

"That sounds great. Give Randy the address. I'll bring some

wine, since I doubt you are getting the bourbon back."

Dani looks more nervous than I do when I get home. "I cleaned everything twice, and I tried to make dinner, but you know I am not good at the cooking thing, so I sent Shane to pick up some take out I ordered. I will put it in some nice dishes and make it seem like I cooked it. That'll work, right?"

"I don't think he cares, Dani. As long as you have some healthy food for him to eat, I think it will be fine." Her eyes widen in panic, which means she ordered the wrong food. "Don't worry about it. We will serve him a salad with a juice box or something." She squints her eyes at me. "I don't know, but don't worry. He loves me; I can do no wrong in his eyes. I promise you." I smile, kissing her cheek, but she doesn't seem to be reassured. Shane comes in through the back door and Dani instantly rushes to get things arranged and set up for company while I watch the road and my cell phone.

Sean and Randy pull in, walk up to the door, and don't even have to knock before I have the door open and ready for them to walk in.

"Relax, Conrad. I am only here to talk to your father for a few minutes. I am not here to judge your housekeeping skills," Sean says, shaking my hand and then Shane's. "How are you Shane?"

"Good sir and yourself? I heard you had a baby. I mean your wife had a baby, but I'm sure it's yours." Sean stands back, sighing.

"I mean, I know the baby is yours because your wife had the baby and she would never cheat on you. I mean you're Sean Grant, and she is your wife, and I am sure she is more than satisfied …errr with that situation. No matter what those crazy tabloids say … ha ha." Sean cocks his head, staring hard at Shane as he continues to ramble himself deeper and deeper. "Your wife is an amazing woman, and you can just look into her eyes and tell how much she loves you."

"You've been looking into my wife's eyes, Putnam?"

"No. Never. I would never look at her at all. Nope, no desire to do that."

"You don't think my wife is desirable?"

"Oh yes, she is very desirable. I desire her all the time… I mean I would think any man would desire her. What I believe, sir, is that desire is a compliment in a way in which a man can form a very far, far, far, but a very safe distance from a woman."

"Shane, shut up!" I say, shocked at his remarkable inability to talk calmly when he is nervous.

Randy laughs with Sean following. "He's a twitchy little guy. I like him, Sean. He makes me laugh," Randy says, smacking Shane on the back and sending him three feet forward and gasping for air before he checks himself for broken bones.

Dani nudges me quietly while I laugh at Shane. "And this is Dani," I say, stepping to her side as Sean takes her hand with a huge smile.

"Hi Dani. I have heard a lot about you."

"I am so happy to meet you. You are one of my favorite

actors. I just love …"

I quickly interrupt her by putting my arm around her shoulders and sliding her away from Social Magazine's, *Hottest Man of the Year*. "Yep we are all big fans, really big fans. How 'bout we eat now?"

Sean never says a word, but I know what he is thinking, and I am running interference before he even considers trying to make me pay for flirting with Ava, once or …a few times. Thankfully, dinner goes smoothly, and Sean does nothing more than make polite conversation with Dani. He seems to enjoy picking on Shane more and making him jumpy. After dinner, I take Sean upstairs to meet my father and leave the two to talk. It's nerve-racking waiting. Randy kicks back and watches the games on TV, Shane sits as far away from him as possible and tries not to make eye contact, Dani cleans the kitchen over and over, and I pace the floor.

Sean finally comes down the stairs nearly an hour later. "Okay, Randy, I think we can go." Sean sighs and looks at me as I stand up to meet him. "I like your dad; he's a good man. I have to be honest. I wasn't sure about your maturity to handle this, Conrad. Since I have known you, you have been kind of a misfit and not one I would consider to be a leader. Your father, though, I can clearly see why so many admire him and love him. Come to find out, he was just as worried about the same issues, but you surprised him and made the place your own. He actually said he has never been more proud of you and believes in you a hundred percent." I smile, looking over at Dani who takes my hand with both of hers. "You were raised by a great man and a great woman from what I understand, so I have every faith you will become the same. I will invest in your business, Conrad, and help you however I can. I will have my attorney's draw something up that will work for everyone. The first thing you need though is more staff and some repairs on that building. See to it that you build up correctly and with people you can trust."

I nod, shaking Sean's hand. "I will, and thank you. You and Ava are welcome to come by anytime, and I will be sure to stop by and see you guys whenever I am in Atlanta."

"Call first. Always call first," he says, shaking his head. I agree with a shrug and a nod. He seems satisfied with that answer and says goodbye to Shane and Dani. I am happy until I see him kiss Dani on the cheek, and whisper something in her ear. She smiles and nods, kissing his cheek with a girlish giggle that I can do nothing more than roll my eyes at. Sean waves to us all before walking out and joining Randy.

Shane walks up and high fives me. "You did it! You actually did it."

"No thanks to you," I say back to him.

"What do you mean? I meant to be awkward and goofy. It made him laugh. I believe I helped relax him and set him at ease with us."

"Uh-huh." I turn to my side and look over Dani. "What did he say to you?"

"That's between him and me," Dani says, cozying up to my chest and smiling up at me.

"I don't like that," I say.

She shrugs and kisses my cheek. "I am so proud of you. So proud I might be willing to do that thing we were talking about doing the other night." My mind blanks, and I stare at her with a large smile as she nods.

"Oh gross," Shane says.

Chapter 18

Dillon

Sean's endorsement and acknowledgment of our small company has brought in interest from all over the world. We have had so much interest, Dani thought it would be a good idea to do some tours of the facility and show how our device works. We set up a mock display of our best furniture with a sleeping baby, sensor and all included. It barely gets built just in time before people start arriving to see it. By the end of the first tour, I have business cards filling up every pocket.

I show up early this morning to do another tour of the facility, and thankfully, the freshly painted exterior is dry before their arrival. I walk around looking it over until I get to the far corner of the building, where there is fresh blood splattered all over the new paint. I follow the trail of blood around the corner of the building until I come upon Colleen, twisted and broken. She is beaten so badly that I can only tell it's her by her bright, purple sneakers she always wears. After I lose my breakfast, I call the police and try to postpone tours until tomorrow, but people show anyway. The tour goes well except for all the questions about the police tape and investigators looking over the crime scene.

As soon as things seem to get better, something else happens. Isn't that the way it always is? I spend two hours talking to police about where I was all night, if I had any reason to kill Colleen, or if

I knew of anyone that might.

"The girl was never a good judge of character, especially of the men she dated, but I can't think of anyone that would do anything like this," I say to them, exasperated by the constant questions without many answers returned. "Can you please tell me if you know anything about what happened?" I ask the two detectives questioning me. They do nothing more than look at each other and thank me for my time as they leave. The murder is all over the news, and we are now known for something horrifying within hours. Sean calls me before the day is up, wanting to know what the hell is going on.

"I don't know, Sean. I didn't know her that well."

"Did you talk to the police?" Sean asks impatiently.

"I did, and they don't have any answers for me right now."

"You better reassure the employees, Dillon, before they all run."

"I'll take care of it."

"Motherfucker! I swear. I can't believe this shit!" Sean screams into the phone at me.

"Yeah, I know. Trust me. I realize how bad this could end up being for us."

"I have to go, but if anything new comes up …"

"I will keep you informed, Sean, I promise. As soon as anything new comes up, you're the first person I will call." I hang up and fall into my palms with a desperate groan.

With Colleen gone, I have no choice. I have to hire Gina back on to take her place, despite Dani's disapproval of the idea. We don't have time to find someone and train them for the job in time to meet production expectations.

Gina shows up at my office a few days later, after her mourning period and with a smug privileged attitude. "Thank you for coming in. We are excited to have you back," I say as she smiles forcefully at me.

"I want a raise. I want ten percent more than what Colleen was making."

"You don't have the same qualifications she did."

"As I see it, I have one very important one. I am still alive and available to take this shit job."

"Nice, Gina. She was your best friend."

"Was, and now she's gone. It's sad and all, but you know, shit happens. I'm sure I'll find a new one. I am very personable you know," she says harshly. "Now, do we have a deal or should I go back to working at the bar for tips?" *What a low life piece of shit this woman is.* I nod and push her the job paperwork to sign. She happily does so as if she is listening to her favorite dance song. "So how is Dani these days?" I don't bother to answer the bitch. "That good, huh? If you ever get tired of old reliable and want a little new and exciting, you know where to find me, Dillon. I know we had that brief moment together, but I have all new parts now." She puffs up her double D's with a joyful wiggle. Gina sashays out of my office running into Shane as he walks in. "Hello Shane. You're looking good today. Hey, now that we are all going to be working together again, maybe the three of us could have a late night meeting?" she laughs, stroking Shane's chest as he squirms to try and get away from her.

"Ewww, tell me rank and stank isn't coming back?"

"I had no choice."

"Damn. Every time I think we have overcome the last hurdle, something else happens." I look up at him wondering the same thing. It does all seem a little too coincidental.

We have managed to weather the last storm with a little help from John Skelton. Our old friend's trial is going horribly for him, and he has recently lost his cool and threatened to kill the senator that has been so dogged in putting him away. Murders happen every day, but a vocal senator getting his life threatened by a known criminal, well that type of news is just too juicy to dismiss. With the media focused elsewhere, we are able to succeed past Colleen's murder. Now, our newly renovated web site goes up in …five…four …three…two …one …and we are live. There is a wild display of cheers and applause behind me, and for a brief moment, I feel like the smile on my face can never be taken away. The factory is running again at full speed with new workers piling in for every shift. I have plenty of supervisors, sub-supervisors, and so on, all of which are keeping an eye on everyone else. But for some reason, I still feel like there is at least one pair of eyes on me, a shadowy judge waiting for me to mess up, turn my back, and then take advantage and send a knife right into my spine. Paranoia I suppose. There is nothing I can do about it; I need to continue on unless that person steps out into the light and tries to do their worst.

"Sales are moving rapidly, stores are calling in to confirm shipments and to ask for more to help meet with demands. You did it, Dillon," Shane says with an encouraging smile. "So why do you look like the end of the world just hit?"

"I guess it's just a feeling, or maybe I know better than to believe that Douglas Portman is ever going to give up his fight for this land or to do me in. We still have to deal with Thomas and the other Portman attorneys trying to push the city to revoke our business license."

"Their reasoning is preposterous." I nod, still feeling uneasy.

"You need to look happy. Otherwise, your employees are not going to enjoy the celebration of the company's 125th anniversary. And I am sorry, my friend, but you are the head of this machine and are going to have to act like it tonight whether you want to or not."

I nod, grabbing my coat and making sure to lock everything up before I follow him out of the factory and down to the local restaurant where we are having a celebration for all employees to enjoy. The factory is closed for one night. All the lights are turned off, and all the machines are shut down, and for some reason, it brings on a reality of what could have been. Driving away from the dark facility, I feel all I want to do is get this night over with and get back to work so the facility looks alive and prosperous again.

When I arrive at the restaurant, I am cheered on to the back area where the celebration cake and champagne await. I hate making speeches, so I simply stand in front of everyone and say, "This celebration is due to many before us and due to all of you. We are successful because of all the hard work done by so many, and I thank each and every one that has helped us get to this day." I raise my glass, and everyone else follows my lead. "Thank you."

I begin to feel good and lighten up about my factory being dark for a night with the happiness of all the workers and my friends. Even Lucas smiles tonight, and I almost think we are friends, but the moment I laugh next to him, he walks away.

"I guess some grudges never die," Shane says. I nod, wishing I knew what to say to fix the strain between me and my old friend.

I decide to chase him down and confront him once and for all. He turns, frustrated to see me again. "Isn't there enough people here to congratulate you? Give you all the attention you crave? You have to come and seek me out. You know I am only here for the free food and drink?" Lucas says.

"I just want to know why you still hold such a grudge against me. Is this still about football? I'm sorry if mutual friends didn't guard you like they should have. I am sure they are too, but I promise you, none of us wanted anyone, especially you, to get hurt. It was always about winning the game, never about us."

"Perfect. You are always absolutely perfect, aren't you Dillon? You can't stand if someone doesn't like you."

"I am far from perfect. Does my life seem perfect to you?"

"Let's see, you graduate at the top of our high school class with little effort, and then your dedicated girlfriend conveniently goes away so you can then go on to college and be the big man on campus there and screw whatever you want without any guilt. After all your joys and fun in college, you carry them on to New York for the big advertising job in the city. You were all big and successful until you were forced to come back here, and like the perfect son that you are, you help your father save his business. Now, here you are again, being celebrated. You are loved and adored by pretty much everyone you meet. So yeah, I think your life is pretty damn close to perfect. I wish my life worked out half as great as yours did," he says, backing me up and walking around me. "Excuse me, I think I have had enough celebrating for one night." Lucas leaves the restaurant and Dani walks up to remind me to smile.

"Ahhh, there's that handsome smile I have missed all day." My girl buries herself within my arms and nothing else matters anymore.

Her warm body next to mine eases a deep sigh from my lips and a powerful beat of my heart against my chest. "You feel so good right now. Let's go home and crawl into bed and…" I say, making her laugh into my shoulder as I let my hands wander.

"I would love to, but you, my darling, are the hero of the night and need to stay until the end I'm afraid."

"Don't call me that, please," I say causing her to lean her head back to look at me. "Don't ask, but I'm not much in a hero sort of mood right now."

"Stop being so depressing. This is a big moment, a moment you should be proud of. I know I am."

"You should be proud of yourself more. I couldn't have made it without you."

"Well that's true." She smiles, kissing me gently and giving me every reason to want to sneak out of this celebration. Before I can even consider the idea, Douglas Portman walks in with his preferred choice of son-in-law, Thomas, at his side. "Daddy, what are you doing here?" Dani says, hugging her father.

"I thought I would come and congratulate you on your hard work and success."

"Thank you. Dillon has done a wonderful job."

"With your help and money, of course," Portman says with a stinging glare my way.

"He used a lot of his money too and was a huge part of this success. You really should congratulate him, Daddy."

"Should? Maybe. But I won't. Instead, I will make one more offer to buy him out before he ruins everything and destroys your life and his father's." Portman hands me a piece of paper.

"It's a more than a fair offer, Dillon. You should take it and run," Thomas says. I toss the piece of paper into the nearby candle, wrap my arms back around Dani, and kiss her on the side of the head. "I hope that wasn't because of what happened the other night. That kiss was nothing. She was scared, and I got excited by her being in my arms. Of course, being all vulnerable and half naked like she was helped too." I stand straighter, looking him over as Dani tenses within my arms. "Oh, so she never told you? I guess us being together in your house while you were out of town is probably something she would want to keep to herself. Oops, sorry Dani," he says, walking away happier than I care for him to be.

Portman is so happy he can hardly contain himself. "Enjoy your night. If you change your mind about selling, let me know." He walks away to go sit with Thomas while I pull back from Dani, waiting for an explanation.

"It was nothing, Dillon. He wanted to talk, and he snuck in a kiss when I wasn't paying attention. I was …"

"Half-naked and vulnerable. Yeah, I heard."

"I wasn't half-naked. You can ask Shane."

"Shane knew about this?"

She pauses, looking around. "I asked him not to tell you, so don't be mad at him."

"He's my friend, not yours."

"No, he's our friend, and neither of us wanted to bother you with something so trivial, with all that has been on your mind lately. Thomas came by, knowing you were gone. He wanted to try and talk me into getting back together."

"Of course he did, but that doesn't explain why you opened the door and let him in my house?" I say, trying to control my rapidly building anger.

"Dillon, I had been watching some scary movies and thought someone was outside trying to get into the house. I was scared out of my mind, and he heard me scream and called out to me through the door and I ran to him …"

"You ran to him, ever hear of a phone, Dani?"

"I tried Dillon, but the phone wouldn't work … at least when I tried it. I was so panicked, I guess I couldn't get anything to work quite right. I was really tired and hadn't been getting a lot of sleep either. I let him in, and I'm sorry. It was a moment, I was scared, and he was there. I thought he was being a friend and then he tried to take advantage. But I turned him down, and he got pissed off and …"

"He grabbed you again? That's where those bruises I found on your arms came from?" She lowers her head and sighs. My control of my anger finally snaps, and I look up, searching the room for the bastard, and when I spot him, Dani instantly presses her hands against my chest. "Dillon, no. This is not the time or place."

"Don't worry, I'm only going to talk to Tommy boy." I smile at her and kiss her hands before walking over to him and Douglas. "Hey Tommy?" He looks back at me with indifference. "Can we talk, Jackass?"

Shane rushes over to me and grabs my arm. "Dillon, let it go. Everyone is fine, and you got the girl remember?"

Tommy stands with a little more concern. "Are you wanting to challenge me, Conrad?" he laughs.

"No, I want to beat the shit out of you."

"Let's go," he says, pushing up his sleeves. I nod with a smile and slug him right in the mouth. The hit felt so good, so I do it again. Someone pulls me back, and Tommy comes at me, getting me in the jaw. I stagger back, but go back at him full force. It takes a couple of guys to pull me off of him, and once Douglas pulls his preferred son-in-law off the ground, he smartly escorts him out of the restaurant before Tommy boy can get his ass beat any more.

Dani walks up on me and cleans the blood from my lip. "Feel better now?"

"A little bit," I say with a cocky smile. "It actually felt pretty good." Dani shakes her head. "Don't tell me it wasn't necessary. You knew damn well that's what would happen, and that's why you didn't tell me."

I wait for her to yell at me or start an argument, but instead, she crashes into my chest and wraps her arms around me. "I just worry about you so much, Dillon. If anyone hurt you, I would probably punch them, too."

I smile in shock and embrace her tightly. "With your right hook, that would be one unlucky bastard." She laughs with a light sigh. "Tired?" She nods. "We can go, Baby." I kiss her before being interrupted by yelling.

"I don't want to hear it anymore! I told you and told you to do it right!"

I step toward Warren as Rafe tries to calm his father down. "Sorry, Dillon. He's a bit fired up tonight."

"And you know why!? You are no good!" Warren yells at his son as he grabs at his throat.

"Maybe you should take a walk, Rafe, and I will talk to your father?" I say, separating Warren's hands from his son's throat. "What's wrong with you? That's your son!"

"Well, I am tired of defending him. I'm sick and tired of helping him for nothin'. He is no good, and you would be smart to get rid of him before his cancer spreads and infects you, too."

"I don't know what you are talking about, but you need to sober up."

"You know! You figured it out just like I did. Some people are just bad, and there ain't nothin' you can do about it." He doubles over, looking pale.

"I think you need to go home and rest. We can talk more when you have a clearer head," I say, trying to help him to a chair. "Can someone call a taxi?" I yell out.

"I'll take him home. I need to go check on your father anyway," Dani says, wrapping her arms around me. "And it will also allow me some time to set up a celebration gift for you, when you get done here."

"I'll come home now," I smile.

"No, you stay here and enjoy your night, and then we can enjoy our night." I help Warren up and out the door while Dani gets in the truck.

"Okay old man, go home and sleep it off." Warren climbs into the passenger side of the truck and almost immediately passes out. "Are you sure you don't need my help?"

"No, if I can't get him out on his own, then I will let him stay in the truck and sleep it off, and you can worry about it tomorrow."

I run around to her side of the truck and kiss her goodbye. "Be careful. I'll see you when I get home." She smiles, starts up the truck, and I have an urge to stop her and tell her I love her, but maybe this isn't the best time with a drunk old man in the truck with her and all. I wave as they leave and walk back inside to finish up this party as quickly as possible.

The rest of the night, I deal with a few more drunks and a bunch of overly loving co-workers. Some women I didn't know had it in them make it known that they are ready and willing to be my office romance. I dodge them the best I can, but Lucas's sister, Gina, is not about to give up. We dated once in high school and really only to get back at Lucas. The whole relationship lasted only long enough for me to come in her mouth. She was always flirtatious and a little easy, especially when she thought it might get her a better position in life. I had no idea what a disgusting individual she really is until Colleen was killed. The moment I get away, I rush to Shane and try to get him to hurry up and get me out of here, but Gina manages to slide into my lap and overtake my attention.

"Gina, please. I think you need to sober up."

"You know I have always loved you. Why do you tease me like you do?"

"I'm not trying to," I say, picking her up and putting her down in her own chair. "I will call for a taxi for you on my way out."

Gina quickly grabs hold of my arm. "You're leaving?" Suddenly, she is back all over me. "Take me home; otherwise, I am going to go find someone else that will. If something happens to me, you know my brother will blame you …forever." I roll my eyes at the drunken disgrace.

"Where is your car?" She hands me the keys with a smile.

"Shane, follow us so I can leave her car at her house," I say, and she instantly huffs. "I'll take you home to keep you from getting into any more trouble, but nothing else." Gina is good for a few minutes, then she slips out of her seat belt and makes her way to me, working her hands down my pants. I jerk one hand out and hold her to the other side of the car. "No. Now put your seat belt back on and don't take it off again."

Once we finally get to her house, I help her inside and lay her keys on the table near the door. I am able to get a few steps out the door before she grabs hold of me. "Dillon, please don't leave me. I am so scared, and I don't want to be alone tonight. Please, I'm afraid. I really am afraid of him." I look out to Shane for help. He reluctantly gets out of his car and comes over to try and help pull her off me. "No, you can't leave. You don't understand. He always knows what I'm doing. I can't get away from him, and now he sees you leaving, I'm sure." Gina continues to whine as she keeps a strong hold of me.

"I don't know who you're talking about, Gina! You need to go to bed and sleep it off. Shane help me!"

"I'm trying. She is surprisingly strong for a small woman!" I finally manage to break free from her and jump in the back of the car as Shane jumps in the front. "Next time, you should try to be less charming." I share a snarling look with him in the rearview mirror. "Actually, I kind of like a woman that likes to get a little rough," he says with a laugh.

"Good, she's all yours."

"Mmm, on second thought, I should save myself for someone

more worthy of my Shane Goodies."

"Your what?" I ask, hoping I heard him wrong.

"My Shane Goodies, you know?" He looks at me with a hopeful nod, as I shake my head at him. "Oh yeah, Dani is the only one who knows that story. Never mind. Sorry I said anything."

"Me too," I say, disgusted by the idea.

"Speaking of, after I drop you off, I am going to go spend some time with Anna-Marie."

"The hottie bartender from the restaurant?"

"The one and only."

"I was wondering where you were most of the night. Well, have fun with that. I am going to be busy myself, so it will be nice not to have to worry about you hearing us."

"Yes, it's nice for me too. Now that you're actually paying me, I think it's time our roommate situation changes. I have had enough of hearing Dillon get his, from the room next door." I laugh as Shane pulls up to the house, only I don't see the truck. "You should have checked with Dani and made sure she didn't already have plans for the night. Did she know you were coming home after the party?"

"Yeah, we talked about it. she should be here. Maybe she thought she would need to come back and get me. Did she see you flirting?"

"Oh, maybe. She might have seen us talking intimately on her break, in her car, too."

"Oh wonderful. She went back to get me I bet. Let me check and see if she answers her phone before you go." I wait through the multiple rings and end up getting her voicemail. "No answer. Give me a second to check on my dad then drive me back up to the restaurant." I run inside to find my dad hobbling around downstairs on his own. "What are you doing up?"

"I wasn't sure when anyone would get home, and I needed my medicine. It's no big deal. I can do it," he says, waving me away from him. *Stubborn old man.*

"Did Dani come by and check on you?"

My father stops and looks me over. "No, she hasn't been home yet. Have you tried calling her?"

"Yeah, but I can try again." I pick up my phone and dial her again, but still nothing. "I'm going to go with Shane and look for her. Warren was pretty drunk tonight, and she volunteered to take him home so maybe ..." He nods at me as I run out the door and jump back into the car next to Shane. "She never came home. Let's go to Warren's and see if she is there."

We drive over while I continue to try her phone. The lights are all off at Warren's, and our truck is nowhere in sight. Shane and I both get out of the car. I knock on the door while he runs around back and checks there. There is no answer. When Shane runs back to me, he simply shakes his head. "Where are they?" He shrugs, shaking his head, and we drive back to the restaurant, finding Warren's truck still in the parking lot but no sign of Dani.

"We should call the police," Shane says, picking up his own phone and calling himself. I nod while I try to think of any place she might have gone or a simple explanation to why she isn't where she should be and she isn't able to answer her phone. There has to be a good reason why she never came home or why she didn't call to let me know if there was any problem with the truck. My hands are shaking, my heart is pounding out of my chest, and I feel like I can't sit down. I can't stand either. My whole body suddenly feels like it doesn't fit in my own skin. I want to crawl out of it, go to sleep, and wake up from what is quickly turning into a nightmare. *Maybe she is at the store, getting some last minute things and she left her phone in the truck? Maybe she had to take Warren to the hospital because he fell or …?* Shane backs up and begins driving slowly down the road, traveling the same route Dani would have driven.

As we drive, we both notice some tracks leading off the road. "Is that the truck there?" Shane backs up and aims the car lights deep into the woods where the bright blue truck shines through. I jump out of the car and run in, searching through the truck and finding nothing but her purse. "They have to be around here somewhere. Walking maybe? So let's get back in the car and search." We both get back in, but something doesn't feel right. We only get a few feet, and I suddenly can't breathe.

"Slow down, I can't see."

"Neither of us can see. There are no street lights here, and it's the middle of the night."

"So, maybe we should get out and walk with flashlights?" I say, instantly digging into his glove box.

"I don't have a flashlight in there, Dillon."

"Why not?!"

"I might have one in the trunk, just calm down and let me pull over to a safe place." As soon as he pulls over, I jump out of the

car and wait impatiently for him to open the trunk. "Here you go."
He hands it to me, and I take off walking. "I'm going to call some
people to come help look for them. Do you want to wait so we
don't get lost in the woods?"

"No, you can wait. I have to find her."

"Dillon. Dillon! Damn it Dillon! You don't even have a coat!"
Shane yells from behind me as I head into the darkness, looking for
her.

I don't know where I am going or what I'm looking for
exactly, but the further I go, the more anxious I get. "Dani! Dani!"
Oh God where is she? "Dani!" Desperation begins to rise up from
my gut and sit in my throat, and I can hardly breathe her name.
The trees begin to close in on me. I sink deeper into my jacket as it
gets colder and ignore my feet that are wet from trenching through
the snow. "Dani!" I scream, listening to the echoes through the
trees. I find footprints in the snow here and there, with wisps of
hair and pieces of clothing and then nothing. *Where are you Dani?*
Where are you? When Shane starts calling me, I ignore him, afraid of
what he may have to say. By his fifth try, I finally answer. "What?!"

"They found Warren."

His long pause forces a dreaded howl from my lungs. "Just
tell me Shane!"

"He was beaten and thrown into the creek. He's dead,
Dillon." The silence sends chills down my spine. "Still no sign of
Dani, but we have a whole crew out there looking for her. The
police are here now. Her father is here too, with some of his
people. You should come back and let us regroup. I have a warm

coat for you now. You can't keep going in that suit jacket. You have already been out there for over an hour."

"No. She needs me. I know it." I hang up and keep searching and searching. I feel like I am going in circles, so I stop screaming for her, crying for her, and begin praying for help, for mercy. I twist and turn here and there and finally see something that I have been missing somehow. I come upon an old paper mill hidden by fallen trees and overgrowth. I move through the thick brush and see a figure in the distance. "Dani?" I move towards it as the wind cuts into me like a knife. I am shivering so hard that I can only walk a couple of steps before falling to the ground.

"Dillon?" I try to run towards them, but my legs are too heavy. "Stay there. I'll come to you." I pause until I see Thomas walking up on me. "You don't look so good pal."

"Don't try and stop me. I need to find Dani," I say, looking around him to search for her.

"I wouldn't dream of it." Thomas pushes me back into the other direction. "Is that her, down there by the water? Back through the brush, can you see her?" he says.

I look toward where he is pointing and believe I do see her. I rush down the hill, stumbling toward the water's edge, only to find nothing but rocks. "It's not her," I yell out, but no one is around. I force myself back up and climb up the hill. The cold begins to sink down into my bones, and my eyes become heavy, but I keep going. I keep searching until I stumble and fall to my knees. I manage to get back up with my head spinning and my heart beating within my ears. "Dani, please tell me where you are." I can't feel my legs any longer and stagger back to the ground. I begin to see lights, and I smile, "Dani?" The images are so blurry that I close my eyes to try and focus, only I can't get them to reopen.

Chapter 19

Dillon

The moment my eyes open, I begin searching for her. "Dani?"

Shane pops up at my side with bloodshot eyes and rumpled clothes. "It's fine. Lie back down" I ease down into what seems to be a hospital bed and look back up at him in confusion. *Was it all a bad dream?* "You're still recovering from hypothermia, so you are going to be pretty light headed and weak for a while. Dumbass! I told you to wait so we could get you a bigger coat. The temperature dropped, and you were out there for hours. We had to form a whole other search team just to look for you. Fucking Thomas said you weren't worth finding. If he hadn't found, Dani, I probably would have slugged him."

I sit up instantly, "He found Dani?"

Shane sits down with a heavy sigh. "Uh… yeah, but no reason to talk about that right now."

"Where is she?" I move the blankets off me and try to jump out of bed, but fall back against it. "She's here, isn't she?" I move towards the door, but Shane stops me. "Let go of me and tell me where she is."

"Get back into bed, and I promise I will." I look back at him with an unyielding warning. "I promise. Just get back into bed before you black out again."

"Again?" I climb back into bed with a sudden realization of

the pain shooting through my head.

"Yes, apparently you blacked out a few times before ending up where we found you. From your footprints, it looked like you were right by Dani, but for some reason, you went right by her and kept going too far. You were nearly dead when we found you … *jackass*. As if the night wasn't bad enough, I had to worry I would lose you, too." I glance over at him in fear. "No. She's not dead, but she is in a coma." I sit up as my entire body tenses. "Someone dragged her to an old paper mill and beat her up pretty bad. She was barely alive when she was found. Her father has her surrounded by the *top medical advisors in the world*. She's holding on so far. No one seems to know if she will make it though, and if she does, what kind of life she will be able to have. It was gruesome, Dillon." I sink down into the bed, feeling my lungs fill with lead.

I can scarcely breathe when I realize, "Thomas found her?"

"Of course he did. He is being praised and honored as the chosen one at this point. You, however, are still the piece of shit that put Dani in this position." I fall back into the pillow, shutting my eyes tight. "Which is not true at all! You know that, right?"

"I don't know anything. I don't even know what I'm doing down here." I lean back, going over the night in my head. "Who did it? Who hurt her?" Shane shakes his head with a shrug of his shoulders. "Was she raped?"

"They don't think so. She was nearly nude when they found her, but they think she put up such a fight that her attacker struck her to get her under control and knocked her out. He must have thought he killed her or heard someone coming. We don't know, but we believe he got scared and ran off. He, or whoever, left her in the freezing cold to bleed to death. Fortunately, the cold slowed her circulation down so much that it gave us time to find her."

"So, she's going to be fine?"

"I don't know, Dillon. I wish I did and could tell you that she is going to be fine when she does wake, but I … I saw her, and she was …" He shakes his head, grimacing.

"I want to see her." Shane starts to argue, but he knows better. "I don't care how or when, but I want to see her. You can help me do that, right?"

"I'll see what I can figure out. It's not going to be easy though. You, in particular, have been forbidden anywhere near her. It's going to take a miracle to get you in."

"You can do it. If anyone can help me, you can. I know you would never let me down."

"Oh, thanks for that. Why couldn't you wake up being an ass? I really wanted to scream at you. I kind of wanted to punch you for putting me through this. The moment I saw you lying there in the snow…" Shane turns his head from me, breathing heavily. "…don't ever do that to me again or I swear I will …" he says, quickly wiping his eyes.

"I promise Shane, and I'm sorry," I say, lying back and sending a weak smile his way.

After talking with my father on the phone and reassuring him that I'm doing well, I told him I would be home soon. Thankfully, some kind neighbors have stepped in to help him until I get back.

Now, I am stuck flipping through channels on the television, waiting patiently for Shane to return with news on Dani. The nurses keep bringing me food and constantly bugging me about eating more, but the last thing on my mind is eating. All I want to do is get out of here and take care of her. When Shane returns late into the night in a doctor's outfit with a wheelchair, I don't bother asking why, I simply smile. *That's my best friend Shane, and he always comes through for me.*

"Don't smile at me," he says harshly. "And don't say a word. Just look sick and get into the damn wheelchair." I do as asked, and he covers me up with a blanket up to my neck and pushes my head down. We casually stroll down a hall and into an elevator. "Okay, I made a deal with a nurse on duty to help me. Dani is pretty much only watched by her guard and one nurse for the next few hours. The other nurse is busy on rounds and poking everyone with needles and the guard is currently having issues."

"Issues?" I ask curious.

"He accidently had a needle plunged into him, with what may or may not have had morphine in it." I look up at him with wide eyes. "Stay down, I didn't do it. Although, I might have accidently caused him to back up into it while a nurse, that I may or may not know, was holding it. No worries, he never felt it. He was too busy cringing from when I pushed the wheelchair into his balls. Considering the pain he was in, the morphine was a nice thing I did for him." I sit back and smile as we roll past the knocked out guard covered by a blanket himself. The nurse ahead of us nods and continues on, "Okay, I am going to stand watch and come get you the moment I have to, so don't you dare fight me when I come for you. I promised I wouldn't get anyone in trouble."

Shane pushes me into Dani's room and leaves me. I get up and nearly fall back into the chair from the sight of her. She is so swollen and covered in bruises and bandages that I can hardly tell that it is …Dani. The breathing machine covers most of her mouth, and the many other wires attached to her are hard to understand. I walk towards her and find her hand, which is swollen twice its normal size with wounds all up and down her arms. I want to vomit at the thought of the beating she had to have endured. I take hold of her hand, kiss her cheek, and wipe my tears away as I wish to see her bright eyes again. I have to close my eyes and breathe, and still nothing comes out of my mouth. I only want her to know that I'm here, so I say what first comes to mind. "You know, when I first met you, I knew we were going to be best friends. It was easy to be sure of that. You were, after all, wearing my favorite player's jersey." I laugh, remembering her in that ridiculously oversized shirt rolled up to fit her small body. "Do you want to know the moment I fell in love with you? It was at that same time, that moment you smiled at me. Your smile is so amazing that I knew, at that moment, I never wanted to be without your smile in my life. Yeah, I know what you're thinking, *but Dillon you never asked me out. You never made a move until I started dating Lucas.* You were my best friend. You and Shane were my family. The idea of dating you and ruining that was something I never wanted to consider. That is, until you told me that you wanted him to be your first. How could I let that happen? You didn't belong with him, and you don't belong with Thomas now. You belong with me, and I don't want to belong with anyone else." I slide in carefully next to her and lay my head against hers, stroking her hand and letting my tears stroll down my face. "I hated you for leaving me. I know you probably thought it didn't matter to me. I was just a stupid kid with a high school crush, right? However, you were my heart, and when you left, you took it with you. Apparently, you took even more than I realized with you. I can't imagine the fear you had, or the pain you felt, and I'm sorry I wasn't there for you to help you get through it. You know I would have been, and I guess that's why you hid it from me, for me." I grip her hand and kiss her cheek. "I'm sure you thought I hated you the moment I saw you at the airport, but that's not the case at all. Actually, the moment I saw you, I wanted to wrap my arms around you and never let go." I swallow a hard lump in my throat. "Thank you for coming back and being here for me. Thank you for being you and loving me, despite my flaws. Yeah, I admit I have a few … but you don't. You're perfect, perfect in every way … for me. Don't leave me, Dani. Don't leave me here by myself. Come out of this, and I promise I won't leave your side. I won't let anyone ever hurt you again. I will make sure you are happy every day of your life." My eyes fill with tears, and I tense with fear as I silently beg her to wake up until the words form and my voice creaks out, "Wake up, Dani, please. Wake up and come back to me." I lie with her for as long as possible before Shane comes in and motions that I have to go. He wheels me out of her room as her guard begins to wake from his painless sleep.

Chapter 20

Dillon

Once out of the hospital, I go back to my daily routines, and thankfully, my father is doing well enough to stay by himself for most of the day. I spend my nights sneaking into Dani's room one way or another, dressed as either a doctor or a nurse or a minion guard of her father's. For several weeks, I manage to figure out something, but tonight, the guard is gone and the nurse that knows me well motions for me to meet her in another room.

'She woke up this morning," she says with a smile. I smile in return, but wait to hear if there is anymore. "So far, she seems okay. She doesn't remember anything that happened. We have been keeping mirrors away from her so as not to scare her. With her memory fragile, we don't want to abruptly bring it back and put her into shock. There is something else, too." She pauses, twisting her hands as if she is unsure whether to tell me or not.

"Just tell me."

"She is not able to walk, but there are signs she will eventually. Right now, she is aware that she cannot move her legs, but she is under the belief it is the pain medicine she is on that is causing the lack of feeling." Sighing heavily, I nod understanding.

"Where is her guard?"

"They moved her, but I can get her out for tests here soon if you want to meet us?" I nod, and she directs me where to go to wait for them.

I pace the room, waiting, until I hear them coming. The moment they come through the door, Dani looks up at me. At first, I worry that she is angry or hates me. Her eyes are so bruised and bloodied, but still I smile, dropping to my knees and laying my head in her lap. "Oh, thank God, you're okay. I have been here every night to see you and talk to you." She doesn't say a word, so I slowly look up and she is crying and smiling. She places her hands on my face and mouths, *I love you.*

"Her throat is tender, so she is not able to speak very well," the nurse says.

"It's okay. You don't need to say anything. All that matters is that you get better and come home, okay?" She nods, gripping my hands as if she never wants to let go. "I love you," I say, and she closes her eyes, holding my hands against her face. We are allowed only a few more minutes before she has to go. "I'll be back tomorrow and every day until you are able to come back home with me," I say, kissing her gently.

I go home on top of the world, only to face my father and Shane, who don't seem nearly as happy about my news. "What's wrong with you two?"

"Do you really think her father is going to let her come here with you? He's already arranging to have her medically supervised at his home in Germany. He is going to take her as far away from you as possible, Dillon," Shane says.

I shake my head. "No, she won't leave, no matter what he wants. She's not a kid anymore. She wants to be with me."

"Okay, so she comes here ... then what?" he asks annoyingly.

"What do you mean *then what*? She comes here and we build a life together," I say simply.

"Dillon, she lost her memory temporarily. Eventually, it's all going to come back, and when it does, how are you going to deal with that?"

"I will deal with it. *We* will deal with it."

Shane shakes his head. "You are so stubborn. You cannot fix what is broken in her by just willing it away. Do you remember how she looks? Do you have any idea what she must have gone through? You can't love that away, Dillon. She can't walk, Dillon. The girl who runs every day, who was one of the top athletes in our school, cannot walk. How are you going to explain to her that she can't do one of the things she loves anymore? Do you understand the long road to recovery ahead of her at all?"

"I understand that I don't care what long road is ahead of us. I understand that I won't give up on her no matter what, and she won't give up on me. We have gotten through a lot together, and we are going to get through this, too. We will be happy again. She will walk again, and she will run again. No matter how much time it takes, no matter what obstacles we meet, I will be there for her to help her accomplish whatever she wants to."

Shane sighs, slamming his glass down on the counter. "You know, I love her too, just like a sister, and I love you like a brother, but sometimes, you think more about yourself than anyone else, and I think that's what you are doing with her right now. She needs more than what you can give, than what I believe you are capable of giving," he says before walking out of the house and speeding out of the driveway.

I glance at my father, "You going to yell at me, too?"

"Nope, I learned a long time ago that you're going to do what you want to do, no matter what anyone else says to you. All I ask is to make sure that, whatever you decide, you consider her needs over your wants," my father says, causing me to consider what I am really going to have to do.

Work is grueling, and you would think it would take my mind off the attack on Dani and the murder of Warren, but with the police still considering suspects, many of them being people that work for me, it makes it impossible to completely put it out of my mind. Things only get worse when the police come to take Shane and me in for questioning. We are asked to go voluntarily to keep from worrying everyone in the factory, not that it matters. The word spreads and everyone here knows what's going on before we walk out the door. The suspicion is that Shane and I came down here to use the factory as a front for drug smuggling, and Warren found out about it. We killed Warren and tried to kill Dani to keep her from talking. That's what Mr. Portman has insinuated, to obviously distract me from getting to his daughter. The police question me for a couple of hours before leaving me, then coming back to question me some more. The longer it goes, the angrier I get, so when they start searching through their case file and purposely let crime scene pictures fall out in front of me, I reach my limit. "Why am I here? You have a perfectly good suspect right there in front of you!"

"And who might that be, Mr. Conrad?"

"Thomas Monroe! He was the one that found her, How did he do that unless he already knew where she was?"

"And why would Mr. Monroe have any reason to harm either victim?"

"Because he wants to ruin me. He hates me for stealing Dani from him. He hates me for making him look bad in front of his boss. He was supposed to easily gain my factory for Mr. Portman, and he couldn't do it. I beat him, and I got the girl, too," I yell at the annoyingly calm man.

"From what I hear, Ms. Portman had plans to leave for Chicago where she and Mr. Monroe were to be married. So, it would seem you have every reason to be angry with him, maybe set him up to look like the killer, only one survived that you didn't expect. She's going to remember sooner or later, you know?"

"I hope she does, and I hope that I get the first crack at the fucker!"

"You're the common thread to all this. Plus another murder - Colleen Farrow, and two other murders at your factory that happened …"

"Before I ever got down here!"

"So, if it is not you, then it is for sure someone you know. Other than Mr. Monroe, who else do you think would have a reason to commit these crimes? I should tell you that Mr. Monroe has an alibi."

"Who? The jackass himself, Mr. Portman? You can't trust him. I wouldn't put it past him to sell out his own daughter to get what he wants. The man bleeds greed."

The detective in front of me, Detective Jonas, sighs into his hand before looking down at his case file. "I'm going to be honest with you, Dillon. I can call you that, right?"

"Call me whatever you want as long as you find the fuck that did this."

"I'm trying to do that Dillon, but I am going to need your help doing that. There was very little left at either crime scene, but we have reason to believe that both victims knew their attackers. They pulled over voluntarily behind another car. Mr. Perry got out to help whoever it was and was beaten with a crow bar then pushed down the hill into the creek. Ms. Portman clearly tried to get away but was ambushed from the side of the truck and pulled from the truck as it was still moving. Where were you? You sent a woman you supposedly love off by herself to help a drunk man home, in the middle of the night?"

"I was going to send Warren home in a taxi, but Dani said she would take him since she had to go check on my father anyway. She wanted me to stay until the end to be respectful to my employees, so I caught a ride home with Shane. I rushed home as soon as the party was over to be with Dani."

The detective begins to go through notes. "Actually, I heard you left with a Ms. Gina Charles, someone that is clearly not a friend of Ms. Portman's and has quickly moved up at your company. Are you sure you two didn't run into Ms. Portman and things took a bad turn?"

"Gina was drunk. I drove her home in her car and left her there soon after. Shane followed us, and I left with him. I can't stand Gina."

"Your blood was found on Ms. Portman's clothes, Dillon."

I shake my head until I remember my fight with Tommy boy. "I got into a fist fight earlier in the night, and she hugged me, so I am sure some got on her that way."

"So you are violent?" I shake my head and growl in frustration. "You were right there Dillon. You were found a mere few feet from where she was attacked. What happened? Did you panic? Did you try to find your way back, but get lost in those dark woods?"

"I was trying to find her! You guys have no idea what you are doing do you? It was Thomas Monroe, I promise you. I don't care what alibi he supposedly has, it was him." The detective looks at me as if he is waiting for me to bury myself in guilt. "Can I go now? I have answered all your questions."

"Let me go check on some tests we are having done on some skin cells we found under Ms. Portman's fingernails, and I will get back to you. That is, unless you want to tell me what we will find beforehand?" I roll my eyes and turn away with a sharp sigh. "Alright then, wait here."

No matter what people tell me happened, I know I remember seeing Thomas that night, and the more I consider the events, the more I doubt that it was a delusion. There is no way in hell I am going to let that man anywhere near Dani when she gets out of the hospital. I spend hours waiting, and I am so exhausted by the time the detective comes back, I don't even care if he arrests me or not. The way he looks at me, I am guessing they didn't get the results back they wanted. "Can I go now?"

"For now, but we will be in touch, so don't go too far."

"Don't worry. I will be checking on you too," I say, walking out and meeting up with Shane who sits waiting for me. There has to be an answer to this mess, but for now, I only want to see Dani. Shane drops me off, and I message Dani that I'm here. She quickly requests her guard to look into something for her. While he is out of sight, I sneak in and close the curtain to hide us from his view.

"You made it!" she labors to say.

"Of course," I say, making myself comfortable before climbing into bed next to her and letting her fall against my chest and sleep until morning. Dani looks so delicate right now, and I have to admit, I am scared of what she may remember. I don't want her to hurt any more than she already does. Shane was right about one thing: I don't know what I am doing. I don't know how to help her through this. I sweep my fingers through her hair and listen as she sleeps peacefully. I have been patient before with her. It wasn't easy, but I loved her enough that I would have waited forever:

It's spring break, and Shane was able to get his uncle's old convertible to take his new girlfriend and Dani and me to the beach. Our parents think we are going on a church trip. I am pretty sure my parents know better, but they still agree to let me go, as long as I call three times a day, every day. The trip down there is amazing. Dani and I spent the ride in the backseat, kissing and holding each other all the while knowing we will be able to spend the night together every night without worrying that we will wake anyone or get caught together. I have waited for her to be ready, and I would wait even longer, but she says she wants it to be on this trip. She has bought some sexy lingerie for the occasion, and I have planned a night out together to make it perfect. We share one room, while Shane and his girl, Britney, share another. We haven't seen them since they stepped foot in their room and doubt we will until tomorrow. I wish Shane was available to talk because I am nervous waiting for Dani to meet me in the lobby. She wanted to surprise me with a new dress or something, so I am left pacing like an idiot in my nice clothes amongst people in swimsuits and flip flops. When Dani finally comes down, I can't wipe the smile from my face. I look her over so closely that she blushes.

I reach out to take her hand and kiss her, "Wow, you look so beautiful."

"You look very nice yourself."

"I felt like an idiot. Everyone keeps staring at me all dressed up like this, but now I don't care so much." She smiles and squeezes my hand tight as she walks with me down the boardwalk to the restaurant. We sit outside, watching the water, and toast with our favorite sodas. After dinner, we take our shoes off and walk along the water's edge, laughing and teasing each other. She suddenly takes off running; I chase after her and pick her up to run through the water together. "How about I jump in right now with you?" I laugh as she giggles, smacking me playfully.

"No Dillon!" she laughs. "Put me down." I set her down, and she runs again, laughing and glancing over her shoulder, waiting for me to catch her.

"I've got you now, and I am not letting go."

"Good," she says, looking up at me with her innocent doe eyes. I pull her in close and kiss her deeply, feeling her body's every curve.

Everything feels perfect and romantic, but by the time we get back to the room, she looks nervous, so I step back. "Maybe we should wait?" She shakes her head and gulps before stepping out of her dress and showing me the tiny, and so very sexy, lingerie underneath. My jaw drops, and every thought leaves my head. I have never seen anything like it before.

I don't know what I did, but she jumps for joy and runs at me, kissing me and pulling me to her. The feeling rushing through me weakens me all over, but it doesn't keep me from kissing her with want. She returns every motion I make with an equally wonderful touch of my body. I follow her into bed, feeling her and kissing her until my mouth gets tired.

"Don't stop," she says, wrapping her legs around me and trying to pull me in on top of her. "Don't you want me?"

"Yes, I do. Can you not tell by the huge bulge in my pants? But Dani, are you sure?"

"I have always wanted to be with you," she says, kissing my neck and nibbling on my ear, making me even crazier.

I stop her and force her to look at me. "You want to have sex with me right here, right now?" She nods. "Why? And if you say to get it over with, then we are definitely not doing it."

"Because you're my best friend, and I can't think of anyone better to lose my virginity to, and … I love you as more than just my friend." She pauses, biting her lip. "I promised myself I would wait for you to say it first, but … I love you Dillon," she says nervously.

I laugh, fingering her hair back into place. "I love you too, Dani." She gasps at my words. I lean down and kiss her sweet, shocked expression away. "Now, tell me you love me again so we can stop being awkward and go back to *being romantic."*

"I love you, Dillon." My heart flutters, and I have no trouble removing my clothes. I actually can't get them off fast enough. I move to her and pause. Take your time Dillon. She's nervous, and I try to give her the attention she needs without making her feel uneasy. Slowly removing each delicate piece of tiny fabric from her body makes me anxious, but I maintain the slow, respectful moves I had been practicing for months in my own head.

I feel down her body and to her only remaining clothing, her tiny little panties that are not nearly wet enough for me. I push my hand down under the fabric and feel her, tease her, and give her a small taste of what's to come while I kiss her deeply. Her breathing becomes labored as she opens her legs even more for me. Once she begins fisting my hair and gripping my arm so tightly that I can barely move it, I know she's ready. I grab a condom and rip it open with my teeth before sliding her panties off and moving in between her legs. "Hey gorgeous," I say, getting her attention on me, "I love you so much." She smiles, and I move her body the way I need and watch as she grimaces. I wrap my arms around her and hold her, whispering whatever I can to help her through the pain she is experiencing. It takes me awhile to get fully in, and she nearly gives up several times before I do, but once I feel her completely wrapped around me, I am in heaven, and I have to constantly remind myself that, right now, she isn't. I can't believe I am with her, that I am inside her. Nothing has ever felt more right in my life. "Does it still hurt?"

"Only a little bit," she says through her teeth.

"Liar," I say as she pulls me in close.

"Hold me, Dillon, please."

I do exactly as asked, "I love you so much, Dani." She kisses me with a large smile and a long breath of relief. I trace the freckles across her nose with my fingers and push her auburn hair from her big, amorous brown eyes. The only thing better is her flawlessly soft lips on mine. Oh damn. I feel everything reach its limit, and I come with her watching me closely. With a goofy smile, all I can say is, "Oh, I love you so much."

Dani laughs and kisses all over my face. "You big, goofy, wonderful boy. I love you forever and ever." I lie down within her arms, sighing with a rapidly beating, but a perfectly content, heart.

I love Dani. I always have, and if I have to, I will wait forever for her again and again.

Chapter 21

Dillon

Dani is getting out of the hospital today, and I am anxious to take her home, but her father is ready to block my every attempt. Little does he know I have been sneaking in to see her every night this week. She is never going to leave with him. I show up at the hospital, waiting outside her room with full confidence and my car keys in hand.

Portman spots me and has nothing better to say than, "Leave before you embarrass yourself."

"I'm here to pick up Dani and take her home, and I am not leaving without her."

"Oh yes you are. She doesn't want to see you. Trust me. It is in your best interest and hers that you leave now."

"I told you. I'm not leaving," I say, pissing him off to the point of him stomping away in a huff. I can hear him loudly arguing with Dani from inside her hospital room. Though I can't make out all the words, I do clearly hear my name several times.

Portman walks out again to meet me face to face. "I'm going to ask you one more time to leave and allow my daughter some dignity as she exits and returns home with me, where she should be."

"I'm not leaving without Dani," I say, standing up to him. I am not that teenage kid that he bullied before. Now, I am taller than he is and certainly more fit. His hard glaring eyes don't intimidate me now.

"Fine, if you wish to hurt her, and you, then so be it." He walks away and returns with a ridiculously covered Dani in a wheelchair; she is hardly visible.

They try to wheel by me and she looks the other way with her face covered. "Dani, talk to me," I beg her, trying to grab for her hands.

"Go away, Dillon. Go away and be happy. I don't want to be in this relationship with you anymore," she says, pushing my hands away from her and her obvious tears.

I tackle her father against a wall. "What did you do? What did you tell her?" I scream at him.

"I told her the truth and simply showed her a mirror. I also told her that she might never walk again. I was honest with her and told her that she is someone that no one of your maturity is going to be able to handle and that you would eventually leave her. She is lucky that Thomas still wants to marry her and take care of her, because there is no way you will do the same for her."

"Fuck you! You don't know me. You don't know anything about me. You never have. I love her, and I will be by her side no matter what." I am forced away from him as security surrounds us, but I don't show an ounce of giving up on her. "I will be by her side no matter what!" He steps back to Dani and wheels her into the elevator with security preventing me from following. "Dani! Dani – I love you!" I scream to her.

As soon as they leave me, I go to Portman's home and knock

on the door. He ignores me while I hear him arguing with Dani inside. I keep knocking and calling out to her until he finally opens the door and stares at me with focused eyes. "Leave before I call the police and have you arrested."

"I won't leave quietly, and do you really want your daughter hearing how you threw me in jail while trying to see her. You think she is going to leave with you so easily knowing that?"

"I'm not going to tell you again. She doesn't want to see you. She wishes you well and wishes you would move on with your life and find happiness with someone else. You can read it in this letter." He hands me a note and slams the door in my face.

Dillon,

Please understand that I have changed and am no longer the woman I once was. You have so much life ahead of you with so much opportunity, and I don't feel that I want to go in those same directions with you. I appreciate your dedication and respect of me, but there is no need to feel guilty any longer. None of this was your fault. Please move on and live the life you are meant to and allow me to do the same.

Sincerely,

Dani

I wad up the formally typed letter and toss it onto the porch. I follow by knocking on the door and demanding to speak to her. "Dani! Dani just talk to me!" I knock and knock and beg for hours. "I'm not going away. I'm not letting you run away from me again. I know you still love me." I bang on the door until my hands swell. Sliding down the door, I sit, holding my face. "Please Dani, please talk to me." The lights in the house go off and so does the porch light. *I'm not letting her go. I refuse.* I am obviously not going to be allowed inside to be near her or talk to her, so I need to figure out another way to be near her. I park my truck in a safe place and pull out my sleeping bag, some water and food, and an umbrella just in case. I search around the house and know I have the right window when I find the only room with a light on. She won't sleep in the dark without me there. I learned that while seeing her in the hospital. I make myself at home right below the window's ledge, huddle up inside my sleeping bag, and post my umbrella in the dirt, using it for shelter before the freezing rain starts coming down. I'm at home for as long as it takes … to get her back.

Chapter 22

Dani

It's been four days since I came home from the hospital, and he is still trying to see me. I hate hearing him scream for me, the heartbreaking sound in his voice breaks me more than I already am. Every time I think of running to him, I look at myself in the mirror. My battered face and body quickly remind me that I am too ugly for him and too damaged to even walk to him. No, Dillon is better off without having to deal with my issues and my anxieties. My father is right. It's going to be a long time before I can be normal again, if I can ever be normal again. *How long would Dillon ever wait for a damaged freak? How much time should he wait?* The way Thomas looks at me, the quick avoidance of my face and eyes, the way he questions my father about whether I will ever be able to fulfill his expectations as a wife, is almost too much to take, even from him. Thomas's fear and disgust of me is something I don't ever want to see in Dillon. I don't want him to feel obligated to be with someone he doesn't want. As it is, my father is paying and bribing Thomas to stay here and pretend to want me, to act as if he believes we have a great future together. I wish he would go away, too, and leave me alone. I will never be what he wants. Not now. My father comes and goes throughout the day, leaving me with nurses to care for me. I hate it. I hate every moment I spend with these people I don't know. I only want to stay in bed and hide. My father forces me to come out of my room and eat dinner with him. I don't know why. I don't eat much anymore, and I certainly don't have anything to talk about.

"I have our flight planned. I reserved a plane to take us back home so you don't have to worry about anyone staring at you. You will have your privacy at home, and I will hire the best counselors to come in and help you get back to your old self and the best doctors to help get you back on your feet. We can even find a great plastic surgeon if the bruises don't heal properly."

"I want to go back to bed, please."

My father finally gives in, wheels me into my bedroom, and picks me up to put me into bed. "I'm going to be right next door, Sweetheart, if you need anything. Everything is going to be okay. You simply have to be patient and trust me. And once everything is back to normal, Thomas will be right there, waiting for you, I promise." My father kisses my forehead, assuming his words are reassuring me somehow.

They said I might get the use of my legs again someday and not to worry. That was shocking enough, not that I wasn't catching on to their, *it's only the heavy medication you're on, Dani*, story. Before I could get used to the idea, my father confessed the trauma that my body took on, just before he showed me a mirror. Images instantly began to flash into my mind. My own screams rattled through my head, destroying every dream I have ever had.

I hear my father walk out of the house, and I immediately begin to get nervous. I don't know where he went or why. I don't like to be here alone. I hate this room I am in. Even with the light on, it feels as if I am suffocating, like I am trapped. If anyone came in after me, there is nothing I could do. I slip down into bed after I take my medication and try to go to sleep without nightmares, without worrying about being here alone.

I can only remember pieces, but it is enough that I don't want to ever go outside or see anyone. I don't want to see him, or hear those footsteps as they come for me. The only thing I can remember is running, running as hard and as fast as I could, trying to get away from the footsteps following me. Then there are the hands, the hand that took hold of my waist and jerked me backwards, and the other hand that grabbed my throat. I remember feeling a harsh, poisonous breath against my ear, knowing death was all he wanted from me. The memories begin to hit hard and run through my head like broken images, but the fear is always the same; the inability to get away, to break free from the grip on me, or to stop the constant pain from coming. I wake up gasping and begin screaming. "He's here. He's here! NO! Daddy, please help me!" I scream, trying to get away, but I fall into the floor and can't get away any other way other than crawl. I scream out in pain, and realize I can't get away. "Help me!" I cry, all alone. "Dillon! Dillon, I need you!" I scream, and suddenly, someone breaks through my window. I gasp, watching Dillon climb through, rush over to me, and pick me up.

I watch him in shock, move me, and wrap me up with blankets to warm me up. "It's okay. No one is going to hurt you, I promise," he says, wrapping his arms around me and allowing me to lie against his still, chilled chest, which, surprisingly, feels safe.

"I'm going to get your things and take you home." Dillon leaves me bound up in warm blankets while he grabs my clothes and starts throwing them into a bag.

The security alarm is blaring and as soon as it is turned off I know my father is coming. "What are you doing in here?" My father screams as he comes into the room. "You set the alarms off, the police will be here any moment."

"I'm taking her home."

"The hell you are. You're not taking her anywhere."

"Where were you?" Dillon asks him.

"What?"

"Where were you? She screamed for you, and you never came. Where were you?"

"She was fine. She was only scared from a nightmare. The house is covered with security alarms as you could hear! I had only gone down the street to pick up a few things. Now, how did you get in here?" my father says, looking at the broken window, rushing to it, and looking outside. "You have been sleeping outside her window? How long have you been out there?" he asks, looking back at Dillon in shock. Dillon doesn't bother answering him. He grabs my bag, puts it around his neck, and picks me up in his arms.

He moves towards the door and my father steps in front of us. "Get out of my way, Doug; otherwise, I may have to make you regret it like I did Tommy boy."

"You're not taking my daughter. She belongs with me."

"Wrong. She belongs with me. She always has, and she always will, no matter what you or anyone else says. She called out for me.

She needed me, and unlike you, I came," Dillon says forcefully. I lay my head on his shoulder, and my father steps out of the way.

Dillon covers me up securely before driving me to his house. I don't say a word as he carries me into his room and puts me into his bed. He instantly begins running around the house perfecting the house layout, the access to my wheelchair, the bathroom, and even him, all for me. When he brings me some ice water, I shake my head at him sighing. "I can get you more, just let me know when that runs out."

"Dillon, why are you doing this? This is too much trouble for you to handle. I can't even walk." He ignores me and gets into bed next to me. "Dillon!"

"I'm not leaving you, Dani."

"But I want you to! I don't want this. I don't want to be with you, not like this." He turns away and ignores me. "Do you understand me? I'm not going to have sex with you. I am not going to be able to do anything! I'm worthless to you!"

He turns to me and takes hold of my face with both hands. "No, the last thing you will ever be to me is worthless." He looks into my eyes, and all I want to do is hide my abused face from him, so I twist away and lay down with my back to him. "The bruises will heal, Dani. The swelling will go down, and your fears will also get better. The doctors said you should get feeling in your legs again eventually."

"That could take forever, Dillon."

"Well, I am not going anywhere," he says, laying his hand on my arm. I jerk away from him. He doesn't know what he is doing.

This isn't going to get better overnight. Within a few days, he will be begging for my father to come get me.

I see flashes of the bright metal object coming at me, then the barbaric pain seeps down into my bones until I hear them breaking. Screams and pleas for it to stop do no good; it just keeps coming and coming. "Dillon!" I scream, sitting up and screaming until he runs in and covers me up in the blankets that have fallen on the floor.

With his arms around me, Dillon holds me while I quiver in fear. "I'm here. Don't worry, I'm right here," he says calmly. I slowly calm, with deep breaths and strokes of his hands through my hair. I want him to go, but I am too weak to let go of him. "Did you remember more?" I nod silently. "Did you see his face?"

I push away from him and crawl back into bed. "No, Dillon. I still don't know who he is. All I see are eyes."

"His eyes? If you know the color or shape, it may help police."

I sit up and push him off the bed and back to his feet. "No! You don't understand. The images don't make sense. All I see is this eye within another eye. It isn't a pair of eyes or someone's eyes, it's only images, insane images. Leave me alone, Dillon, and stop asking me questions. I don't remember. I don't want to remember."

"Okay, we won't talk about it. Do you want to work on your

physical therapy now? The therapist said if you do the exercises she gave you a few times a day that your sessions with her will be a lot easier," he says and immediately sighs when I look up at him angry. "You need to do them Dani, whether you want to or not."

"Why? So you don't have to feel guilty about leaving me? Just leave, Dillon. I don't care if I ever walk again." I fall hard onto my pillow and wish for him to go away.

He covers me up and kisses my head. "We can do them a little later when you're more rested then, but we will do them today." He leaves, shutting the door behind him, only to return what seems like a few minutes later. "Okay, let's get you up and moving." I shake my head as he reaches in, picks me up, and carries me to the basement workout area, where all my therapy equipment is.

"Dillon, stop. I told you I don't want to." He won't listen, and I have very little I can fight him with. "Dillon, take me back to bed. I don't feel well."

"You haven't felt well in days. Maybe if you tried getting out of bed once in a while you would feel better." I cross my arms, and he pulls out the equipment the therapist left and waits for me to unfold my arms. "You can sit all day and all day tomorrow for all I care, but we are doing this. So, whenever you're ready, we can start."

"I hate you," I say.

"Good. Now take this and let's get to work," he replies. I scream and cry through the painful exercises until he is finally satisfied for the day. He asks if I want to stay downstairs and watch TV with him and his father, which I don't. Eventually, my silence is understood, and he takes me back to his room.

His room is like a Dillon memory box. Old pictures of high school friends, of us, of trips taken together, nothing but happy memories. I pull out an old photo album from his nightstand and open it up. The trip to the beach, the weekend we ran away together. Our parents never knew we weren't going to a church event. Shane, Dillon, and I and some girl Shane brought along that he was dating at the time, we all packed and left to meet up with our supposed church group, which we never did. We all saved money for months to be able to go. The best part was the old convertible Shane's uncle let us borrow for the trip. Shane drove with his girl at his side, and Dillon and I sat in the backseat, sitting close and finding new ways to enjoy each other without being too obvious to the passersby. The wind in my hair and sitting perfectly within his arms with nothing but excitement for the life ahead of us.

No one should feel and smell this good. I don't think we could kiss any more than we already have this trip. Now, we are going to spend days together, waking up in each other's arms, and going to sleep the same way.

Dillon leans in, nudging me, "Let's never go back." I look up at his smiling face and can do no more than smile back. "Yeah, let's run away and find our way through life together. We can be like gypsies, traveling from one place to the other."

"And how will we make money for this ongoing trip?"

Dillon ponders my question for a few seconds before smiling again. "Alright, I will pose nude for Playgirl, for the sake of our future, but I am going to have to warn you, I can't be held responsible for the ladies swarming all over me." I shake my head, while fighting my laughter. "No? Okay, I'll think of something else. How about I..."

"No, nothing that involves either one of us being nude."

"Damn, and I had some really good ideas. Fine, I will just love you until we can afford to run away without worries or fears."

"That could be a long time, Dillon."

I watch as he lays his hand on my leg and opens it up. I take it, and he squeezes my hand hard and whispers, "As long as we are in it together, I'm good with wherever life takes us."

I look up into his handsome eyes, "Me too."

"That was a great trip. We should do that again one day," Dillon says, walking into the room. I quickly put the photo album up and lie down. "Don't lie down. I'm preparing a bath for you."

"You are not bathing me," I say, but he picks me up, carries me into the bathroom, and undresses me before setting me gently down in the water. All of my bruises and marks are visible. I sit in the water, avoiding him. "I said I could bathe myself."

"Then do it, Dani. Stop pouting and feeling sorry for yourself. What happened to that tough, independent girl I once knew?"

"She died, and now there is only a cripple left here. Why don't you get that?!" He tosses my favorite shampoo and soap on the floor next to me and leaves, slamming the bathroom door behind him. He is obviously getting tired of dealing with a cripple all the time. He will soon hate me, I am sure of it, but I am going to hate him first. I am not going to let anyone hurt me again.

Chapter 23

Dillon

I don't know how to help her. I fear she is going to plunge so far into a depression that I am never going to be able to get her back. I wait outside my own bedroom door while Dani sits with a psychologist, not that she was happy about doing that either. She never wants to see anyone that might help her and, as expected, it doesn't take long before the latest doctor comes out frustrated. "I don't know what to tell you, Dillon, but until she wants help, there is nothing I can do to help her."

"And how do I get her to want help?"

"That answer is different for every case. I wish I could help you more, but I would continue to be there for her and wait until she gets tired of being cooped up in that room all the time," Doctor number five says, giving me little hope for progress.

I get an idea and go in with a smile. "So, she seems nice." I get the typical death stare with no words. "I saw where the old drive-in has that movie you were wanting to see …"

"No, I don't want to see any movie."

"Why not? We will be in the car, so no one can see you. It will be just you and me. We can cuddle like we used to and enjoy a nice night out, some place out of this room and out of this house."

She throws a pillow at my head. "I don't want to go anywhere, Dillon! The idea of spending a night cuddling with you in a car makes me sick to even think about. I don't want to do anything with you. I don't want to be near you. I want you to go away. I want you to send me back to my father's and leave me the hell alone."

"No," I say, enraging her more.

"I hate you! I hate you! Why can't you get that through your damn head? I don't want anything to do with you!" She waves her arms and throws whatever she can reach at me until I can get a hold of her.

"I tell you what. You work on your therapy and you give at least one of these psychiatrists a chance and when they say you are capable of living on your own again, then I'll leave." She looks at me hard. "You get to where you don't need anyone again, Dani, and I'll go and let you live your life however you want."

"Liar. You feel too guilty, and I will be stuck with you forever... no matter what." I let go of her and walk out of the room, shutting the door behind me before crashing against it and holding my face in my hands. "I hate you, Dillon! Leave now and do us both a favor! Do you hear me? I hate you!"

"Dillon?" My father says, stepping a few feet out of his own room. I look up with tears in my eyes and shake my head. He sighs, "She doesn't mean it. She's just in pain and confused right now."

I close my eyes as tears stream down my face. "I don't think so. I think I've lost her, Dad. This time, I have lost her for good." The pain penetrates deep as my heart pounds against my chest and shatters. My father steps to me cradling my head against him without words.

Dani tosses and turns all night, struggling and crying in her sleep. She will wake up fighting for breath and begging for the pain to stop. I haven't slept more than couple of hours at a time since she's been here, so it isn't a shock that I find myself sleeping on the floor at the bedroom door. I am not sure what woke me up, but when I do, I hear her beginning to whimper again. I rush into the room and climb in next to her; pulling her into my arms. "Dani," I whisper. "Dani, Honey, it's okay." She wakes and clutches me so tight that I wonder if she even realizes it's me. I hate to admit something so awful, but these are my favorite moments now, when she needs me and wants me.

This morning, Dani's father stops in and, as usual, he has little to say to me other than asking about the psychologists he has been sending over. There is nothing new to tell him, and I assume that any day now he is going to tell me he knew I couldn't handle this and demand that she leave with him, but he never does. I don't know if he doesn't want the responsibility or if he likes to see how miserable I am. While Portman is seeing his daughter, I spend time at the factory, checking on things. Shane has been primarily in charge since Dani was released from the hospital, and he is looking completely drained these days.

"I only have a couple hours, so fill me in as much as you can,"

I tell him.

He sits back in his chair with a scowl. "Wow, a whole two hours? I don't know what to do with all this attention to your business."

"Shane, I don't have time for the attitude."

"You don't have time? I have no life, Dillon. I am killing myself to do my job, your job, and Dani's all while trying to make sure this whole thing doesn't fall apart, but you want to come in here and tell me to hurry up because you don't have time? Fuck you!" I rub my head as he sits silently, staring away from me.

"What do you want me to do, Shane? Leave her with strangers?" He doesn't answer. "I love her. I can't throw her away and leave her out to fend for herself."

"You mean like you have done to me?" he says, getting up and walking out.

I gather what information I can on my own and do what I can before I have to leave. When I return home, I begin preparing lunch for Dani and my father. "You know I can make my own lunch now?" My father says, hobbling in on his cane and grabbing some things from the fridge. "And I am sick of all these natural foods and *good for you* crap." I step back and look over what he has in his hand.

"You are not supposed to eat that. It has salt in it, and sugar," I say to him.

"I don't care. I'm a grown man, and I am going to eat what I want to eat." I throw up my hands and let the bullheaded old man make his own lunch and go back to preparing Dani's. "So, how is the factory doing?"

"It's okay I guess. Shane is exhausted and hates me now, too. I don't know what to do. Which one do I choose? My best friend that I love like a brother and would kill for, or my other best friend that I have loved since the day I met her and would kill for? I'm working one to death and losing them both, no matter how hard I try to at least save one." I go back to concentrating on lunch, and my father stares at me until I look his way. "What?"

"I think it's time I come out of retirement." I shake my head and dismiss his suggestion. "Don't shake your head at me. I may not be able to run a marathon, but I can do the job I did for longer than you have been alive."

"And I say *no*. You are not supposed to be under any kind of stress, and I own the business now, so that is that."

"I don't have to run the floor. Shane can do that, but I can keep the day to day going. Shane needs help. This isn't the job that boy wanted, but he is doing it for you. The least you could do is send him some qualified help. You know I am going to do it anyway." *Unbelievable! The man is absolutely a pain in my ass.*

"How are you going to get there? You can't drive."

"Carpool."

"Carpool? Wonderful." I look over at him as he stands inflexibly at my side.

"I work for free, and for the right to make my own damn meals once in a while."

I laugh as he takes a bite of his huge sandwich and moans with joy. "Fine, but if I see you under any kind of stress or showing any signs of any kind of illness, you're done, old man." He smiles and walks away with his sandwich and soda to go watch his favorite show.

With my father helping Shane out, it makes my day a little easier, but Dani is still trying to push me to give up on her. She threw her breakfast in my face this morning for suggesting she should try eating in the kitchen in front of the bay window, where she can appreciate the beautiful day more. I don't even know what I said this time to set her off, except that heaven forbid she leave the damn bedroom once in a while. I find some cleaning detergent and try to scrub out the stains on my clothes, when the doorbell rings. I look back at the window to see who it is, but the figures are too odd to make out. I open the door to find Sean and Ava both standing at the door. "Hey… what are you guys doing here?" I let them in as Sean sighs and points to Ava.

"Sean talked to your father the other day. He told him what happened, and then he told me, so I made him bring me here," Ava says, hugging me and looking me over like my mother used to.

"She wouldn't let up until I agreed, but if anyone can help you, it's her," Sean says, kissing his wife on the cheek with one arm wrapped around her waist. "She's been through a lot and may be able to talk to Dani like most couldn't."

I shake my head. "I don't know. She's not really ever in the mood to see anyone. She throws every psychologist we get for her out before they can say much of anything."

Ava pats my chest, nodding, "Of course she does. Trust me, Dillon, and tell me which room is hers." I shrug and give her directions. She grips Sean's hand quickly before rushing up the stairs to Dani.

I glance back at Sean as he looks me over closely, "You know, I can bring you some bibs that we aren't using for the kids if you need some?"

I look down at the mess on my clothes, look back up at him, and roll my eyes. "I didn't do this. Dani threw her breakfast at me."

"Oh, nice, kind of wish I had been here to see that," he laughs.

"Ha ha. I am not sure what Ava is expecting, but Dani is really stubborn, and I doubt she is going to listen to anything."

"Then there is no one better for her to talk to. Ava's middle name is stubborn. It's really annoying." Sean sits down, and I follow.

"I don't understand why she won't listen to me? Or why she won't let me help her?"

Sean laughs. "Yeah… good luck with trying to figure that out."

"You don't have any advice for me?"

"Sure. Get good at dodging flying objects aimed at you." *Gee thanks, that's helpful Sean.* "I will say, that if you ever have kids, never suggest that she get on a long plane ride with two little ones by herself to come visit you on set." He shakes his head. "No, don't ever do that, because when they finally get there, she will hurt you and not in a good way. Ava scared Randy; he wouldn't go near her for weeks," he says as I shiver considering the idea. Sean looks me over again. "If you go change into something decent, I will buy you lunch somewhere if you want?" I nod but look upstairs. "Don't worry, they'll be fine. You, however, look like you need to get away for a little while. I promise… Ava has got this handled."

Sean does as promised, and the moment I step out of the house, I feel like I can relax without scrutiny. I don't say much. I simply enjoy sitting back and having a beer and good food. "I'll tell you, Conrad, Ava and I have been through hell and back, but we made it, and we did it because we wouldn't give up on each other."

"Dani hates me. She said so. I don't think we will ever be the same."

"Don't give up; don't ever give up on yourself or on her. There will be a moment that comes along that will give you the opportunity to get everything back, and you have got to be there, ready to take it."

"I didn't know you were so philosophical, Sean?"

"I'm not. That line was in a movie I did awhile back," he laughs.

"Great, thanks."

"But seriously, it's the truth. The best you can do right now is be there for her and wait for that moment."

"Well, I hope she doesn't knock me out with a vase or

something when it happens and I miss it." Sean laughs out loud, causing me to finally laugh along with him.

When we return back to the house, Ava is making tea for her and Dani and goes back upstairs to continue talking. I am shocked, but suddenly hopeful. When Ava eventually comes down, she pulls me aside. "She's doing better. I know someone that I think can help her more, and she says she is willing to talk to her." Ava hands me a card. "Call her, and she will help you, I promise. For now, give Dani some time and try to be patient. I know it's difficult. She doesn't want to be this way towards you, but she hates what you remind her of, the life that could have been. If she can believe that life can still happen, the anger will calm and she will find her way back to you." She hugs me and leaves with Sean, promising to call and check on us.

The woman's name on the card is Robin Vandiver. It doesn't say much more, but I call her anyway.

Chapter 24

Dillon

Robin shows up with a personality that lets you know, at once, not to question her methods. She takes over Dani's physical therapy and day-to-day routines. She demands I go on with my life as I would normally. No matter what she says, I'm not leaving, and as soon as I hear Dani scream for me, I run to her, but Robin stops me. "Do you want her to get better, Dillon?"

"Yes, of course," I say, trying to get around her.

"Then force her to do things on her own once in a while."

"She's screaming for me."

"She's screaming for you because she knows you will come and stop whatever is causing her pain. You are so desperate for her to need you and want you that you are not considering what is best for her. I want you go back to work and get back to as much of a normal life as you can." I shake my head, not wanting to consider the idea of leaving her alone all day. "She needs the independence, and she will never get that with you around here to be her crutch. She should be walking by now Dillon."

"She's faking?"

"No, but there is no reason that she shouldn't be able to other than she doesn't have to try."

"I promise I won't go running to her. I will stay out of the way, but I will be here in case you need me."

"No, Dillon, you won't. You will run to her every time she calls your name, and I am not in the mood to deal with a brokenhearted boyfriend on top of a bitchy patient. Go back to your normal life, and she will be more apt to follow. You can be there for her at the end of the day when she will need you to remind her that you are still there for her."

It's easy to understand what she is trying to tell me, but it isn't easy to abide by. I take a breath and agree to do whatever it takes to help Dani, no matter how much it hurts.

The hardest thing to do is to get up, go to work, and pretend everything is normal. Dani seems to believe I am playing a terrible joke on her. I make it to the front door before Dani starts screaming for me.

"Dillon! Dillon, don't leave, please. I'm sorry. Please don't leave me," she cries out over and over. "Dillon, please." Her distressing pleas are tearing me apart, so I turn around and start to go to her when Robin comes at me and points back to the door. "But she …"

"Go, she's fine, and yes, she will forgive you," Robin insists.

I have to brace myself when Dani calls out for me again, pleading with me not to leave her. Robin pushes me out the door and locks it behind me. *Maybe I will stay out here on the porch for a while?* I hear her cry and I realize that there is no way I can listen to her all day without climbing the side of the house to get through the window to her. No, if I am going to do this I have to go now.

It took me more than an hour of going back and forth down our street before I finally make it into work. I sit at my desk for another hour, thinking about calling the house to see if they need me. I spend another half hour picking up the phone, dialing, and then putting it back down before getting up and going to a meeting. I gave Shane some time off, so I have to meet with the supervisors on my own today. All goes well until shortages are recognized in product. Gina's team is behind in their efforts. "You need to pick up the pace, Gina. If you can't meet the demand then you need to let me know before we get behind so I can find you some help."

"I am not the one behind. We spend most of our time waiting on Rafe and his team. Rafe's team is the one that is always behind," she says bluntly.

"You Bitch! I told you the machine went down. There is nothing I can do about that. Don't blame me for your work issues. You spend too much time talking and arguing with your boyfriend to get your job done."

"I do not! Maybe if you got laid once in a while, Rafe, you wouldn't be so desperate and drooling over every woman that comes within eyesight. He spends all of his time drooling over Amy whenever she is around; it makes her uncomfortable. He should be disciplined for sexual harassment in the work place."

"Would both of you, shut up!? I want the issues fixed. If you have to stay late, then stay late, but I want the shortages made up before the end of the week or I will find replacements for you both," I say before dismissing everyone.

Gina stays behind to talk to me alone, which makes my day that much worse than it already is. "I am not going to listen to excuses, Gina. If you have had issues with Rafe, you should have come to me before you got so far behind."

"I would have, but I was trying to be nice."

"You? You were trying to be nice? Yeah, I bet."

"Well his father did die, so I was giving him a break." I roll my eyes, knowing that wouldn't matter to the ice queen for a minute. "Fine, so if I stay late, will you stay here with me and protect me?"

"No."

"Can I have access to your office so I can lie down and take a nap at lunch?"

"No."

"Can I rest for a little while now?"

"No!" She huffs. "I am not paying you to sleep, Gina, or to stand here and waste time talking to me about nonsense."

"Well, I would at least like to talk to you about transferring to another department."

"What department?"

"The technology and development department? And before you say no, I think I could be of a great benefit testing product and giving a woman's point of view on things, especially since Dani is gone now."

"First of all, Dani isn't gone forever."

"Dillon, come on. She's not coming back, not here. It was probably someone here that attacked her anyway. Whoever it was is probably waiting for the opportunity to finish the job."

"What?!"

"Oh come on, don't tell me you haven't considered the idea? Dani, I am sure, has considered it; she is never going to come back here. She's probably some crazy ass freak already. Coming here isn't going to help that. Now, let me talk to Shane and see …"

"No, now get back to work!" I yell, pointing the way out my door. She grumbles her way out the door and all the way back to her station. I walk to the window overlooking the floor and consider the possibility that someone here may be a murderer. The idea that someone that works for me could have done this is too awful to consider. Still, it doesn't stop the thoughts of potential criminals running through my head, especially Gina. She hated Dani and wanted Colleen's job, she has no morals, and certainly no boundaries. She could have talked any of her low life boyfriends into helping her, I'm sure. She suddenly becomes a strong possibility, and I keep an eye on her throughout the rest of the day. She spends more time on the phone than she does at her station, but when she is there, she is delegating her work to others so she can fight and argue with Rafe all day. I can't imagine why she would want to be in development, she would have to actually work.

As expected, Gina works five minutes past when she thinks I have left and then heads home. She is so dedicated to catching up on her work that the lazy ass stays a whole extra five minutes. Gina happily leaves the parking lot with me following her in the distance. She arrives home, and I sit outside, watching her house, trying to figure out why I am here. What did I expect to find out by following this horrible woman? *Do I want to go in and talk to her? Or wait for her to leave and break in and look around? Great Dillon, you did this without any kind of plan. I don't know what I expected her to do, lead me to some guy she paid to have Dani attacked or* ... as I argue with myself, a car pulls up into her driveway, and Tommy boy gets out and walks inside. *Huh? Well that's something I didn't know.* I have absolutely no reason to trust this woman. She will be fired tomorrow if not tonight. The two fall in front of the front window all over each other. *Tonight. Definitely tonight.*

Dani doesn't speak to me when I get home, or even look at me, which is supposed to be progress, but it feels more like a punishment. I think I liked it better when she was pitching things at my head; at least there was some kind of communication. I am not even sure I am allowed to sleep in the same room with her anymore, let alone the same bed. I try to take a few things to go sleep in another room, but she suddenly pops up and opens her mouth. "Do you have something to say to me?" She shakes her head and lies back down, turning her back to me. "I guess not." I leave her and make up the bed in the guest room. Now that Shane has found his own place, I might as well make use of it. It's not the most comfortable bed, but I still manage to fall asleep without issue.

"No! Go away! Dillon! Leave me alone! Dillon!" Dani screams as I rub my eyes and jump out of bed to find her trembling, drenched in sweat. She falls into my arms as soon as I get near her. "He was here. I saw him."

"Who was?"

"Him! You know who, he was here, outside, looking in."

"Dani, you're on the second floor, no one is looking in."

"He was. I saw him. He's come back to kill me."

"Okay, I'll go look outside," I say, but she holds me tighter. "You have to let go of me Honey if you want me to go see."

"No, I don't want him to hurt you," she mumbles into my shoulder. "Don't leave me." Dani pulls me deeper into the bed with her. As usual, her desperate grasp for me to stay with her, to be with her, feels to wonderful to consider moving even an inch away from her.

Dani was so loving last night that I hated to get up and go to work this morning. I could have stayed in bed all day. I walk to my truck, fighting my urge to return to bed and her. I breathe a long sigh and instead of running inside, I decide to walk around the house and see if there is any chance Dani did see something outside her window last night. The tree between the two houses has grown considerably since we were kids, but it blocks anyone from the opposite house from looking in clearly. I look up into the tree and back down, and find marks on the side of it. The bark is rubbed off at different spots up the tree, as if someone was climbing it. *Maybe Dani wasn't dreaming.* I decide to stop by the police station on my way to work and have them investigate it and perhaps get some full time protection for Dani. I ask for the detective handling her case, and as soon he walks out, I jump up to meet him. He directs me back to his desk and politely tells me to have a seat, but he doesn't look too excited to talk to me. "Have you got anything yet? Someone was at our house last night spying on Dani."

"Who?"

"I don't know who. I didn't see them, and all she saw was a shadow or something. I'm beginning to think it was Johnathan Skelton or one of his people, as a payback."

"A payback?"

"Yeah, I might be partially responsible for his latest legal troubles."

"Well, you know, he and anyone connected to him have the FBI all over them. I doubt they are worried about some small time factory worker. And I seriously doubt a known leader of an organized crime syndicate, has people climbing trees and peeping into your home," he laughs.

I roll my eyes. "Alright maybe it wasn't, but it was someone. What about Lucas Charles, he left right before she did. He could have been waiting for her. He has always held a grudge against me."

"Are you saying you think both attacks are to seek revenge against you?" he asks as I consider the idea more clearly.

"Yeah, I guess so. I mean… why else? Dani doesn't have any enemies, everyone loves her except Gina Charles. She would have every reason to help her brother attack Dani and get back at me."

"Gina Charles?" he asks, surprisingly interested in what I have to say all of a sudden.

"Yeah, I think she was the one giving information to Portman about my business."

"Why do you say that?"

"Because I saw her with Thomas Monroe last night. The two were all over each other."

"You saw them together last night?" I nod. He quickly picks up the phone and makes a call. He's so frenzied when he hangs up that he slams his fist down on his desk at me. "You may have just solved this case Dillon."

"I did? How?"

"Gina Charles was murdered last night." I sit up straight in my chair with my jaw open. "Yeah, she was beaten to death and thrown into a ditch near her home. It wasn't Lucas Charles. It was Thomas Monroe."

"But I thought he had an alibi for when Dani was attacked."

"An alibi that has been suspect from the beginning, you said so yourself. If we can find evidence that he killed Gina and Colleen, then we have three killings and one attempted murder with similar M.O.'s, and Mr. Monroe's alibi becomes a little less solid without some other kind of collaboration. We got him this time. With your eye-witness account and hopefully some DNA to confirm our suspicions, he won't stand a chance." He receives another call and eagerly grabs for it. "You sure it's him? Alright, stay with him, and as soon as I get the warrant, we will be there." He hangs up and pats me on the back. "We got him, and we are going to bring him in now. I guess you don't have to worry about anyone looking through your windows anymore."

"No, I guess not," I say, watching him run off to arrest Tommy boy. For some reason, I don't feel good about this. I have hated that prick since the day he waltzed into this town, but I don't want to believe he would have anything to do with this, that Dani would feel this man's wrath because of me. I make a quick call to my dad and Shane and let them know I am going to hang out here and wait for them to bring him in. I need to see his face. Hours go by, and I nearly pace my legs off before they finally bring him in. Tommy walks into the station in handcuffs and meets my eyes immediately. The numbness I have been feeling is suddenly overwhelmed by rage. I charge at him and throw him to the ground, punching him until I am dragged away. The police get Tommy back to his feet and drag him away, ignoring the blood dripping from his nose and mouth.

"I didn't do this, Dillon!" he yells back at me. "There is no way I would ever hurt Dani."

"Sure you wouldn't, just like you didn't leave bruises on her while I was gone?" I yell back at him. I turn around, grabbing my coat and run right into Douglas Portman. "You happy now? You brought him into her life. You forced him on her." He doesn't say a word. "Don't you dare lie for him and say he was with you because you know damn well he wasn't. You actually were going to leave him alone with her while you went out of town. What kind of father are you?"

"I trusted him. I admit it wasn't my best decision. I believed him when he said he was nowhere near there when it happened, so I gave him an alibi to keep the company name from being involved."

"Oh, how nice of you to protect your daughter's attacker so your precious livelihood wouldn't be affected."

"My daughter means everything to me. She's all I have. I would never do anything to purposely hurt her."

"Okay, so you didn't do it on purpose. I'm sure Dani will feel much better about that," I say, walking away and taking a long drive before going anywhere specific.

After a lot of driving and cursing, I stop by the bar for a while so I can think of something that makes sense to tell Dani, something that won't hurt her any more than she already is. I buy one drink, and then have another and another. Still, I have not managed to think of anything of value to say to her. No. Instead, I keep thinking about how I can sneak into jail and torture that son of a bitch to death. Two men come in and try to sit near me at the bar, stumbling into me and laughing as if it is no big deal. "Excuse me," I say, annoyed.

I turn around and realize one is Paul, Dani's ex-stepfather. "Oh I'm sorry. Did we hurt you, little boy?" he says laughing along with the other. The drunk bastard hasn't changed a bit. "Hey, I heard about Dani. I guess the whore should keep the S&M down to a minimum next time," he laughs. I jerk the bastard off his stool and knock him on his ass with one hit. I stand over him, kicking him until his friend attacks me from behind. I toss him off my back and don't hesitate to fight them both. My anger intensifies until someone drags me out of the place and throws me against a truck.

I turn around, ready to battle again until I realize it's Lucas. "What the fuck do you want? Do you want to go at it to now?"

"Settle down Conrad, and get in the truck before the police get here."

"Why, what are you up to?"

"Just get in the damn truck! Now!" he yells at me. I don't know why I listen to him, but for some reason I get in, holding my mouth as it bleeds down on my shirt. "You need to get it together and stop with the constant fighting every time someone pisses you off. Not every situation calls for someone to get their ass beat."

"I assure you this situation called for some ass beating."

"Paul is a drunk moron, not worth your time or frustration. I'm sorry about your father and Dani, and I am sure you feel like it's your fault. Hell, it probably is." I glance his way with a growl of impatience. "You have acted like a jackass most of your life; running off and doing whatever you want to do with no worries or concern about anyone else."

"I told you I had nothing to do with you getting hit in that game. I didn't then, and I don't now, know anything about it. It was an accident, Lucas!"

"Shut up, Dillon! Just shut up! I don't care anymore. I care about how I am going to spend the rest of my life, and you should too. I don't know what that was about in there, or do I care. All I know is that it isn't helping Dani any."

"Like you care about Dani."

"I care about her more than you, obviously, because if she was my girl, I would be there with her right now, and every day until she got better. Not worrying about my stupid factory or some dumbass at a bar. She deserves better than you."

"Fuck you, Lucas! I haven't left her side for one minute that wasn't for her own good." I shake my head, not wanting to say another word to him, but I can't help myself. "You have no idea what it's like. You're not there listening to her scream at night, crying and begging me to help save her. You're not there when she pleads with me not to leave every day, even after her therapist says it's for the best to let her struggle and learn to fight rather than to lie in that bed and give up. You have no idea what it's like to find out your son died and you didn't have the opportunity to even hold him for one damn second, or be there with his mother because her father is a jackass who would rather her be with a murderer than you." He looks over at me as I turn away, punching the dashboard. "Don't tell me what I should be feeling or doing when you have no idea what it is like to be losing the woman you have loved since you met her. You act like you know so much about me, but you don't know anything. All you care about is placing blame for your life on someone else. You say you are over what happened to your knee, yet you still do very little to better yourself. You won't even take Warren's old job because it was me that offered it to you. It's an opportunity that you could really do something with, but no, you would prefer to sit at a station and order a select few around and hide from me all day. And then what? Hope Dani comes back and realizes she would rather be with you than me? Is that the only reason you stay; to get back the girl you think I stole from you?" He has nothing to say suddenly. He pulls up to my house and puts his truck in park. I jump out, sick of his bullshit. "Thanks for bringing me home, and I'm sorry about your sister, but at least they got the guy today."

He snaps his head in my direction with wide eyes. "What?"

"Thomas Monroe. He was sleeping with Gina. She was helping him steal information about the factory. I saw him with her last night."

"You were there and saw him, you're sure it was him?" I nod. He shakes his head. "She was never good at picking men. She wasn't really my sister, you know. My father married her mother when we were both young and forced him to adopt the idiot. Her mother is just as big of a loser. *I hate that woman.* She kept my dad from paying for me to go to college because it wouldn't leave her enough money to go on nice trips. A football scholarship was the only hope I had to get out of here, to get away from her and everyone else." I stare at him, suddenly understanding him a little better.

"You guys seemed like the perfect family."

He laughs. "Family secrets, Conrad. My family was the best at them. I don't know. Maybe you're right. Maybe I stay here and work shit jobs so I can enjoy being miserable. Or, maybe it's so I don't have to worry about failing again, disappointing my father again, or giving my step-monster more ammunition to use against me." He looks down at the dashboard quietly.

"That job is still open you know?" I say as he nods slowly. "Well, think about it and let me know tomorrow. Right now, I need to go inside before I get sick."

"Do you need me to help you?" he asks as I rush inside.

Chapter 25

Dillon

I spent most of my night sick, doing my best to take care of Dani without letting her know why I was sick. I didn't tell her anything about her ex-fiancé. Every time I tried, my stomach started to churn. To tell Dani her ex was the one that tried to kill her, that the one her father was ready to leave her alone with was the cause of her nightmares, the one that took her ability to walk away…how do I dare? I have no idea, but I am going to take a day to think it through and figure out who to move into Gina's position, which turned out not to be too hard. She pushed most of her work onto someone else. Once I figured out who that was, I had my replacement.

Business is really beginning to take off, but it's hard to enjoy the rising success with so much else on my mind. My trip home is so full of *what if's* that I vaguely remember anything between work and home. Dani is up, working with Robin, and from the look on her face, she is already in a foul mood before she even looks up at me.

"Dillon, welcome home," Robin says joyfully. "You will be happy to know we have made quite a lot of progress today."

"He doesn't care. He is the one that leaves me here and rids himself of the bother every day. I am surprised he comes home at all. It must be the guilt of leaving the woman he supposedly loves all alone, all day, with a human torture device," Dani says, causing Robin to laugh hysterically, but I don't find the statement nearly as funny.

"Thanks for that, and that makes this information much easier to share now. Thomas was arrested for killing Gina Charles, Colleen, Warren, and the attack on you. Your father picked out a real winner there for you," I say, taking a second to actually look at Dani as the information begins to sink in. With her jaw open and her eyes staring blankly at me, I suddenly realize what a complete ass I really am. "I'm sorry …"

"I remember him," she says.

"What?" I ask.

"I remember. I was driving Warren home and Thomas was waving us down because there was something wrong with his car. I pulled over, and Warren got out and helped get his car started. I was talking to him while Warren worked, and we started arguing. He grabbed me, and I smacked him. He got angry … and I, I don't remember much else."

"That's good, Dani. That's huge progress," Robin says, as I stand dumbfounded that the information caused her to remember something so important.

"But I don't remember what happened after that."

"What were you arguing about?" Robin asks her.

"He kept going on and on about how far up the ladder he could move at my father's company with me at his side. He was upset and swore that Dillon was all wrong for me. He believed I was blinded by an old childhood crush I never got a chance to get over properly," Dani says, looking up at me. The way she looks at me, I wonder if she believes that too.

"Well, at least you don't have to worry so much about your safety now and can concentrate on getting better," I say, looking deep into her eyes before needing to walk away. I don't want to know if her love for me is truly gone.

Thomas's DNA was found under Dani's nails. The case against him is building, and I become more confident by the day that he will pay for what he has done. I just don't know if it will be enough to satisfy me. Since Gina is gone, I am forced to move people around and take over one spot until I can find someone else. The old locker room is managing to hold up, but barely. For sure, the next thing I need to do when we have the money is to have this torn down and rebuilt.

"So Boss, I hear that the police are pretty certain that Monroe guy is the one that killed my father?" Rafe asks with his usual shy approach as he opens up his own locker.

"Yeah, it looks that way," I say to the side of his head as he quickly turns away before I can look him in the eyes.

"So how is Dani doing?" he asks softly.

"She's getting better."

"Is she remembering anything? I mean maybe if she remembers more, they can make sure to put this guy away."

"She's remembering some, a little more each day. At least we got the son of a bitch though."

"Yeah, that's for sure. My father and I rarely got along, but I still miss him."

"Me too, it's going to be hard to find someone else to spit on my shoes when they talk to me," I say, causing him to laugh. I pat him on the back and finish changing into my work clothes as he begins. "You know, we should …" I say, looking over at him and noticing a tattoo on his arm.

"We should what?" He asks with a goofy laugh that I rarely hear from him.

"That's an interesting tattoo. It almost looks real."

"Oh yeah, I paid a mint for it, so it better look good. My mom used to tell me I had a great imagination, that my mind's eye was one of the most creative she had ever seen. It's like I had an extra visual force inside of me. So, I sketched out an eye within an eye, and this guy said he could make it look like it was actually coming out of my arm," he says, putting his shirt on and covering up the odd tattoo. "So, what should we do?"

"Huh?" I say, lost in thought.

"You were saying we should do something, but you never finished."

"Oh, I was just going to say we should put up a plaque or a dedication of your father somewhere."

He looks me directly in the eyes and smiles, "That would be great, really great. Thank you, Dillon."

"Sure, not a problem," I say, watching him walk away with a sharp agony in the pit of my stomach. I race out of the locker room. "Lucas, I need you to find someone to take over position twelve today."

"I thought you were doing that?" he yells as I leave work and drive to see the one person who can clarify the newly formed questions in my head.

The last thing I want to do is to see this man, but I have to know, and for some reason, I think I will see the truth in his eyes. Thomas doesn't get many visitors and none outside of his attorneys, so I am not sure how he will feel about seeing me today. They bring him out in his prison uniform and handcuffs. His usual well-styled hair is barely combed through, and his smug face is accompanied with an overgrowth of facial hair. He begins shaking his head as soon as he sees me. He walks in and sits down in front of me, avoiding eye contact.

"What do you want? To gloat or to see me at my worst?" he asks.

"Neither. I have a few questions I would like you to answer. Your choice on whether you do, but if you answer them and I believe you, then I may be able to help you get out of here." No sooner do my words leave my mouth than he takes a sudden interest in what I have to say. "Don't get too excited. You have to answer my questions first." He nods, shifting his body square with mine. "Dani remembers your car being broken down and pulling over to help you. She said you got into a fight. What happened after that?"

"She hit me, scratched up my arm to release my grip on hers, and I was done. I told her that I was done with her and she said, '*Good! Because she has all she needs now*'." He glances up at my eyes, and I look away, waiting for more and letting him know I am not interested in discussing my relationship with Dani right now. Warren got my car started, and I offered him some money for the help, but then he started getting sick and ran into the woods. I yelled at the old man to be careful because he was stumbling around in the dark. I told Dani to just leave him, and she yelled at me and said I was a bastard and that's why she never loved me. So, I left her to deal with him on her own."

"You left her there, on the side of the road, in the dark, by herself?"

"It's not something I am proud of. When I found out she was missing, I felt sick and would have done anything to find her. I offered money to anyone that could give me an idea as to where she might be, and some guy walked up to me in private and told me about the old paper mill. When I went down there, I saw you and pushed you in the wrong direction so I could be the one to find her. I told the cops this, but they don't believe me. They, of course, think I knew where she was because I was the one that tried to kill her. I mean, how stupid would I have to be to go back to the scene of the crime if I was the one that did it?"

"Who was the guy that told you about the paper mill?"

"I don't know. He led me part of the way there, I handed him some cash, and he was gone. It was dark, especially in the woods."

I look him in the eyes, and for some reason, I believe him. I sit back, trying to figure out something that makes no sense. "Why are you asking me this?"

"Dani remembered something else. I thought it was crazy nightmares …at first."

"At first? What is it? You have to tell me, Dillon. I swear I might have been doing everything I could to try and shut you down, but I didn't kill anyone."

"She said she saw two eyes staring at her, one inside the other."

Thomas looks down and jumps suddenly with wide eyes. "The guy that told me about the paper mill, he had a tattoo. It was realistic and bright; it was really the only thing I could see in the dark.… I couldn't believe he didn't have a coat on. He wasn't even shivering. I was cold as hell, and I had a coat on. It was like heated adrenalin was running through his veins." I nod, and he closes his mouth, sitting back in his chair silently. "He was right there, the whole time. I had him and …"

"Tell your attorneys to check out Rafe Bolton," I say before standing and walking away.

"Dillon!" I turn back to him. "Thank you." I don't feel good enough about helping him to acknowledge his appreciation, so I continue on my way out the door with nothing else said.

After talking to the police, I wander off to a park I used to play in as a kid, working my anger down to a manageable level. I don't think I can see that man without killing him. I certainly don't want him working for me one more day, but how to fire him without letting him know I am on to him? I am hoping there is evidence that he still has, proving he did this and making a solid case for the police to put him on death row. I have to maintain control until the police have what they need. I have no choice. I can't tell anyone in fear they might give my suspicions away. By the time I get home, Thomas's attorneys are at our doorstep, wanting to talk to Dani. She doesn't understand, and I make sure they don't mention any names, to keep from scaring her. She does fine until they hand her a sketch of Rafe's tattoo. Instantly, she begins panicking. She buries herself so deep into my chest that I know the questioning is done for now.

"I think that's it for today gentlemen," I say as my father shows them out.

The next day, I stay home with Dani, avoiding the possible murder I might commit if I go to work. On top of everything else, seeing the tattoo again caused Dani to have nightmares more vivid than ever. Even Robin thought it best I stick around today, but I think it is less for Dani and more to keep me out of trouble.

I set up in the basement with a punching bag and take out all my frustrations on it. When I finish, I have to walk through Dani's therapy area and decide to take a moment to stand back and watch.

She isn't complaining, and she is actually moving her legs. It's nice to see Dani seeming to get better and stronger. Her being able to move her legs at all brings a smile to my face, and for a moment, causes her to smile back.

"She's doing well," Robin says from behind me. I nod with a smile. "How are you doing though?"

"I'm fine. I wasn't the one nearly beaten to death."

"No, but I bet it feels like you were sometimes. If you want to talk, I am open for business."

"I'm fine. There isn't anything to talk about. You just worry about helping her," I say, motioning towards Dani before leaving them all to go get some work done in the den.

"Okay, if you say so," Robin says to my fleeing figure.

I don't get more than a few minutes in and the detective handling Dani's case pulls into the driveway with his partner. I rush to the front door to meet them. "It's not a good time right now."

"We need to talk to her. We can't solve this until we do."

"She talked to those attorneys last night, and she had nightmares all night. I don't think she can handle much more."

"If we don't get to talk to her, then we can't get a warrant for his arrest, and we will be forced to continue our original focus on the case."

"You're going to continue with your charges against Thomas and leave Rafe out there to kill again? How can you do that?" I ask in shock.

"We can't get a search warrant without probable cause, and we can't have that without Dani's statement. If you want us to come back later, fine, then we will wait, but that only means we have to wait that much longer to investigate Rafe closer."

I have no choice. "Alright, but try to be considerate and not tell her what your suspicions are yet." I allow them inside and have them take a seat before I go get Dani. I bring her in and help her sit on the sofa where she can be more comfortable. She looks the detectives over as her hands begin shaking. "They want to ask you a few questions, Dani," I say, taking hold of her hand.

"About what? That tattoo?" The detectives move to the edge of their seats towards her. "I remembered a little more last night. It wasn't Thomas, was it? It was the guy with the tattoo, and Thomas doesn't have any tattoos. He's scared of needles."

"That figures," I laugh, and she glances over at me with a pointed glare.

"Do you remember what he looked like?" The detective asks.

"No, it was too dark, and I didn't see his face. I only remember running." She looks down at my hands around hers and squeezes tight. "After Thomas left, I started the truck up, waiting for Warren to finish getting sick in the woods, but when I heard him yell out, I thought he fell, so I jumped out of the truck and went looking for him. And I found him …" She closes her eyes tight, trembling. "He was lying face down and wasn't moving. I thought he had passed out from drinking. He wouldn't move, so I tried to shake him and call out to him. Then, I saw the blood, and this figure moved in near me with a metal object that was dripping with blood. I screamed and started running and running. I didn't know who it was, and I didn't care to know. I only wanted to get away from him. When he caught me, he drug me to this place with his arm around my neck and ... that's when I saw the tattoo. I think I remember him, but ..." She pauses, gripping my hands with quivering lips. "That tattoo has haunted me more than anything, but everything happened so fast. I didn't even remember it being a tattoo until recently. So, who was it?" she asks, looking up at them as they look over at me. She turns to me. "Who was it Dillon? It was someone I know, wasn't it? Tell me Dillon." I look up at Robin, and she nods.

"We think it was Rafe. He has that exact tattoo on his arm," I say.

"As it turns out, Warren owns a small cabin not far off that road. He called the number at that cabin with his cell phone about the time you would have pulled over to help Mr. Monroe with his car. Rafe has been living there for the last few years. He was probably looking for Rafe to come get him since he wasn't feeling well. I am sure Rafe heard the yelling between you and Thomas and took advantage of the opportunity. That's our theory anyway. It fits. We know he didn't get along with Ms. Charles. There are numerous accounts of them fighting; his name came up by other employees at the factory before we even suspected him of doing anything."

"He didn't get along with Colleen either. They had numerous confrontations. Gina threatened to get him fired, he and his father got into a fight the night Warren was killed," I say, adding to their notes.

"And I threatened to fire him while Dillon was gone because

he wouldn't do as I said," Dani says, closing her eyes tight.

The two detectives look at each other briefly, "There is more. When we thought it was Monroe, we assumed it all revolved around getting back at Dillon, but after we talked to Monroe's attorneys, we thought maybe we should check out nearby cities and towns for similar deaths. There has been many over the years with the same DNA that we found on the two girls and you Ms. Portman. Not to mention, the two gentlemen that were killed months ago outside the factory. As it turns out, Rafe was about to be fired by the man that was in charge of your factory at that time. We need you to keep this to yourselves until we can get an arrest warrant. He is sure to run if he knows we suspect him."

"Of course. When do you think you will do it?" I ask, anxious to get this over with.

"As soon as we can." They stand, and I shake their hands before walking them out the door.

I call Shane over so I can talk to him and my father at the same time. I let them both know what is about to happen. The news is a hard blow to them both, and we all decide it best that I don't come into work until he's gone. The day is a rough one, and after I make sure Dani is okay, I get ready to watch the game with my father. The game barely gets going when there is a knock at the door. I open the door and find Rafe standing in front of me. My whole body freezes over as soon as I lay eyes on him.

"Hey Boss, I hope you don't mind, but I thought I would stop by and see how Dani is doing."

"It's not really a good time right now," I say, gripping the door so tight I begin to lose feeling in my hands.

"Oh, okay, but is there any way that I can talk to you for a few minutes?"

"Maybe tomorrow at work, but like I said, it's not a good time right now." He nods and waves as he starts to walk away. I sigh and then, *bam*! He comes barreling through the door and right at me. He gets me hard in the head before I have a chance to react. He grabs the poker from the fireplace and strikes me in the arm as I try to get away from him. "Rafe, what are you doing?"

"Getting rid of the evidence."

"It's too late. The cops already know. They know that it was you."

He shakes his head, "No, if they did, they would have released Monroe. You're the only one that knows what happened; Dani is the only one that can prove I was there."

"You're going to kill all three of us?"

"I have done worse," he says coldly. I catch sight of my father coming at him from behind with a bat, but as soon as he gets ready to take a swing, Rafe knocks him back on his back. I run at him and jump him, taking as many swings as I can, anything to get him to slow down. The man seems to be on some kind of drug. He is wild with blackened eyes. He twists and pounds me up against the wall. I slide down it, grimacing while bracing myself for the slashing blow coming at my body. The iron rod hits my body, ripping into my skin and going straight into the bone.

I scream out, but he gets me in the back of the head before I can recover and move out the way. My blurry eyes watch as Rafe runs up the stairs … "Dani!"

Chapter 26

Dani

After a long day of therapy and questioning, I settle in for the night and take out a book to read, but I can't seem to get the images of Rafe out of my head. Now all my nightmares have a face, it is impossible to think about anything else. I have not turned a page in my book in an hour, yet I still keep trying to get through to the next page. I don't want to face my dreams right now, not without Dillon in bed with me. I begin again on the same page when a sudden commotion downstairs causes me to set my book down and pay closer attention. I can hear the enraged voices, but I can't make out what they are saying. A scuffle at the stairs leads to a pounding up the stairway to outside my door. I scoot back in the bed, waiting as the door swings open and Rafe stands in the doorway salivating.

"Do you remember this?" he asks, holding up the fireplace poker. "I wanted you so bad that night and that prick came wandering in, right in the middle of my conquest. I did all that work, messing with your phone line and sabotaging your cell, only for him to come in and save the day. You were lucky that night. I wasn't ready for Monroe, and again, you were lucky when I was interrupted by Dillon screaming for you. I wanted you, but it was more important to kill you before it was too late. But tonight, tonight, I am ready for whatever I need to do to get to you and finish the job," he says with a rabid hunger in his eyes. I glance towards my cell on the nightstand. "Don't bother. I have set up a jammer to disable the signals from within this house." He takes a step towards me, and I lose any breath I had with which to scream within a single gasp of fear. I can't run, and I can't cry. All I can do is accept my death. He holds up the iron rod and gets ready to take aim at me. I close my eyes hard until Dillon comes flying in and onto Rafe's back, pushing him into the floor. Dillon punches him in the spine and shoves his face into the floor once and then twice. Rafe goes still, so Dillon slowly gets up.

"Dillon!" I scream as Rafe tries at him one more time. The struggle between them is such that it's hard to comprehend who has the upper hand. With my breath back, I scream. "Dillon!" I scream for help, I scream for Dillon to be okay, and I scream to distract Rafe as much as I can. The levels of my voice carry and the nosey neighbor raises the blinds to look through her window and into mine. I don't know if they can see much for the tree, but I keep screaming, hoping they fear for the worst and call the police for us.

Dillon struggles to catch his breath in between fighting for his life and protecting me, but he finally gets some help from his father who comes in swinging a bat into Rafe's back. Rafe screams out as he falls to the ground and looks up to a gun in his face. "Don't move. I won't hesitate to shoot you," Matt says, checking on his son. Dillon is clearly hurt, and I watch him closely as he sits, cringing and holding his broken arm.

"Dillon?" I call out to him, hoping he is okay. He tries to get up, but falls back down to the ground. I reach out for him as he looks over at me and tries to get to me. His body suddenly slams down onto the floor, and his eyes close hard. "Dillon!"

When the police arrive, they arrest Rafe and check on Matt and I while EMTs see to Dillon. They manage to get him awake just so he can fight them about going to the hospital. Matt goes over to him and talks to him, but again Dillon shakes his head. There is a lot of arguing before he starts coughing up blood.

They strap him into a stretcher, and he looks back at me as he is rolled away. "I'll be back, I promise," he yells out to me. Matt comes and sits with me, putting his arms around me.

"I called your father. He's on his way," Matt says.

"Is Dillon okay?"

"I think so. He told me to stay here with you. Shane will meet him at the hospital and hopefully talk the stubborn fool into staying there and getting the proper care that he needs. He has a concussion and some pretty serious wounds." He looks down at me as tears begin to form. "He'll be fine though, and he'll be back, annoying us both with his overprotective ways, I am sure of it." I force a smile and sigh as I lean against him, worrying about Dillon.

I am sound asleep when I feel someone near me. I turn quickly and see him. "It's just me. "I'm sorry for waking you. I only wanted to check on you."

"I'm fine. How are you?" I ask him, looking at his arm in a

sling and bandages on his head and chest.

"I'm good, barely a scratch." He feebly smiles his crooked smile.

I shake my head, touching his arm lightly. "Liar, you're a mess." He doesn't say anything as he runs his fingers through my hair and along my face. "You saved me." He doesn't seem as pleased with that fact as I do. "You saved me twice. It was your voice that kept him from killing me before too, you know?"

"I shouldn't have let you leave without me," he says, looking towards the floor.

I scoot over and pat the bed, and he moves in close with his body still cold to the touch from being outside, proving his first concern when he got home was to check on me. "I'm sorry. I have been so mean to you."

"It's alright."

"No, it's not. I don't know why I am so angry and why it is so much easier to take it out on you. I guess I look at you and wish for things to be different between us."

"Do you ever think you will be able to look at me and not be angry?" he asks, but I don't know the answer.

"I hope so. I want to be able to do a lot of things again."

It's been months since Rafe was arrested, and I am able to stand on my own now. I can even walk, sort of. I have to use crutches or someone has to help me, but I can get around the house now and feel useful. I won't dare leave the house, but I will step outside on the porch though. I remember almost every detail of the night I should have died. Now, I even remember Dillon calling for me. I tried to call out to him, but Rafe had his hands around my neck and was readying himself to rape me. But, Dillon's presence convinced him to kill me instead. Rafe denies it all, and there is very little evidence other than DNA that can be explained with reasonable understanding. He is so sure of beating the case against him that he is threatening to sue Dillon for attacking him for simply trying to visit a sick friend. We are lucky that the judge denied him bail, so he has to remain in jail until trial, a trial they want me to testify at. I can't even leave the house, and they want me to face him and talk about that night to a room full of people. I don't even like to talk about it with Robin. Dillon, so far, has avoided asking me about it, and I am thankful for that. My mother and father, however, are determined to get me to not only testify but talk more about what happened and what I saw. They want to know every detail of the heart-crushing terror I felt. I keep getting pushed to go here and there. The bruises have healed, and my legs are getting more useful, but my head still tells me that I am damaged. One look in the mirror, and no matter the time that has gone by, I still see my swollen bruised face with all the cuts and wounds. My reflection always reminds me of the rage that was inflicted upon me. I try to stand up straight in front of the full-length mirror and see what is really there versus what I feel is there. I brush my hair and angle my face into the light to find some sort of beauty within it. There is a lot of me to see, but nothing I want to see. I am so full of anger at how this could happen. How could I lose myself so easily and want to give up so badly? I want to scream out to myself to snap out of it and see the renewed skin that covers me. I drop my robe and look at my nude body. Horror overpowers me. The tears rush to my eyes as the resentment and pain capture me tight, not allowing me to see anything other than broken disgust. The disappointing form in front of me is agonizing. I want so badly to see me again, to be the woman Dillon wants me to be. If only I could be what I was then, maybe, I could feel worth his time, worth all the effort that he puts into helping me. There is nothing here to be proud of. There is not a woman to see, only wreckage. I close my eyes and cringe, wishing that I could break the hold that my dark memories have on me.

"Dani!" Dillon screams at me as he runs into the room. He takes hold of me and covers me up as he takes my hand. "What are you doing to yourself?" I look down as blood pours from the palm of my hand. Dillon digs my metal comb from my skin and runs to the bathroom before bringing back some bandages and treatments for the wound. He repairs my hand gently and wraps it up, all the while glancing at me with concern. "Why did you do this to yourself?"

"I didn't know I did," I say in a daze. Dillon helps me put my pajamas on while I try to avoid looking into his disappointed eyes. When I do look into his eyes, I want to plead with him to let me go, to give up and run to something better, to someone more worthy of him. I want to scream at him, shake him, anything to get him to see what a mistake he is making with me. Instead, like a selfish bitch, I sit here, holding onto him, smiling at his warm touch and the sight of his comforting bare chest and hopeful, handsome face.

"The attorneys need you to testify in court against Rafe. They don't think they can win against him if you don't," he says suddenly. *I wonder how long he has waited for the right opportunity to say that.*

"Well I am not, so they need to figure out another way," I say, harshly folding my arms and turning away from him. "I don't know why everyone keeps trying to push me to do something I don't want to do. I don't want to see him. I don't want to be there!"

"Okay, then what do you want to do? Do you want to hide out in this house forever? Do you want him to make you a prisoner instead of you making him one? Do you want to give up? How do you want to live the rest of your life? What do you want, Dani? Whatever it is, I will make sure it happens for you."

I turn to him and want to punch him for being so unbelievably considerate and nice. "You know what I want, Dillon? I want to run away from everyone. I want to forget this place and never come back!" I scream at him, wanting to hurt him as much as I hurt and then hate myself for it.

Dillon stands tall and inhales deeply, "Okay, then let's runaway." I sit back, confused. "You want to leave this place? You want to tell everyone to fuck off and forget them? Then let's do it. I'll take you wherever you want to go."

"You're crazy."

He nods with a slight laugh. "Maybe, but no matter how crazy

I am, I still would do anything for you." He says walking away. I assume the issue is settled, until the next morning, when he comes into the bedroom with suitcases.

"What are you doing?"

"Packing," he says oddly.

"You're packing my stuff. Are you kicking me out?"

"No, Dani, we are running away like you wanted." I look him up and down and find no reason to laugh at his bullshit. I shake my head and refuse to respond to this craziness. Dillon continues to pack, asking me questions in between about what I prefer, but I ignore him. Not that it matters, the jerk dismisses me and makes a judgment call. "Oh, by the way, I am taking condoms, but that's only in case one of us gets lucky. Don't take that to mean I plan on getting lucky with you."

"You would only be so lucky."

"Yeah, because Lord knows I enjoy every second we spend together."

"I hate you."

"Good, I hate you too. Now, do you want to take your bikini or a one piece swimsuit?"

"Fuck you!"

"Two piece it is then."

"Dillon!"

"Dani! You'd better change out of your pajamas. That's no way to travel." He walks out of the room with a large annoying smile and a suitcase full of my clothes and another full of his. I shake my head and curse his name under my breath until he comes back. "So are you ready?" I stare a hole into him, daring him to make a move towards me. "Alright, going to be lazy, are you? Fine, but don't take this to mean that I am flirting with you." He comes at me and scoops me up into his arms.

"Dillon put me down!" I yell at him as he carries me through the house. I catch sight of my father quickly turning away and pretending to be interested in something on TV. "Daddy, help me!"

"I'll get her crutches. Have fun, Sweetheart," he yells at me.

"Matt, tell your son to stop this foolishness now!"

"Have fun kids," he yells, with a wave.

Dillon puts me in a car almost exactly like the one we went to the beach in when we were in high school. "Is this supposed to be a joke?" Dillon smiles and climbs into the driver's seat next to me. "Someone help me!" My father brings out my crutches and waves goodbye before quickly disappearing again. "He hates you. He would never let you take me away, so you can stop this ridiculousness now. I am on to you."

"Yeah, he used to, but we worked things out though, so buckle up." Dillon puts on his sunglasses, starts the car, and drives off. I keep waiting for him to stop and turn around, but he never does. He drives to the main road and stops. "So, which way, right or left?" I cross my arms and ignore him. "Left it is then." He takes off down the road, and I look at him in shock.

"What are you doing? Take me back! I'm in pajamas!"

"I told you to change," he says with a *very* annoying smile.

I sit in my seat, crossing my arms with a growl. "Where are we going?" He shrugs, which only frustrates me more. I sit, ignoring the sights to prove a point, but after a while, I get distracted by the back roads and the scenery going by. I try not to let him know I'm interested or enjoying myself in the least, because I'm not. However, it is hard to ignore the open fields of animals and other interesting sights going by. A few hours in and Dillon pulls us into an open field and parks. "What are you doing?"

"Taking a break. I'm hungry."

"You're always hungry." He gets out and brings out a cooler and a blanket from the trunk.

"If you want to join me, feel free. Otherwise, continue to sit in the car and pout like a child."

"I was kidnapped and forced to come with you against my will!" I snap at him. He laughs, shaking his head. "It's not funny."

"Okay, if you decide you're hungry, I got some great stuff from the deli, and oh look—your favorite cookies." He waves them at me as if I am a child who will instantly come running for a stupid cookie. I'm not. Although, I am hungry. I didn't eat breakfast. I can't fight him and stay determined for him to take me home unless I keep up my energy. Besides, I don't like being alone in this car. I don't know why he had to set up so far away. I look into the back seat, find my crutches, and fit them on before getting out of the car. The rough terrain makes it difficult to walk, and I nearly fall a few times. I look up at Dillon, and I know he notices, but he acts like he doesn't. It takes forever for me to get to him. "Could you set this up any further from the car?"

He looks around the area and then nods. "Yeah, I guess I

could have."

I practically fall to the ground and am sure to huff and groan to make him aware of my impatience with him. "Cookie?" he asks, handing me one. *I love these.* I bite into it and smile without realizing. I look up at his glowing enjoyment of my misery and turn away from his view while I eat my cookie.

"I thought we would go to Myrtle Beach and enjoy the water. Is that okay?"

If he thinks I don't realize what he is doing, then he is crazy. "What are you asking me for? I was kidnapped and forced to come on this trip." I say with my best angry tone. Dillon laughs at me and goes on like I made a joke. *I hate him.*

When we arrive at Myrtle Beach, Dillon pulls into a hotel and checks us in. "You had a reservation?"

"No, they have heard of me. I guess word about my amazingly handsome smile has spread beyond the borders of North Carolina. Now, are you going to sit in the car all day or come up and change so you don't look so ridiculous in your pajamas anymore?" I get out of the car as a couple passes by and looks me over with judgment in their eyes. I eye them back with disdain, before looking back at Dillon shaking his head.

"What? They seem to have a problem," I say.

"You have skull and crossbones pajamas on and …" he says, stepping forward and pulling out my shirt, "part of your lunch on your shirt. It's a good thing you weren't hungry." I huff, grabbing the room key from his hand, and snatch my bag from the trunk, putting it over my head before taking hold of my crutches and going to find the room on my own.

I walk into the room amazed. It's actually nice and has a great view of the water. Dillon follows me in, looking around the place and seeming pleased himself. "This is nice. Pretty nice view, too."

"It's better than nice, and you know it. Did my father pay for this?" He looks back at me with a scowl. "You paid for this?"

"No, I told you they adore my handsome smile here," he says, smiling obnoxiously.

I roll my eyes and disregard his typical Dillon actions. Since it looks like I am staying here for a while, I might as well clean up and make myself at home until he decides to stop this foolishness and take me back.

While I sit in a corner of the room reading, far away from Dillon he suddenly looks at his watch and jumps up with a smile. *Oh no.* "So, I am thinking I am going to go down to the boardwalk and walk around for a little while before dinner. You're welcome to come or you can stay here and watch the fun from the window if you like."

"You'd leave me here? By myself?"

"Don't worry. There is a lot of security at this hotel, room service if you're hungry, and most people are out enjoying the festival so there shouldn't be anyone to bother you," he says, acting like he would really leave me here and go and have fun by himself.

"I'm good here." I crash down into the sofa, crossing my arms and daring him to leave.

"Okay. Have fun. Call me if you need me," he says, waving goodbye and walking out. One …Two…Three …and …nothing. I get up and look through the peephole, but I don't see him. He didn't leave. No way. I will just sit here and wait for him to come back.

It's been two hours of sitting here by myself. I'm beginning to think he isn't coming back. Another half hour goes by and still no sign of him. *I can't believe he isn't coming back! He knows I'm scared to be by myself and especially in an unknown place!*

I pick up my cell and call my father, but no answer. All I get is a text that says, *"Enjoy yourself."* The same goes for anyone else I call to come get me. Damn him. He has turned everyone against me. *I'm calling him, and I am going to tell him …*

"How's it going? Having a good time up there?" Dillon says happily.

"Shut up, Dillon! I can't believe you left me here alone. You come back here right now!" I say through my teeth.

"I'll come back, but only if you agree to come out and have dinner with me."

"Errghhhh! I swear."

"Is that a yes? I'm sorry, I only speak English. I know a little Spanish, but only the dirty words." He begins saying a few, just to piss me off.

"Yes, fine. Whatever. Just get back here!"

He comes up flashing his crooked smile. "I am so glad you changed your mind."

I grab my crutches and hobble past him, making sure he understands my bad mood as I pass him. "Oh, you are the most aggravating person," I say but holding up once I step out into the hall alone. I suddenly have trouble catching my breath until he shows up at my side.

Dillon places his hand on the small of my back. "I'm right here with you." I take a breath and walk slowly alongside him to a quaint restaurant right on the water. They seat us right away at a great table with the perfect view to watch the sun go down. "Wow, it's beautiful. How did you get us in here? This place is very expensive."

"Don't worry about it," he says.

"Is my father behind this?"

"Dani, damn it," he says with an angry tone. "No, your father has nothing to do with any of this. This was all me. I am paying for everything. The hotel, the restaurant. Hell, I even own the car. The company paid off its debt and is now making a profit, a great profit."

"When did that happen?"

"A few months ago."

"Why didn't you tell me?"

"You don't ever really give me much of a chance to discuss my day," he says, taking a sip of his wine and taking in the view with enjoyment. I look him over, seeing someone I have never seen before, seeing a man, an incredibly handsome, mature man. When the waitress comes over, she makes polite conversation before telling us the specials and smiling nervously when Dillon looks up at her to listen.

"I'm sorry. I lost my train of thought there. So, would you like to start off with an appetizer?"

"Sure. What do you recommend?" Dillon asks and she giggles.

"We'll have the crab cakes," I say abruptly.

"Oh, okay. I will be back to take your dinner order," the pretty, young blonde says, giving an extra wide smile towards Dillon. I roll my eyes and imagine her falling head first into someone's dinner. I look back at Dillon who seems to be enjoying himself way too much. I'm not going to even bother asking what he thinks is so funny.

Dinner was tolerable, but then he forces me to walk along the boardwalk. "We should go out to the water," he says.

"I'm on crutches. I can't get through the sand on these."

"I can help you with that." He takes my crutches from me, swoops me up, into his arms, and carries me out to the shore before setting me down and helping me take a seat next to him. I watch the water edge up to my toes and back out again while listening to the mesmerizing sounds of the waves. I would complain, but I am too content.

I'm actually smiling, which Dillon notices with pride. He helps me take off my shoes so I can feel the water rushing up between my toes. He follows, seeming to enjoy the sensation as well. "Can we come back here tomorrow?" I ask.

"Definitely," he says.

We stay until I can barely hold my eyes open, and then, Dillon carries me back to the boardwalk and escorts me back to our room. Once I get in bed and he assumes I am safely asleep, I hear him make a call. "Hey, yeah she's asleep now. She seems to be doing well. We had dinner and sat by the water. She wants to go back tomorrow. Yeah, I know, but I can't rush her back after one day. I don't know, it will be when it has to be. Sure, I'll check back in tomorrow." He hangs up and crawls into the other bed near me.

The next morning, I wake up to a bright sun, and despite knowing that I am being tricked into something, I still want to go to the beach. I grab my crutches and maneuver myself to the sliding doors, unlocking them before trying to get them open. The doors are tough to open. I have to let go of my crutches and pull back on the door with both hands before it finally opens. The morning air and sounds of the ocean send instant excitement through my body.

"You ready to get out there already?" Dillon asks from behind me. I simply nod, trying to tone down my excitement. The moment we get to the beach and I get my feet into the water, I laugh out loud like a child. Dillon looks at me as if he sees something wonderful, so I break up the awkward moment with a splash of water at him. "Oh, now you've done it." He splashes me back and the water war begins. He wraps his arms around me and twirls me through the tides while I laugh and hold onto him with all the strength I have. Dillon grasps my waist and carries me right into an oncoming wave, causing an exhilaration to rush through me like I haven't felt in a long time. He stops and looks me over as we come through. "You ready to do that again?" I nod with excitement, holding tight to him and waiting for us to go again.

After some time playing in the water, we take a break and walk along the boardwalk. As we look through the shops along the way, we pick up odd souvenirs to show to each other with amusement. The moment Dillon sees a fair, he hustles me over to the games and challenges me to Whack a Mole. He hands me my mallet, and when they begin, I go nuts, trying to hit everything I can while Dillon does the same. I glance his way, watching him take it way more seriously than I ever would. It makes me laugh, watching him, and even more so when it ends. He wins and stands up shouting like he is king of the world for winning a stupid game. It is something he would always do growing up.

I laugh so hard tears come out of my eyes. Dillon wraps his arms around me from behind and kisses my cheek, "Okay. Pick whatever you want, gorgeous."

I look at all the crazy toys and giant stuffed animals, spotting a giant white tiger and pointing. "That one," I say as the man gets it for me and hands it over. We move onto another game and then another, losing most but enjoying them all the same. We get some junk food and share some popcorn as we walk through, trying to decide what to do next. I see the Ferris Wheel, and all I have to do is glance Dillon's way before he makes it happen. We sit down and float up towards the top where I can see for miles. I look over at Dillon smiling, and he winks. Grabbing hold of his shirt, I pull him to me and kiss him. I sit back and look into his eyes with an old feeling growing inside. Dillon recognizes it immediately and grasps my face into his hands. He takes hold of my lips so softly that I moan against his. I don't know whether it's the bad boy tattoos along the muscles in his arms, the feeling of his abs under my fingers, or if it is simply his lips that know how to make my knees weak and my body crave him. We kiss again before I sink down against his side and feel his head against mine. "Dillon?"

"Hmmm"

"Will you … will you sleep with me tonight?"

"If that's what you want." I nod, pushing my fingers in between his and gripping his hand. The room is comfortable, and the bed is even more so, but when Dillon climbs in next to me, I make sure he does without his clothes on. My hands explore his nude body without any pressure to react to his desires of me. I kiss him, and he kisses me back. I sit back, staring at him with shaky hands and tears welling up in my eyes.

He quickly takes hold of my hands. "It's okay. We don't have to do anything. I'm here whenever you need me."

"No, I want to, but can we go slow …very slow?" I ask, and he nods with a soft gulp.

"I can be as patient as you need me to be. You know that," he says, brushing my hair off my shoulder and kissing down my neck before slowly helping me out of my shirt. I release my bra and exhale as I open my arms to him. I look up into his eyes, hopeful to see something that will make me feel attractive to him, and I do. "You are so beautiful Dani," he says, looking at me in amazement. I release my fears with a lively smile and welcome his lips, his hands, and his entire, incredible body on mine. My panties slide off and are tossed to the floor. I am able to feel his erection against me. It edges across every delicate part of me before it slides its way deep inside of me. I lift my hips up and welcome the sensation enveloping me. The warmth of his body wraps around mine, and the softness of his lips lead the motions of mine into a fiery passion. The delicate twists of his tongue against mine ease my tension as his hands reach down and take hold of my butt, pushing my hips up into him more. I feel down his strong back and then cradle the back of his neck before running my fingers deep into his hair. Dillon looks down on me, similar to how he did our first time. The pleasure of him rushes to my core and then back out again, curling my toes and releasing a velvety delight from my lips. I grip him closer as he tenses and groans, "Dani, I missed you."

Chapter 27

Dillon

I wake, thumbing the tiny box underneath my pillow with eager anticipation. She's back. I know it. I feel it. We had sex several times since last night's great dinner by the water, and each time was better than the last. I wake up with her in my arms, feeling the sun on my face, and never wanting to move from this place. She wakes up smiling, and I can't take my eyes off of her. *Yeah, this is the moment. Don't screw it up, Dillon.* I open the box and wrap my arms around her nervously.

"Can we go back to the beach today, or can we go to the park, or how about …" She is so excited, so happy, but I realize something isn't right. This isn't right, no matter how much I want it to be. I don't want to make her do something she doesn't want to do, but I am the only one that's willing to give her the push she needs, the only one to help her break from the cage she has built around herself. *She'll understand. She'll listen to me and …understand why.* "What's wrong?" Dani asks.

"We can do whatever you want Dani, but just not today. The trial starts soon, and they want you in town and ready to testify, Dani. They say they want to start preparing you for questioning." Her mood tumbles into an instant depression. "I don't want to do this to you, but they have subpoenaed you. You don't have a choice. You have to be back in town by tonight. All your doctors say you are more than capable of handling it …"

"What do they know?!" She screams at me. "No, I won't go. We are running away, remember? You promised me," she pleads, gripping my hands, "Dillon please, don't make me. I don't want to see him. I don't want to remember it. You don't want to hear the details of that night. You won't love me anymore if you do. You won't look at me the same. I'll always be a victim to you. Every time I look in your eyes, that's what I will see."

I sit down with her and clear her face, "I will love you no matter what. Nothing you can say can change how I feel about you or how I will look at you, Dani. It's going to be okay. I'll be right there with you the whole time. He won't be able to hurt you, not while I'm there."

She pushes me away. "You lied to me. This was all a setup, to trick me. I knew it, but I thought I could trust you to help me, to protect me."

"You can trust me, Dani. I promise; I will be there with you."

"I don't want you with me. You're a liar. You only care about revenge. You don't care about me."

"That's not true!"

"Yes it is! You fight everyone that challenges you, and you never let anything go. You won't let this go until Rafe is convicted, no matter what it does to me." Her quivering lip and swollen, pained eyes stare at me with gut-wrenching sorrow. "I want you out of my life, Dillon. For good," she says, pushing me away, tearing my heart out of my chest, and crushing it all over again. Staring at her naked back, I realize the truth of what's to be and push the diamond ring back into its tiny box and pack it away with the rest of our things to return home.

I never wanted to do this to her, but no one else was going to be able to do it. No one else wanted to be the one to tell her that she has to testify because they knew she would hate them forever. I knew it too, but for her, I was willing to be the bad guy and help her get to that moment she can finally let go of her crutch… me. I only wanted one last chance to remember my Dani, the way we were together, to hear her laugh and to see that look in her eyes when she sees me and makes me feel like I will never find love as wonderful as hers. One last trip, one last set of memories to hold onto before I have to let her go.

As soon as we get back from our trip, Dani demands that her father come get her and move her out of the house. She won't speak to me or even look at me. Her mother tries to reason with her with no luck. Dani comes down the stairs, carrying her final bag. "I think I have everything of mine now."

"You look beautiful, Darling," her father says, kissing her cheek.

"Yes, you do," her mother chimes in, trying to be cheerful despite Dani's rigid demeanor.

"Can we just go? I want to get this over with." She hugs my father and glances back at me with a chilling glare.

The house feels empty without her. I don't know where to go or how to be in my home anymore. My father is doing much better on his own and really doesn't need me here. I feel as if I need to have my own life now, and I think the first step to doing that is buying my own home. There is a house nearby that needs some work, a lot of work actually, but something about it reminds me of her. I fell in love with the old house the moment I walked through its squeaky door. It feels like a home to me. I buy it and begin working on it immediately, using it to keep myself busy and keep my mind even busier. Shane stops by once in a while to help out, but when Lucas comes by with some beer and some tools, I begin to search the sky.

"What are you doing, Conrad?"

"Looking for the flying pigs? That's what I was supposed to wait for right? Before you helped me do anything?"

"Shut up, jackass and take a beer before I change my mind," Lucas says, laughing. He helps through most of the day before we call it quits and order some food.

"Thanks for helping me today."

"You're welcome. I expect that you will help me with my new house when I'm ready, right?"

"Oh damn, I didn't know I was going to have to return the favor and shit; otherwise, I would have pushed you off the roof at the end of the day," I say.

"Ha ha! I forgot how funny you are." He says sarcastically.

"Really? How could you do that? It's one of the best things about me."

"I always thought Dani was one of the best things about you." I turn away from him with nothing to say. "I saw her the other day. She's doing really well and looking good. I know she is being really stubborn right now about testifying, but you have to be there."

"I'll be there, but she doesn't want me there."

"Yes she does, and you need to make sure you are right up front so she can see you. Don't you dare give up on her now or I am going to have to come back over here and beat the shit out of you. I just started believing you two are meant for each other."

"She hates me; the last person she wants around is me."

"Sure she does. She hates you so much that she asked me how you were doing and made me promise to come check on you."

"I knew you didn't come over here on your own. Wait. She asked about me?"

Lucas nods, laughing at me. "I, of course, told her that you have aged horribly over the last couple of months, gained a lot of weight, lost your hair, and shrunk, too." Lucas glances over at me. "And that I heard you were planning on having a sex change soon. You know, since your penis never really developed you might as well."

"Ha ha." I push the asshole over laughing with him before seeing Shane walk up to the house with beer in his hand and looking concerned.

"What's happening here?" Shane asks, pointing at us.

"I've decided I am in love with Dillon and we're getting

married after his sex change," Lucas says. "Don't worry, you can be a bridesmaid."

Shane narrows his eyes at us before finally shrugging and nodding. "Oh. Alright, but I am sick of tired of always being the bridesmaid. Unless! I can wear something that's form fitting and shows off my abs? I have been really working out a lot lately." He lifts his t-shirt up to show off for us.

"Oh, I have changed my mind, I think I will go with the one that's already had a sex change." Lucas jokes as I laugh. Shane looks back at us unamused.

I show up at court, running into my father and Shane as Dani comes through with her parents. She glances my way, noticing my suit for court. "What are you doing here?"

"I told you I would be here for you," I say expecting her to scream obscenities at me, but instead, she turns away with a slight nod.

"Do what you want Dillon," she says, seeming to want me here. Maybe she's right. I won't want to hear the details of that night, and she believes it will only cause me to regret forcing her to do it.

My father encourages me to follow them, and I shake my head until Dani's father waves me to come with them as well. We all follow Dani and sit with her outside the courtroom, waiting for them to come get her. She glances up at me constantly, and I meet her eyes more than once, believing I even see a smile here and there. I want to say something to her, but I don't know what.

"So, Dillon, how's the new house coming?" Mr. Portman asks, shaking me out of my daze.

"It's good. I am only getting some time at night and on weekends to really get much done, but it's really coming along."

"You bought a new house?" Dani asks.

"Yeah, the old Seiber place."

"Oh, I love that house." I nod, and she fidgets with her hands some before looking back up at me with half a smile. "Congratulations."

I wrestle with the change in my pocket for a few seconds before working up the courage to ask her if she would like to see it. "Dani would you …" She looks up at me with her beautiful doe eyes, and I lose every thought I had in my head.

"Ms. Portman, we are about ready for you. I would like to go somewhere private and go over a few things before you go up to testify," one of the prosecuting attorneys says as he exits the courtroom. They take her to another room to talk while we go find a seat in the courtroom. They bring in Rafe, and the son of a bitch looks right at me and smiles with a gleeful nod.

I flinch and Dani's father pats my arm. "Calm down. Dani needs you more than he does." Never would I have believed that Douglas Portman would ever treat me like someone he cared about. *I kind of wish he would go back to hating me. It was more fun.* I sit nervously, vibrating when the prosecution announces Dani as their last and final witness. She comes through the door with some assistance from a guard, walking in on crutches, which makes the journey even longer for her. The room is so silent that you can hear every creak and crack of her crutches and every struggling breath she makes, trying to hold back her fears. I do my best not to run to her and carry her out of here. *I only need to wait until she gets there,* I keep telling myself. *She is going to be okay. She's tough, and she is going to be able to do this.*

She looks really nervous, but I stay focused on her, hoping somehow I can transfer any strength I might have to her. They ask her some simple questions at first and then dive right in. "Ms. Portman, can you tell us what happened after you found Mr. Bolton dead?"

"Um …I …" I brace myself, preparing to run to her as she searches for the right words. She looks up trembling, searching the room frantically until she meets my eyes. I nod to her, and she nods back. She takes a deep breath and begins telling her nightmare, all the while, staying focused on me. I don't look away, and I don't look the least bit affected by what she is saying. I keep nodding and mouthing support to her through every horrific detail until she gets through it.

"Thank you, Ms. Portman. Your strength is inspirational," the prosecutor says. The defense stands up, and I steady myself to not choke the life out of them, but they decide not to question her, and she is excused without having to endure another second. She looks over at me and smiles with relief.

Before we leave for the day, she approaches me. "Are you going to come back for the verdict?"

"I was planning on it, if that's okay?"

"I would like that," she says before leaving with her father. *And I love you, Dani.*

The verdict is in, and we all sit together in the courtroom waiting. Dani sits between her parents while Shane, my father, and I sit behind them. Dani glances over her shoulder at me many times, seeming strong, persevering, and more beautiful than ever. The jurors are back quickly, which leads us to believe they had an easy decision to make. When Rafe comes in, he seems to be worried for the first time since I have seen him. He sits at the table, bouncing in his chair before turning towards us all and waiting for Dani to look his way, but she won't do it.

"Hey Dani, do you still dream about me?"

I jump out of my seat and over the barrier between us, taking hold of his throat. "You don't talk to her! You don't look at her!" I yell at him, managing to get in one good punch before being escorted out of the courtroom by two guards. "So, am I being kicked out now? He's a murderer, but you're treating me like I'm a criminal. He is protected, really? He doesn't deserve to be protected!" I yell at them after I break free.

"Calm down. We understand your feelings, but you can't attack someone in the courtroom, Sir. Now, if you promise to behave, you can stay out here and wait, but you are not allowed to go back in. Do you understand me? Stay out here and wait."

Otherwise, you're going to have to go to jail," one guard says before they both go back into the courtroom.

I pace back and forth impatiently until I hear people gasping and clapping. One guard leans out of the courtroom doors and nods at me. He's guilty. She did it, and he's gone forever. I feel good and excited and then… fear all over again. *What now?* She, for sure, doesn't need me anymore, or does she have to stay in this town anymore. The place of her nightmare. *Why would she want to stay here, Dillon?* I must be out of my mind for even considering the idea. I take a deep breath, wondering if I should wait to be rejected or go and relieve her of having to walk away from me, or rather, relieving myself of that heartbreak of watching her walk away, again. Pacing from the courtroom doors to the exit stairs and then back again, I finally decide to go.

"Dillon! Dillon!" Dani yells at me before I can make it to the stairs. "Dillon wait!" I stop and turn towards her. "He's guilty," she says, nearing me.

"I heard. That's great. You were great, amazing even. I couldn't have done what you did."

"Oh yes you could. You would have. I was only able to do it because of you. There is no way I would have made it without you. I realize that now."

"You are more than strong enough to handle anything on your own, Dani. You don't need me."

"Maybe, but I …I want you. Are you willing to forgive me?"

"For what?"

"For forgetting how much I love you and how much I want

you in my life. I'm sorry, Dillon. I never wanted to hurt you; I only wanted better for you. If there is any way you can forgive me and give me a chance to make it up to you, I promise I will never ever let you down again." I watch her as she pours her heart out to me and offers to repair mine at the same time, but do I dare take another chance on having it crushed again? I have trouble finding the right words to say. "I understand, if it's too late. If it helps any, I never hated you. I only wanted to be perfect for you, and I hate that I am not. I hate that I am not good enough, but I will be. I promise. I am doing everything I am supposed to, and I will be back to the Dani you loved. I will …"

"Shut up," I say, causing her to look up at me. "Shut up, Dani. You clearly don't understand what I see. Since I knew what love was, I knew I loved you. No matter what has happened, that hasn't changed. Whether you ever walk perfectly again or get grey hair and saggy skin, I will still think that you are the most beautiful woman I have ever seen. You're my best friend and the love of my life. If you decide to return that love or not, is up to you. Do you understand, it's all up to you? Our relationship has always been up to you. I love you that much," I say as she fights tears and holds her hand over her mouth.

"Can I ask you a question before I decide?"

"Sure, anything," I say.

"What if I asked you to marry me?" She asks with a playful smile.

I laugh, shaking my head, recalling that moment perfectly. "I would say that is a very serious question, Dani." She smiles wide with laughter. "And I would hope you considered all the points of concern, such as, do we enjoy the same things? Can we agree on the important things in life, …money, and children?" I step closer to her and look down into her eyes directly, sweeping the hair from her face so I can clearly see her amazing smile. "We would have to be husband and wife and not only the best of friends anymore. We would have to live together in the same house, and…" I laugh, remembering the words, "And share stuff." Her bright doe eyes smile right up into mine. "And what about vacations, Dani? We would have to go together every single time. We would have to spend a lot of time together." Taking her hand in mine, I pull out the ring I had bought for her when the factory started making money again. I knew it was the right one as soon as I saw it. I had hoped that I would get the right moment to give it to her one day. I get down on one knee in front of her and open up the tiny box. "We would have to be together …forever. You know?"

She gasps, crying and trying to catch her breath before speaking. She takes in a deep breath while her smile stretches from one side of her face to the other, wider than I have ever seen. "But that's why I would ask you, Dillon. I couldn't think of anyone better to spend my forever with." She accepts my ring, and I get up and pick her up in my arms, carrying her to our home where she belongs.

Epilogue

Dillon

Dear Dani,

I am sitting in my truck on the other side of town with Ellie, getting ready to mail this letter to you. I can only imagine what you and Matty are doing right now, he was not in the best mood last night. I don't think he likes my jokes. I am sure he will grow out of it though, because everyone loves my jokes. Right? Right.

So onto my reason for writing this letter to you. I am not sure where to begin. How do I pick one moment in time that means the most to me? How do I pick only one moment that I spent with you? There was the time we first met, which was proof of your stubbornness even then. You are annoyingly stubborn, you know? Alright, maybe I have my flaws too, but not everyone is perfect. Although, I am pretty close, you have to admit. Besides, my flaws are endearing according to what Mrs. Green said. She was a brilliant old woman, don't you think? Wait, or did she say enduring? Damn it. I think I should be offended. That senile old woman never liked me. She loved you though, everyone always loved you. My mother adored you, treated you as if you were her own. My father the same. Neither could let you go, like I did. Despite what you think, watching you go was the worst moment of my life. There were many bad ones, a lot of rough ones, and some downright torturous moments that we shared, but losing you was the one moment I hate the most. But now, all those bad moments are in our past, and I do want to prove to you that I still love you. Even as I sit here on the other side of town from you, I miss you. What is my favorite moment that we have shared together? I promise, my beautiful girl, that I have done my best and thought long and hard on that question. I have considered this moment and that moment, and after great consideration, I can honestly say, I don't have one. I mean, how can I choose one moment in time that I spent with the most intelligent, the most caring, the most exquisite, and the most wonderful wife and mother I have ever known? No, I don't have a favorite moment with you, but I do have a favorite life, and that is this one, the life I have with you. Every moment spent with you is better than every moment I have spent away from you. You have given me the life that every man would be jealous of. I wouldn't trade my life for anything. I love you, Dani. I love our children, and I love the life we have built together.

Forever only yours,
Your husband – Dillon

P.S. – Please stop reading those women's magazines. I feel like a damn fool driving all the way out here to mail my wife a letter that I could have given to her this morning. And please don't tell anyone I did this. I do have a reputation to keep up you know?

P.P.S. – Ellie says, "I love Mommy, too."

Jennifer Loren

The Author

 @JenniferLorenDE

 https://www.jenniferloren.com

 https://www.facebook.com/JenniferLoren.Author

 http://www.youtube.com/user/LorenJennifer

Jennifer Loren

www.ingramcontent.com/pod-product-compliance
Lightning Source LLC
Chambersburg PA
CBHW061323170626
46817CB00001B/286